Candles Over
the
Septic Tank

Chris Phipps

Published by Eleven Jewels Publishing

This is a work of fiction. To create a sense of place, the Sierra Nevada foothills of Northern California is used as a backdrop. The town of Miner's Ridge, The Tavern, and the gambling house in the country are all fictitious. While the other towns mentioned exist, the structures, characters, their names, and incidents are products of the author's imagination and experience or are used fictitiously.

Cover by Karen Phillips of Phillips Covers
ISBN: 978-0990914174

This one is for Nita
With love and admiration for your courage,
strong faith, and optimism as you fight
the toughest battle of your life.
I hope this story will provide a few laughs
and brighten your days a little.

Acknowledgments

I'd like to thank those who helped bring this book to life:

Supportive fellow writers in my online Inked Voices Mystery Writers Group, who critiqued chapters as I wrote, and offered constructive comments and suggestions;

Fellow writer Joli Roberts who offered encouragement and suggestions all during the writing process and, along with Robin Rice and Windy Bakarich, later read the entire finished novel, ferreting out inconsistencies and errors.

Christiana Bakarich, who did her usual great job of painstaking editing; and

Karen Phillips for working so hard to get the cover right.

Thanks to all of you, for making the book so much better than it might have been.

Chapter 1

I came fully awake knowing something was wrong; I just didn't know what. The room was still dark, no hint of morning light creeping through the open window. What had awakened me?

I lay still, my ears straining for any unusual noises, trying to separate them from the normal creaking and settling of the old house. Then I heard it: a faint shuffling scrape. A footstep? Eyes shut, I concentrated, trying to pinpoint not only the sound but its location, hoping my imagination was playing middle-of-the-night tricks on me.

No, there it was again.

I reached for my cell phone on the nightstand, my hand scrabbling around lamp, books, water bottle, and my alarm clock, displaying 3:12 in glowing numbers. The phone wasn't there. I'd probably left it in my jeans pocket.

I slipped out of bed and crept to the chair where I'd left my pants and shirt, then searched through them with shaking hands. The pockets were empty.

Could the phone have fallen out? I dropped to my knees and patted the floor around the chair. Nothing but my shoes and socks. I ran my fingers inside the shoes, then under the clothing. Nothing.

I stood still, listening for a creak in the old hardwood floors, aware of every sound, every scent. A gentle delta breeze had cooled the room when I went to bed, carrying a faint scent of honeysuckle and early-blooming roses through the open window. Now it was colder, chilling my bare legs and feet.

Or maybe it was fear raising those goosebumps.

The room offered few hiding places. The bed was so low, I doubted I could wedge myself under it, and the closet was old-house small and packed tight with clothes.

The dog next door barked. I turned, staring into the darkness outside. Maybe I should get out through the window. The clips for the screen were on the outside, but they were old, always slipping loose. They'd give way if I pushed hard enough.

Before I could move, I realized the sounds weren't coming from inside the house. There was no way an intruder could avoid all the creaking floorboards. He must have been at the front door, trying to find a way inside. I closed my eyes, listening, hoping—praying he'd given up and left. The minutes ticked by.

He's gone.

Another sound came, a slight thump, then...nothing. Where was he? Another slight scuffling noise, a little closer, from the side of the house. A footstep on concrete? Was he working his way around to the back, toward my open window?

Maybe there were two of them, one at the front, another at the back.

I had to close and lock that window but, more often than not, it got stuck partway down, taking me a few minutes to work it loose. Right now I didn't have a few minutes. And I didn't have a weapon.

Then I remembered something. Edging away from the door but staying close to the wall to avoid creaking boards, I worked my way toward the closet and the baseball bat I'd been nagging Randy to move out of the house, along with the rest of his junk.

By the time I found it, the Border Collie in the neighbor's back yard was growling. Staying low, I crept to the wall and stood on one side of the window, the bat raised high. A sliver of pale moonlight helped me focus on the window sill.

The dog seemed to be running along the back fence now, barking. I tensed, my hands gripping the bat, waiting. Was the intruder still there? Maybe the dog had scared him away.

A low squeak at the window removed all doubt. Somebody was lifting the screen. A tiny thump as it was set on the ground, then two man-sized hands appeared, pressing down on the sill.

He was ready to climb inside.

Heart racing, I waited a few seconds, giving him time to get his head in the opening, then brought the bat down. Hard.

I had misjudged. I was too close to the window for a good swing. The edge of the bat scraped against the window frame and the blow landed on the back of his shoulders, not his head.

He let out a grunt and jerked back, his hands still gripping the sill. I brought down the bat again, aiming for the fingers, but he had pulled away, falling backward.

The motion light came on and, even before its light revealed him, sprawled on the ground, I knew it had to be my ex-husband. Nobody else was familiar enough with the motion lights to avoid turning them on as he had worked his way around the house to my window. He knew the screen clips were exterior and that I liked to sleep with the window open; we'd had enough arguments about it.

He struggled into a sitting position, moaning as he rubbed his shoulder. "What the hell did you hit me with?"

"Your baseball bat. I told you to get it out of here."

"Marcie..." Whimpering, he worked his shoulder back and forth, testing for damage.

"I was scared," I said. "I thought a burglar was trying to get inside. Or a rapist. Or a—"

He held up a hand, or tried to, before he winced and let it down. "Okay. Okay. I get it. I tried the front door, but you had the chain on." His voice sounded accusing, as though I owed him an apology.

"I had to. I couldn't afford to change the locks. If you really had to get in, why didn't you ring the bell or knock like a normal person, instead of sneaking around in the middle of the night?"

"I was trying not to wake you. Sometimes you have trouble going back to sleep."

That was true, usually because he'd made me so mad I couldn't settle down. I suspected the same thing was going to happen now. "You just knew I wouldn't let you in so you were trying to sneak through the window. Did you think I wouldn't wake up?"

"I thought...why are you sleeping in the spare room?"

He didn't need to know I'd felt lost in the king-size bed we'd shared, too restless to sleep. "It's cooler in here, with the cross breeze." Then, thinking about those windows, comprehension dawned. The latch on one of them, the one I'd already opened, was broken. He'd planned to get in that way—climb into a room he thought was vacant. And then...what?

"Why are you here, anyway? What do you want this time? And why at this time of the night?"

He brushed a hand across his tight blond curls and studied me with the blue-gray eyes I'd once found so appealing. Well, maybe I still did, a little. They were clear and held a child-like innocence, without a trace of guile. He smiled and my heart quickened. I tamped it down; I didn't need more trouble in my life. He'd already brought more than I could handle.

"Knock it off, Randy."

"What? I'm not doing anything."

"Yes, you are. You're trying to lay on the charm and I'm not buying. I've been down that road too many times and it always ends up at the dump."

"Aw, babe, you don't mean that. Did I tell you how good you look in that old nightgown? I bought that one for you, didn't I? And I like your red hair all messed up like that."

I'd forgotten my skimpy nightwear, made a little shorter when I raised my hand to smooth my hair. "It's not red. It's auburn."

He tilted his head and studied me. "Red, to go with those green eyes."

"They're not green. They're hazel."

Randy grinned. I pressed my lips together to keep from smiling, but he was no longer looking at me. He'd turned his head toward the barking dog on the other side of the fence. "Don't you think you should let me in before that mutt wakes up the entire neighborhood?"

"I've got a better idea. If I scream loud enough, maybe one of them will call the cops."

"You really want all those guys you work with seeing what I'm seeing? All that bare skin and bedroom hair? And I gotta tell you, babe, that nightgown is kind of thin."

I could put on a robe and comb my hair before anybody got there, but I didn't want the guys from work to see Randy and know even more about my miserable life than they already did. And I knew Randy. He wasn't going away until I talked to him. I might as well get him inside and find out what he was trying to pull this time. "Okay, put that screen back on first. Then go to the back porch and I'll unlock the kitchen door. But be quiet about it."

I put the bat in the closet, then grabbed a robe before I headed for the kitchen and the door leading onto the screened-in porch.

"Got any beer?" Randy asked as soon as I opened the door.

"It's three o'clock in the morning. And, no, I don't have any beer. Or wine. Or soft drinks. Or anything else. Not even coffee. Thanks to you, I can't afford it."

"Why not? You've got a good job."

"You think so? My pay is almost as low as my clerical position on the organizational chart. Not nearly good enough to pay all the bills you left. Especially after the IRS hit me with penalties for the overdue taxes you told me you'd paid."

He dropped into one of the chrome dinette chairs, his sneaker-clad feet tucked around the front legs. "Aw, babe, I'm sorry. I meant to pay them. Honest. I just...well, like I told you before, I was a little short and—"

"Spare me. You're always a little short. Probably because you lost it in a poker game or at a blackjack table or to a pool hustler. Or lost your job because you were too hungover to go to work."

He ran a hand through his curls. "You've got it all wrong. I don't gamble that much anymore. I don't drink that much, either, since..." He stopped then, probably realizing he'd just asked me for a beer, then plowed on. "I didn't have it because Billy needed help paying his rent." Randy spread his hands. "What was I gonna do? I couldn't have my little brother out on the street with nowhere to go."

"Your little brother is twenty-four. Old enough to take care of himself." But I believed Randy. He had a lot of flaws, but he had a big heart. He'd give away his last dime to help somebody else, even if he didn't know where his next meal was coming from. But lately, it had been my dimes he'd been giving away.

I sat down on the other side of the table. "What about me? I'm the one who's going to be on the street if I can't come up with the house payment. Randy, when Grandma left me this house, it was paid for. Then I let you talk me into taking out a mortgage so we could make a down payment on that condo. Now I have monthly payments I can't afford and the condo is long gone."

" I just thought...this place is so old." He looked around at the Harvest Gold Formica countertop, avocado-green linoleum, and faded yellow-flowered wallpaper. "And it's kind of out in the sticks. You need to be in something closer to town where there's more action. A place that's not so much work and where you'd be safer, with more people around."

"You mean where I wouldn't have prowlers crawling in one of my windows at three o'clock in the morning?"

He gave me a lopsided grin. Randy always had a reason and, somehow, it usually involved my welfare. He'd traded in my reliable old 2007 Acura TL for a newer model bright-yellow Chevy Camaro convertible I didn't even like. He said he was worried about me breaking down and being stranded somewhere; I needed better transportation. That Acura had never broken down on me. I suspected he just didn't want to be seen in it, that he'd spotted the convertible on a used car lot, thought it looked cool, and made the trade without another thought. It wouldn't have occurred to him that I might not approve, that I couldn't afford a car payment. Lesson learned: never add your husband's name to your car title.

"Marcie, babe, I didn't mean to leave you with all those bills, but it wasn't my fault. How did I know I was going to lose my job?"

"Maybe when you punched your boss? That'll usually do it."

"Yeah, I let my temper get away from me again. I couldn't help it when he made that nasty crack about you."

"What crack? What did he say?"

"Nothing you need to hear. Just forget about it."

"Forget about it? How can I forget about something that was bad enough for you to hit him?"

"It doesn't matter now. It's past history. I punched him and I'd do it again. The only thing I regret is losing my job over it."

I stood up. The conversation was pointless; it wasn't going to help me pay my bills. "Randy, right now I have to make a choice. Do I skip the house payment, the car payment, or the grocery store? If I don't have the car, I can't get to work. If I lose the house, I'll be living in a cardboard condo. And I don't think I'd last very long without food. The cupboards are already pretty bare. Even the Top Ramen is getting scarce. So, unless you're here to help, get your butt out of my house."

Randy scrambled to his feet, took a step toward me, then stopped. "Marcie, I've only got a little over forty dollars, but it's yours." He reached into his back pocket for his billfold. "It'll at least buy you some groceries."

He opened the wallet, pulled out the bills, and handed them to me. Forty-two dollars.

"Is that all you've got?"

He gave me a frown of disbelief. "You want my change, too?"

"No. I just...how are you going to manage without it?"

His face relaxed into a smile. "I got a job. A really good one, running heavy equipment. It's the kind of stuff I like to do, so I'm not going to mess this one up. As soon as I get a paycheck, I can help you with all those bills."

I studied his eyes. Guileless, as usual. "Are you being straight with me, Randy? Because if you aren't..."

He raised his left hand. "Swear to God. The pay is good and they have medical insurance."

"How long before you get paid?'

"Every Friday. Except...well, the first week. They have to have time to calculate overtime and everything, so the pay is always a week behind."

I couldn't restrain the sigh. He'd had my hopes up for a minute or two. "I can't hold off on the bills for two more weeks. If I let the house payment go any longer, they may call in the entire loan. And the car payment is already late. I'm afraid they're going to repossess it."

"Let me see what I can do. Now that I've got a good job, I might be able to borrow a little."

I didn't think that was likely. Randy's friends and acquaintances might be glad he had a job but, with his history, they wouldn't use that as collateral for new loans. They'd just hope he hung onto it long enough to pay back money already owed.

He knew it, too. "I'll hock some stuff. Is my guitar still here?"

"Randy, I appreciate the thought. I really do. But all your stuff put together wouldn't raise enough money to help."

He let out a soft sigh. "I'm sorry, babe. Sometimes I think I screw up everything I touch, but you don't deserve this. I know some people. Give me a day or two—"

"And what? Get it from some loan shark? No."

He looked so bewildered then, so defeated, I had to fight the impulse to put my arms around him. I took a step back. "Randy, why are you even here?"

His shoulders slumped and he dropped his gaze to the floor. "I...I guess I just needed somebody to talk to. Grandpa got killed, and I thought, since you knew him..." His chin wobbled.

Without conscious thought, I folded him into my arms and let him cry. He'd been close to his grandfather, maybe because the two of them were so much alike: both charmers who had never quite grown up, who were always looking for the next sure thing, and who had such big, loving hearts.

"What happened?" I asked, wondering if his grandfather had finally pushed somebody too far.

"A hit and run and...and they haven't found the driver." He pulled away from me enough to swipe at his eyes with the back of his hand. "Marcie, I hate to ask, but there's something I need you to do for me."

I dropped my arms and stepped away. Every time Randy asked for a favor, it ended up costing me, one way or another. I was out of money and through with favors.

"It's Grandma," he said. "She's going to be all alone in Miner's Ridge next week, and I can't go up there. I need this job too bad. If I don't show up Monday morning, I'll lose it before I even get started."

"Where are your sisters?"

"Katie is working in D.C. and it's going to take a few days for her to get away. Natalie is with Grandma now. She went up as soon as we heard, Thursday morning. But, see, here's the thing. She had to take the kids with her, and she can't keep them out of school any longer. She has to go home Sunday. So...anyway, I know you have vacation coming. You never take any time off. Could you do it? Not for me, but for Grandma. I think she always liked you better than me, anyway. Just stay long enough for her to get through the worst of it."

And just like that, he had me again. I liked his grandma too much. I couldn't let her down. And Randy had to keep that job if I were ever to get out of my financial mess.

"Okay. I'll call work and ask them, but I'll need that forty-two dollars for gas."

His smile was back again. "You can use your grocery money. You won't have to buy any next week, and I'll need some here."

"Here? You think you're going to stay in my house while I'm gone?"

"Babe, I don't have anywhere else to go, and you won't be here, anyway. I can kind of look after things, maybe fix some stuff like those window latches. It'll just be while you're gone. And look at it this way. They won't be able to find the convertible to repossess it if you take it to Miner's Ridge. That means you can delay the payment until I get paid. With that money and what you'll save on groceries, you can make the house payment with plenty to spare for gas. Then we can catch up on everything in a couple of weeks, when I get paid."

He grinned as if he'd miraculously solved all my problems. It might even work. But, then, Randy's plans always started off with high possibilities before everything fell apart. Even knowing that, I didn't have a lot of choices, not with Grandma Edith up there alone. I tried not to think about what might go wrong during my absence. Something would; with Randy, it always did, and I had a sneaking suspicion there was something he wasn't telling me.

Chapter 2

I left Galt and was on the other side of Sacramento, picking up I-80 east in a little less than an hour. Sunday afternoon traffic was fairly light, nothing like the slow-moving tangle it became on Friday afternoons when commuters were heading home from Sacramento, Roseville, or even the Bay Area.

Despite the circumstances, I was looking forward to the trip, to getting away from the too-crowded valley with its ever-increasing smog, into the foothills, away from work and all my financial problems. Grandma Edith was a great cook, Randy had told me that Miner's Ridge was a pleasant little town with friendly people and, best of all, I liked Grandma Edith. It would be great to see her again.

It was a beautiful day. The Camaro's flaky check-engine light hadn't come on, and hillsides were still green, forming a backdrop for patches of golden-orange California poppies. I almost wished I could put the top down on the Camaro.

Randy had lowered it a few days after he bought the car. It was late spring then, and the weather was beautiful, the sun warm on my shoulders and the clouds so wispy they looked like fading contrails.

I'd been cruising along, enjoying the breeze ruffling my hair, when sprinkles started to fall. I pulled off the street and dug out the instruction manual.

First, I had to make sure the car was level. I wasn't sure how to go about that. I had parked on a paved street with no potholes in the near vicinity. It was the best I could do because I was fairly certain there was no carpenter level in the trunk.

I went back to the instructions but, no matter how many times I went through the procedure, nothing happened; the top wouldn't budge. The clouds, packed a little closer, turned gray. The sprinkles increased, then turned to fat drops, and finally to a downpour. Everything inside the Camaro—including the instruction manual—and me—was a sodden mess. I turned around and drove home, trying to ignore the stares and honks from other drivers. I was pretty sure they weren't flirting with me, considering the wet hair plastered to my scalp and my mascara-smeared face, so I could only assume they were trying to tell me my convertible top was down and it was raining.

It took Randy and one of the next-door neighbor's teenage boys several hours to get the top back up. After that, no matter what the forecast, I never lowered it again and every time I thought about that top and my old Acura TL, I got mad all over again.

Once past Roseville, the freeway began its climb into higher elevations and more open land. I turned onto Highway 49 at Auburn and soon saw more evergreen trees than oaks, and more vegetation along the roadside.

A deer emerged from the brush just ahead of me, apparently ready to cross the road. Two more stood on the other side. I slowed, watching for more wildlife.

I had left Highway 49 and was cruising along, just enjoying the ride, when a sign appeared on my left. "Welcome to Miner's Ridge." I'd barely finished reading it when I saw another, telling me I'd left the town. About a quarter-mile from the sign, I turned right onto a narrow, two-lane road. A ditch ran alongside it, on the driver's side, so choked with tall weeds I caught a glimpse of the water only when I crested a slight rise in the road. There was a narrow bridge ahead where the ditch apparently fed into a stream. Several cars were coming toward me in the opposite lane, one already on the bridge.

Lights flashed behind me and I glanced at my rear-view mirror. A patrol car was creeping up on me. With the bridge so close, I didn't have a place to pull off so I peered ahead, trying to see a wide enough spot on the other side.

The driver of the patrol car flipped on his siren and motioned for me to pull over. The problem was, where? Couldn't he see the bridge? While my eyes scanned the roadside ahead, my mind tried to sort through a jumble of questions. Were they going to repossess the Camaro? Did police even do that? And, if they did, how did they know I was here, on this road?

If they'd shown up at the house, Randy wouldn't have told them where I was. I'd let the neighbors know I'd be gone for a few days, but I didn't think I'd told them where I was going. I couldn't remember whether I'd mentioned my destination to anybody at work, but I didn't think so. Just that Grandpa Dan had died and I wanted to take some vacation so I could be with Grandma Edith.

I crossed the bridge and spotted a narrow space ahead between two trees. I signaled for a right turn and had barely pulled off the road when the cruiser passed so close I thought he'd clip my bumper, siren blasting as he picked up speed. So it was pretty safe to assume he wasn't there to take the Camaro.

I was shaking my head, almost laughing at my irrational thoughts about vehicle repossession when I heard another siren and looked back at a second set of flashing lights. That vehicle passed so fast I could barely read the Miner's Ridge Police Department logo on the door.

What was going on? Miner's Ridge was a small community. I suspected most of their crimes consisted of jaywalking, running the stoplight or, possibly, chicken theft.

I waited a couple of minutes, just in case a third cruiser was barreling down the road. Nothing happened and it occurred to me that Miner Ridge's Police Department probably had only two vehicles; their full force had just passed me, racing toward something big. Maybe an accident up ahead, somebody killed.

I pulled back onto the road and headed for Grandma Edith's house, half expecting a delay from an accident scene. I reached her street without incident, though, and breathed a little sigh of relief as I turned into it.

Grandma Edith's house sat on the front of an acre, nestled among other like-sized lots on the short street ending in a cul-de-sac. The property at the end, two lots over from hers, was a double, creating more than two acres since it wasn't divided by the width of the road.

Intent on watching the sidewalks for darting kids or pets, it took me a few minutes to notice those flashing lights were now down the street. The patrol cars were parked haphazardly in front of Grandma Edith's house. Neighbors stood on their lawns or porches, front row observers to whatever was going on.

Building lots in the foothills were rarely flat, and the embankment between Grandma Edith's driveway and her neighbors' yard was populated with a mixture of evergreen and ornamental shrubs and medium-sized trees. Several cops were huddled there, looking down at something. A wheelbarrow stood on the driveway nearby, half-filled with shredded bark. More had scattered onto the driveway. Grandma Edith was an avid gardener, spending hours in her yard. Had she been working on that slope? Slipped and fallen?

I scrambled out of the Camaro and was halfway across the street, running toward them, when one of the cops grabbed me. "This is a crime scene, miss. Move back to the other side of the road."

A crime scene? Not an accident? A chill crept up my spine.

As I tried to twist away from the cop, I stood on tiptoe, looking over his shoulder. One officer, partially shielded from view by the low-hanging branches of an evergreen, was bending over something on the other side of a big boulder. A foot protruded from the shrubs. Then I saw another, this one attached to a leg. It stuck out at an odd angle.

"Grandma Edith! Is she..." I couldn't utter the word "dead," my irrational mind balking. If I didn't say it, maybe it wouldn't be true.

The look on my face must have alarmed the cop. He gripped me tighter, one arm around my shoulders. "Miss. Miss? Are you okay?"

No, I wasn't okay. My heart felt like it was exploding in my chest as I tried to make sense of the scene. I couldn't think; the image of those legs lying on the ground pushed out all rational thought. I took a deep breath, then another, trying to calm down. What kind of crime was the cop talking about? And if those legs belonged to Grandma Edith, why? Who would want to hurt her?

The officer gave me another light shake. "Miss? Are you okay?"

"I...what? No. Yes, I think so. Is Grandma Edith...?"

"Your grandmother lives here?" He pulled me to him, pressing my face against his shoulder. "You don't need to see this. Let's get you to your car."

I twisted to look back at the slope just as a woman emerged from the low limbs of a deodar cedar. I couldn't mistake that figure; it was Grandma Edith, a trim, slender woman with graying, sandy-blonde hair, wearing denim pants and shirt, both soiled with dirt and clinging bark. She looked down at the officer examining whomever was on the ground, her hands in motion, pointing to the wheelbarrow, the slope, and the feet I'd seen. I was too far away to hear what she was saying and, even as I breathed in a long sigh of relief, glad she was safe, I wondered who those legs could possibly belong to. And I couldn't push away the words the cop who was still holding me had said: "This is a crime scene."

Chapter 3

The police officer Grandma Edith was talking to rose and looked around, brushing the bark off his knees. Then he started laughing, a full-throated blast of mirth, like he'd just been told the best joke he'd ever heard. He came down the embankment, his gait awkward as he watched his steps, struggling to maintain his balance.

At the bottom, he looked up, still laughing, then strode toward us, his shoulders shaking. "It's...pantyhose," he gasped, before his entire body erupted in a spasm of laughter again.

The cop holding onto my arm stiffened. "Cliff, are you okay?"

"I'm...I'm fine. It's just...It's just so damn funny, and I don't know how I'm going to write this one up. I can just see the headlines when the paper gets hold of it: Entire police force dispatched to ...to...inspect pantyhose." He shook his head, still laughing.

"But Grandma Edith is all right?" I asked.

He seemed to notice me for the first time. "And you are?"

"Marcie Clifton." I motioned toward Grandma Edith. "She's my...my grandmother. I just need to know if she's okay."

"Oh, she's fine. Nothing wrong with that lady."

The cop who had grabbed me released his grip about the same time Grandma Edith spotted me. She was coming down the bank—too fast. Afraid she'd slip and fall, I ran and grabbed her arm. "Grandma Edith, what's going on?"

Holding onto me, she worked her way down the slope. "Fools. Marcie, I'm surrounded by fools. And that stupid Jack Loudon over there is the worst of the bunch." She inclined her head toward a man standing in the street, farther down toward the end, wearing khaki cargo shorts and a blue polo shirt. He stared back at us, arms crossed. I couldn't see his face; he was too far away and wore a black Oakland Raiders ball cap, the brim pulled low against the setting sun. He appeared to be in his mid-to-late fifties and reasonably fit.

Giving Grandma Edith a belated hug, I asked, "What did he do?"

"Called the cops. Lord only knows what he told them. Any fool can see those aren't bodies." She nodded back at the bark-stuffed pantyhose, then stopped and tilted her head, studying them. "Huh. They do look a little like human legs from a distance, don't they?"

For a few minutes, I wondered if Grandpa Dan's sudden death had loosened a few screws, making her slightly unhinged. I supposed if you'd been married as long as they had, losing your husband unexpectedly could do that. I'd even heard of old people who had died a day or two after losing their life partner. Not that I was likely to ever find out for myself.

I studied her face. She looked tired, her eyes a little puffy with dark shadows under them. "Grandma Edith, are you okay?"

She patted my shoulder. "As right as I can be with Dan...with the way things are now. The house is too quiet. That seems strange because I never minded being alone in there before. It helped, having Natalie and the kids here. But after they left...I don't know. I just knew I couldn't stay inside, moping. I had to get busy and it's better out here, working in the sunshine and fresh air."

"I was so sad to hear about Grandpa Dan. But I'm glad you weren't with him. You might have been hit, too."

"Not much chance of that. I think he was out working a case." She bent to scoop loose bark back into the wheelbarrow. When I tried to help, she pushed me away. "You'll get your nice clothes dirty." She grabbed the handles and started wheeling it up the long driveway toward the back of the lot, brushing off my attempts to take it from her. "This stuff isn't heavy, and I need the exercise." I doubted that; from the looks of her yard, I suspected it gave her more of a workout than I got in my all-too-infrequent trips to the gym.

"What's it for? The bark?" I nodded toward the wheelbarrow's contents.

"Couple of things. It's shredded, so it tends to stick together. You put it down thick enough, it smothers all the weeds. And on a place this big, that's important. It's good mulch, too, retains moisture around the plants, saving irrigation water. But you're really asking about the pantyhose, aren't you?"

I couldn't help smiling. "Well, I am a little curious."

"It's simple. I needed bark on that bank. Not just for weed control, but to stop soil erosion. Trouble was, the stuff wouldn't stay put. It just slid down the slope. That's when I got the idea of those old pantyhose I used to wear to work. I stuff them full of bark and fasten them down in tiers with landscaping pins. That holds them in place. Then, when I lay bark in between those tiers, the pantyhose keeps it in place. Works like a charm, and they hold up well to the weather."

We came to a wide gate at the top of the long driveway. She stopped to open it, then pushed the wheelbarrow through. "I had filled up some of the pantyhose and had them on the bank when I went in for lunch. I saw Jack Loudon walking down the road, but didn't think anything of it. He's a Bay Area transplant, playing farmer. He had no idea what I was doing and didn't bother to ask. He just called the cops and told them I had a bunch of dead bodies on my property."

She parked the wheelbarrow beside a huge pile of shredded bark. This part of the lot, probably half of it, was her work area, separated from the rest of the property by a vine-covered fence. It held a big, deer-fenced vegetable garden, a work shed, a greenhouse, and a large shop, complete with a bathroom where she brushed herself off and washed up. "Where's Randy, Marcie? Why isn't he with you?"

"Um…he's starting a new job early tomorrow morning so he—"

"Couldn't come up for the weekend?" She studied my face, which always made me feel as though she could see straight through me. She had an uncanny way of knowing exactly what I was not saying.

She sighed, a slight little rise and fall of her chest. "He never could handle this sort of thing, and he did love his grandpa." She reached for my hand. "Well, come on. Let's get inside and see if we can find something cold to drink."

She unlatched the gate leading from the back work area into the rest of the yard. I stopped, drawing in my breath, staring at the profusion of yellow flowers climbing the wrought-iron boundary fence on my right. Next to them, boughs of white blossoms cascaded toward the ground.

"It looks like a bridal veil," I said, more to myself than to Grandma Edith.

She laughed. "That's what it's called. Bridal veil spirea. And the yellow is a Lady Banks rose."

"Your garden is always beautiful." She'd planted it so something was always in bloom from early spring until late fall, making her yard not only colorful and full of birds, butterflies, and tree squirrels, but ever-changing.

We'd reached the big brick-colored patio by then and she stopped to take off her gloves and kick off her shoes. "I've got to get the mess out here cleaned up. Dan's been neglecting it and I was kind of counting on Randy to help." She opened one of the double glass doors and led me into the kitchen.

"I can help with the patio or anything else you need, Grandma Edith. If it's okay with you, I plan to stay a few days."

She opened the refrigerator. "Of course you can, dear, and it's sweet of you to offer, but I wish Randy had come. We could use the muscle." She looked over her shoulder at me. "Bud or Corona?"

"Corona."

She pulled out a couple of bottles and turned to face me. "I know Randy hasn't been very steady, Marcie. He's too much like his dad and his grandpa. But he's getting better all the time, thanks to you. I'm so glad you married him. I rest a lot easier now, knowing you two are together."

So that nagging little voice had been right; there was something Randy hadn't told me. Grandma Edith thought we were still married and this was not the time to tell her about the divorce. Not so soon after Grandpa Dan's death. The least Randy could have done was to let me know. Maybe then I wouldn't feel like I should have taken better aim with that baseball bat. "I...I need to move my car," I stammered. "I'll be back in a minute."

I stepped out the front door and came to a halt. A police officer stood in the street, observing the Camaro. The car sat at an angle to the road, glaringly yellow in the late afternoon sunlight, its back tires protruding a least a yard into the street. The cop wasn't writing a ticket, so why was he examining my car? Surely it wouldn't have been reported as stolen. Not after one late payment. But, then, for all I knew, law enforcement might help locate cars for repossession. I should have checked for answers before I agreed to Randy's scheme.

The cop turned as I walked toward him. "Nice car."

"You think so? Are you looking to buy?"

His smile brightened his entire face, including the bluest eyes I'd ever seen, startling with his tanned skin. "Not really my color," he said.

"Mine, either, but it gets me where I'm going. Most of the time." I opened the driver's side door. "Sorry I left it like this. I'll get it out of the street."

"You were pretty rattled when you jumped out of it," he said. "I'm sorry about grabbing you the way I did. If I'd known..." His words trailed off as though he didn't quite know how to end the sentence. Rather than try, he said, "You're Edith Clifton's granddaughter, right?" It was more a conversation starter than a question.

I nodded but before I could explain that I was her ex-granddaughter, he continued. "I...well, I just wanted to tell you how sorry I was—we all were—to hear about your grandfather and to ask how Mrs. Clifton is doing." He held out his hand. "I'm Eric Roberts, by the way. We're a fairly small community, and we try to look out for each other, so if there's anything we can do, just ask."

"Marcie Clifton." I shook his hand. "And Grandma Edith is doing fine, from what I can see. She's always been a strong woman."

He released my hand. "If you feel up to it, I'd like to ask a few questions, maybe clear up some things."

"About the pantyhose?"

He grinned, putting crinkles at the corners of those blue eyes. "No. I think that's pretty clear." His expression sobered, the grin slipping away. "It's just...well, we've never had a hit-and-run in Miner's Ridge. At least not since I've been here. We're a small town...not much traffic, especially late at night."

A movement to my left caught my attention. Grandma Edith's neighbor, the Bay Area transplant, was again standing across the street, watching us.

Roberts, probably sensing he'd lost my attention, followed my glance. "Who's the guy?"

"From what I gather, the proverbial nosy neighbor and possibly one of your best informants."

"You think he's waiting for us to start moving bodies?"

I almost laughed, trying to picture the expression on the neighbor's face if we started hurling "bodies" at him.

Roberts nodded toward Grandma Edith's front porch. "Let's find a better place to talk."

"Okay, but I need to move my car."

I parked the Camaro on one side of Grandma Edith's driveway and grabbed my overnight bag. Roberts met me at the bottom of the steps. We walked up together and settled into red-cushioned white wicker chairs. He took off his service cap and set it on the table, revealing sun-bleached dark-brown hair, closely cut. This guy spent a lot of time outside, not all of it in uniform. He looked fit and trim, maybe in his early to mid-thirties.

I turned to face him. "You were saying hit-and-run is unusual in a town with little traffic, especially late at night. How late are we talking about?"

"Six minutes after eleven when we got the call, so a few minutes before that. And the collision happened in a fairly well-lit area. Miner's Ridge has only one stoplight, and that's where Mr. Clifton was crossing."

"So somebody saw what happened. Couldn't they describe the car?"

"Not saw. Heard. The doctor from over at the clinic got called out of the late movie. He heard the crash but by the time he got to the scene, the car was gone. He did what he could for your grandfather while his wife called 9-1-1." Roberts shifted in the chair, making the wicker creak. "Do you know why your grandfather was in town Wednesday night? He wasn't one of the movie-goers. The restaurants were closed, and he hadn't been drinking, so it wasn't likely he'd been in one of the bars."

"I'm afraid I can't help you. I just got here—haven't even had a chance to talk to Grandma Edith about it."

"Talk to me about what?" Grandma Edith stood in the doorway, holding an open Corona. She handed it to me then turned to Roberts. "You want one?"

He shook his head. "No, ma'am. I'm on duty." He watched as I lifted the bottle to my lips and let the cool liquid trickle down my throat. "Maybe some cold water, if it's not too much trouble."

I put the Corona on the table. "Sit down, Grandma Edith. I'll get it while you talk to Officer Roberts."

I found several bottles of water chilling in the refrigerator and grabbed one. When I opened the door to the porch, Grandma Edith was asking, "Why are you shouting at me? Do you want the entire neighborhood in on this conversation? I may be old, but I'm not hard of hearing."

Visibly flustered, Roberts lowered his voice. "I'm sorry. I was asking about your husband's activities in the days before the accident, but I probably didn't make my questions clear enough."

"I understood your questions, Officer Roberts. What I'm having a problem grasping is your reason for asking them. What does any of this have to do with Dan's death?"

Roberts took the water from me, nodding his thanks. "Maybe nothing." But he was speaking to me, not Grandma Edith. "We have no description of the car that hit him, so haven't been able to ask for help from other jurisdictions. All we can do is keep an eye out for a vehicle that has recently sustained damage. Thus far, we've been unsuccessful, so we're trying to learn everything we can, hoping to get a lead on the car. There's not much going on in Miner's Ridge on a weeknight, so maybe your grandfather and the driver of that vehicle were either heading to or coming from the same place."

I tilted my beer bottle toward Grandma Edith, who was scowling at Roberts. "Then you'd better talk to her, not me, because I can't answer any of your questions. As I told you earlier, I just got here."

Grandma Edith studied his face, her eyes narrowed. "Is the back room at O'Malley's open on Wednesday nights?"

Roberts flushed. "What do you know about—"

"Oh, come on, Officer Roberts. Everybody in Miner's Ridge knows you look the other way when it comes to that card room. The same people have been playing poker there for fifty years, probably more, and they didn't stop just because the state suddenly decided it was illegal."

"Playing poker is illegal?" I asked. "I thought Grandpa Dan played all the time."

"He does...did," Grandma Edith said. "Quite a few people in Miner's Ridge play, or have played at one time or another. Just locals, having a little fun once or twice a week. After all, there's not much to do for entertainment. Then the Indian casinos came into the state and suddenly it was illegal to play anywhere else, other than licensed card rooms. And those licenses aren't easy to get. I think there are only seventy in the entire state. That equates to about one in every two thousand miles. Most are probably in southern California or the Bay Area, with some sprinkled along the Central Valley."

"I don't understand why they would do that—make it illegal."

"Tax money, Marcie. The state wasn't making anything off those friendly little poker games being played all over the state. Now, with everything regulated, they can tax the winnings, small as they may be. Do you know it's illegal in California to even place a bet on a pool game?"

I doubted Randy knew that. He tended to consider his winnings on pool games a secondary source of income. "But you said Grandpa Dan played poker all the time."

Grandma Edith glanced at Roberts, but he didn't say anything, so she explained. "It's not too likely we'll ever have anybody coming to a little place like Miner's Ridge to check on us but, to be on the safe side, O'Malley's switched things around. Card tables went in the back room with the door shut, pool tables in the front. Nobody but the regulars know what goes on in the back room."

"But the cops..."

"Look the other way," she said. "The chief and the mayor aren't stupid. They're not about to risk losing their jobs over shutting down that card room."

She turned her attention back to Roberts. "Is that it, Officer? Are you trying to find out from me whether my husband was in that back room Wednesday night because you were so busy looking the other way you don't know if there was a game?"

Red spots blossomed along his cheekbones as he reached for his cap. I noticed he was left-handed, with long, slender fingers, like an artist or a musician.

Grandma Edith put her hand over his. "I can tell you this. My husband's job as a private investigator often took him out of the house at night. I think he may have been working one of his cases, but I have no idea which one. He rarely talked to me about them."

Officer Roberts neither raised his voice nor slowed his speech when he asked Grandma Edith his next question. "What about his friends? Maybe he discussed it with some of them."

For a moment, I didn't think she'd heard him. She stared off into the distance, frowning, then took a drink from her beer before speaking. "I can ask Nate Riordan. We were close to him and his wife before she died. Other than that, I'm not sure I even know who Dan was spending time with lately."

She glanced at me, then continued. "I like to work in the yard, something my husband doesn't—didn't—enjoy. He took long walks around the neighborhood, more often than not by himself. He was too slow for me. I like to walk. He liked to stroll. Anyway, he was getting to know people I never met, other than three men he played poker with on a regular basis. They'd meet on Thursday nights, sometimes here, sometimes at one of their houses. I don't know if those games are still going on, but I doubt it. They haven't been here in a long time. Dan was also playing at O'Malley's, so he might have decided he liked the stakes there a little better. I can dig out the phone numbers and emails for those poker buddies if you like, but it may take a day or two."

Roberts rose to his feet, adjusting his service cap on his head. "I think that's all anybody can ask of you, Mrs. Clifton. Thanks for your cooperation. I'd like to express my condolences again..." His phone rang. He glanced at it, then raised it to his face as he turned toward the steps. "Yes, sir...Yes. I was just leaving..." He stood still, listening. "Oh, wow! When did...Yes, sir." He glanced our way, his eyes wide. "Okay...Yes, I can do that."

His voice grew fainter as he walked toward the steps. "It shouldn't take long. Mrs. Clifton and her granddaughter seem to..." He looked over his shoulder at us, lowered his voice, and hurried away.

"I wonder what that was all about?" I asked Grandma Edith.

"I don't know, but that young man knows more than he's telling us and, for the life of me, I can't figure out what that could be."

Chapter 4

Grandma Edith slapped at a mosquito that had landed on her arm. "Time to go inside."

While she picked up the beer bottles and I pushed the chairs back into place, I puzzled over Officer Roberts's questions and what connection the poker games might have to Grandpa Dan's death. If there was a connection. After all, this was a small-town police force. Even by Officer Roberts's admission, they'd had little experience investigating hit-and-run deaths.

"Is it true that Grandpa Dan never discussed his cases with you?" I asked as we walked back to the kitchen.

Grandma Edith dropped the bottles into the recycling bin. "Not for a long time now. He used to, but I guess I lost interest somewhere along the way. When he first started the business, I thought he was just bored and looking for something to do after retirement. But nothing was ever that simple with Dan. I think he had dreams of some big case that would make him rich or famous, or at least provide some excitement in his life. All I saw was nickel-and-dime stuff—mostly nickels. Following a husband or wife suspected of cheating, somebody faking a disability, or petty theft cases. It all seemed pretty tedious to me, and I don't think he was making any money. I was a little surprised he stuck with it, that he didn't lose interest. I suspect that's why the penny-ante poker games stopped. Not enough excitement."

She might have been describing Randy; I could envision him getting caught up in the same things. He, like his grandfather, craved excitement and was always looking for the next get-rich-quick scheme.

Grandma Edith pulled a couple of plates out of the cabinet. "It's been a long day and I have a lot to do tomorrow. What do you say we have an early dinner and turn in? You must be tired after your drive up here."

The drive wasn't that long. I would have preferred learning more about Grandpa Dan, but I didn't want to stir up any painful memories. Besides, I was looking forward to one of her home-cooked meals.

She opened the refrigerator and stared inside. "I should have asked that young officer to come in and eat while we talked. I don't know what I'm going to do with all this food. The neighbors keep bringing it in faster than I can eat it and I'm running out of freezer space. Would you prefer a tuna casserole, baked mac and cheese, shepherd's pie, or whatever this is?" She pulled out a bowl, took foil off the top, and gave it a sniff test. "God only knows, but I wouldn't recommend it. If I didn't know better, I'd suspect Alma Reitman brought it over. She can make anything taste like four-day-old leftovers."

"How do you know she didn't bring it?"

"Her baking dishes are CorningWare, with a design on the side—yellow and orange flowers." Grandma Edith laughed. "Nate says it's the neighborhood skull and crossbones symbol."

I'd met Nate Riordan several times, so I knew he lived next door. From what Randy and his sisters told me, the Riordans had been Grandma Edith's neighbors for almost fifteen years, ever since Randy's grandparents had bought their lot. Nate and his wife, Sheila, transplants from Arizona, had moved into their house a few months earlier.

The two couples had become close friends, sharing dinners and frequent rounds of bridge at one house or another until Sheila's death three years ago from pancreatic cancer. During those last months, when Grandma Edith had spent most of every day at the Riordan house, doing what she could to help, the love she and Nate had shared for Sheila had cemented their relationship into an enduring bond. Nate was one person Grandma Edith could always count on.

She dumped the bowl's contents into the garbage disposal and turned her attention back to the refrigerator. "How about a spoonful of each casserole so we can figure out which ones are best?"

"That'll work." So much for those wonderful home-cooked meals I'd been looking forward to. I wondered how long I'd fit into my jeans on a diet of mac and cheese and tuna casseroles. Not to mention all the pies, cakes, and cookies that lined the kitchen counter.

The thought of my clothes reminded me that I'd left my suitcase on the porch. "I'll be back in a minute." I hurried to retrieve it.

"Jack Loudon is finally gone," I told her when I came back in. "I was beginning to think he was going to watch the house all night, waiting for something else to happen."

"He probably went up on the bank to look at those bodies after we came inside." She was dishing spoonfuls of food onto our plates. "No, come to think about it, he wouldn't do that. He's too lazy to climb up that slope."

"You don't like him. Is it because he comes from the Bay Area?"

"Good heavens, no. We have lots of people coming here from there and most of them are nice, friendly people just looking for a good place to retire. I simply don't like stupid, lazy people and Jack Loudon is both. He won't put down bark. It's too much work. So he has tall weeds growing up all over those two acres, creating a fire hazard for all of us, and blowing seeds into our yards. Even when he gets out the weed eater, he does it in fits and spurts, never getting all of it cut."

She pulled a food-filled plate out of the microwave, set it on the table, and added flatware while she waited for the second plate to heat. "Everybody on this end of the street knew I was putting down fresh bark. Several of them offered to help. So Jack knew what I was doing and he couldn't miss that wheelbarrow in the driveway. But rather than ask questions, he called the cops and stirred up a lot of problems for everybody."

She folded paper napkins and put them beside the flatware. "A lot of the people who move up here, especially on big lots like ours, are interested in starting vegetable gardens, maybe planting a few fruit trees, and raising chickens. They've never done any of that before, so they ask questions. Not Jack." Her hands stilled and she let out a low chuckle. "That is, not until the one time I wished he hadn't asked for advice. Somebody told him the chickens would lay better if he had a rooster."

"Is that true?"

"I've never raised chickens, but I've heard that's true. Anyway, that rooster was almost as dumb as Jack, which is not easy, even for something as lame-brained as a rooster. It crowed every time a light came on. If we had to get up in the middle of the night, we fumbled around in the dark, afraid to turn on a light. It got so bad everybody turned off their headlights when they came down the street, trying to keep that rooster from waking up the entire neighborhood."

I laughed, sure she was exaggerating. "Does he still have the rooster?"

"No. He either realized his mistake and very quietly found somebody who needed a rooster or..."

"Or?"

She shrugged. "Who knows. Chicken pot pie? But you won't have to worry about a rooster waking you up in the middle of the night. And if you're up to it in the morning and have some work clothes, I could use your help getting the rest of that bark down. It shouldn't take more than a few hours with both of us working. That'll give me time to finish up with the memorial service arrangements. And then I suppose I can dig into Dan's records and see what I can find for Officer Roberts."

We said goodnight and headed for our bedrooms, at opposite ends of the house.

Thanks to Randy trying to climb into my window, I'd had little sleep the night before. Despite that, even after a hot shower, I couldn't relax in the unfamiliar bed. My thoughts drifted from Randy and what might be going on at my house in Galt, to Grandpa Dan, wondering what he'd been doing on that street late at night, and finally to Officer Eric Roberts and his questions.

Sometime in that maze, my brain apparently admitted defeat and shut down, lacking the energy to even shift to dreams.

I awoke to an ominous crack of thunder, followed by a flash of lightning. Rain beat against the windows. I wondered what it was doing to the bank where Grandma Edith had been working, but nothing could be done about it. We wouldn't be working out there today.

Grandma Edith had coffee ready when I walked into the kitchen. "Change of plan," she said, motioning her cup toward the rain-streaked window. "We'll go into town instead. James Gallagher called from the mortuary. He says he has to see me. I don't know why we couldn't take care of it over the phone, especially on a day like this. Natalie already helped me pick out the urn, leaflets, flowers, and music, so I can't imagine what else he might need. But he says I have to come in."

When we stepped onto the porch, a gust of wind hit me. Rain pounded on the roof and came down the sides in almost solid sheets. Grandma Edith handed me a couple of umbrellas, then locked the door. She looked up at the sky and paused before we walked down the steps. "I hope this lets up. I've seen April storms where the ground gets so saturated, the water collects in big puddles. From the sound of that wind, we'd better pray it doesn't uproot any trees."

She spoke little as she drove her white Malibu the few miles to Miner's Ridge, a community of about thirteen hundred people. I could remember being there only once, with Randy, and then only for a quick trip to pick up something for Grandma Edith. As we drove down the main street, I spotted the police station, a movie theater, a newspaper office, a red-brick post office, and a bank. I motioned toward the buildings. "Looks like you have one of everything."

Grandma Edith looked puzzled for a minute, then smiled. "Oh, no. We have two grocery stores, two bars, two restaurants if you count the coffee shop, and probably a half-dozen churches. There's even a little department store and a drug store with an old-fashioned ice cream counter. Everything we need. Oh, and there's a super Walmart."

"Really, in a town this small?"

"Hey, it's an unwritten rule in this country. You have to have a Walmart and a golden arches every fifteen or twenty miles. But the Walmart is actually out on the highway, not in town."

She parked the Malibu in front of a low white-stucco building. "This is it. You can wait for me in the car if you want." She leaned over the center console to get one of the umbrellas I'd stored by my feet.

I really didn't want to go inside, but I unfastened my seat belt. After all, I was here to give her some support.

She was out of the car, moving toward the building at a fast clip by the time I got my umbrella open, no easy task with the wind threatening to snatch it from my grasp. Ducking my head against the wind-driven rain, I made a dash for the double doors just as she opened them.

I followed her into the foyer, a little unnerved by the silence. Then I stopped, drawing in the cloying, too-heavy scent of flowers. Or maybe air freshener to camouflage less welcome smells.

Grandma Edith hesitated, then squared her shoulders and walked into the empty reception area. I followed. Everything in the room was understated: beige walls, light brown carpet, walnut chairs and reception desk. Even the floral arrangement on a side table held muted colors: white, pale pink, light yellow. No red or orange to add a splash of color.

"Mrs. Clifton?" An impeccably dressed man in a dark suit—I assumed the funeral director—came from an inner office. He turned and gestured toward a pedestal draped in a silky taupe fabric. Displayed on it was a slender, bronze-toned Grecian urn. "It's ready. I think your husband would have liked that classical design."

Grandma Edith raised her eyebrows. "There was really no need to bring me out in the middle of a storm for this elaborate display. I know what the urn looks like. After all, I picked it out..." She put a hand over her heart. I suspected she realized then what he was trying to tell her, in a round-about way. The cremation had already taken place. Grandpa Dan's ashes were now in that urn.

She walked toward it while I tried not to think about the cremation process. Instead, I dredged up every memory I had of Grandpa Dan's smile, his laugh, his life-of-the-party stories and jokes.

The funeral director's words and expression—even his stance—intruded, pushing aside my memories. I watched him, wondering if he practiced in front of a mirror. Did funeral directors attend classes, their final presentation a formal, black-suited demonstration, proof that they'd nailed the look—pleasure at the urn's design, tinged with sympathy for the loss? Did everybody applaud when they finished and bowed to their classmates? Was that a requirement for graduation?

A giggle bubbled its way up through the tightness in my chest. I clamped my lips shut, wondering if I lacked a compassion gene. Why was I having these inane thoughts when Grandma Edith was grieving for her husband?

She didn't look sad, though; she looked irritated. She opened her mouth but before she could speak, Gallagher cleared his throat and his expression changed to one not so well-practiced. "Um...uh, Mrs. Clifton..." He put a finger under his collar and pulled at it, pushing his bow tie askew. "There's a slight problem. It's undoubtedly a simple mistake, easily rectified, but...well, your check didn't clear the bank. It came back marked 'insufficient funds'. You understand, we can't let you take the urn until the check clears?"

Grandma Edith turned, her hand still on her chest. Her mouth opened, then closed. I stepped a little closer, afraid she might be having a heart attack, but she dropped the arm and raised her shoulders, drawing her spine into a straight line. "I have never had a bounced check in my life," she snapped. "The bank has obviously made a mistake. I'll take care of it."

I think she'd forgotten about me. She stormed out of the building so fast I had to run to catch up, stopping only long enough to pick up both umbrellas before I sprinted toward the car. She was sloshing back to the Malibu, skirting puddles, her shoes sinking into the spongy grass bordering the parking lot. The rain had let up but the dark undersides of the clouds promised more to come.

"It figures," she muttered, as I caught up with her. "First, Gallagher's card reader wouldn't accept my American Express card, now this." She opened the car door, then turned to look at me. "I'm sorry. I just can't deal with all the scripted sympathy, especially now. Why on earth—or any other planet—would Gallagher suggest that Dan knows or cares what kind of container holds his ashes? It wasn't something we ever talked about but, given a choice, he probably would have preferred a coffee can. Better yet, a beer can. A big one with a few dregs left in the bottom."

I couldn't help laughing. She smiled then and got into the driver's seat. "It's good to have you around, Marcie. Since Dan died, I've avoided people as much as I can. I know they mean well but I get tired of their pitying glances and clichéd condolences. You can't escape it in a small town like this, where everybody knows what happened, especially with it being Dan's hometown. He knew everybody."

She started the car and pulled out of the lot. "Dan used to tell me that, in Miner's Ridge, they know everything about you, your parents, your grandparents, and your great-grandparents, not to mention all the family offshoots. And if they don't know, they make it their business to find out."

"Or make up?"

She smiled again. "I suspect there's a lot of gossip. I always figured I had an advantage. I knew the stories of everybody in town, through Dan, but they didn't know anything about me, and I planned to keep it that way."

I didn't respond and, after a few moments of silence, she continued. "You know, remembering those stories, I think I might have figured out why my check bounced. We have a new bank manager, L.B. Corringer. Dan once told me that Lesley—that same L. B. Corringer—was so terrible at math, he almost flunked eighth grade. There was a final exam he had to pass and the girl in front of him was really smart. He leaned over her shoulder, trying to see her answers, but she thought he was trying to look down her shirt. She yelled 'pervert' and stabbed him in the thigh with her pencil."

"How did the teacher handle something like that?" I asked.

"Dan said she grabbed Lesley by an arm and marched him, limping on a leg probably forever branded by the punched-in pencil lead, to the principal's office. Lesley had a choice. If he admitted to cheating, he'd probably flunk math and have to repeat eighth grade. He decided it was safer to back up the girl's claim. Most of the boys in both seventh and eighth grade claimed they'd seen the girl's boobs, which had grown exponentially that year. Dan said he couldn't remember what happened to Lesley after that, other than a new nickname of Lead Butt."

The big clock over the Miner's Ridge Bank struck ten o'clock as we approached. I was trying to stop laughing at Grandma Edith's story as we pushed through the front door. She leaned toward me and whispered, "Apparently Lead Butt still isn't very good at math."

Once inside, I had to give her some privacy to straighten things out with the bank, so I settled into a seating area by the front windows while she found a teller.

The bank looked like it might be a century old. Its relative quiet and lack of color reminded me of the mortuary. Here, everything was dark and aged wood rather than beige walls and muted colors, but the effect was the same, stilling any inappropriate bursts of laughter or even raised voices.

Except Grandma Edith's, crisp and clear. "First of all, I am not your sweetie. Second, I did understand your explanation, but it didn't answer my question. You are not listening to me. I may be old, but I am not senile, and I was working on computers before you were potty-trained. They may not make mistakes, but the humans who program them or enter data do. Is there anybody here who can help me?"

The teller murmured something so low I couldn't hear, unlike Grandma Edith's response. "That's not possible unless you have powers I don't know about. Again, you are not listening to me. There is no way my husband can come in. He is dead. And James Gallagher is holding his ashes ransom until I get this...this banking fiasco fixed so I can pay him."

The teller looked from one side to the other, then out on the floor, to the desks. "Perhaps I can get somebody else—"

"How about Lead Bu...Lesley. Lesley Corringer. Where is he?"

"Oh, no. He's much too busy. You'd have to make an appointment. I'm sure somebody else..."

I didn't hear any more because Grandma Edith had turned and was making her way toward a row of offices at the end of the room. As I watched, mesmerized, she rapped on a door, opened it, and walked in.

Chapter 5

I watched the door Grandma Edith had gone through for a few minutes, half-expecting a security guard to rush into the room and escort her out. Nothing happened. The bank was quiet again—until my phone rang. It was my next-door neighbor, Lucinda Arnold, the mother of two teenage sons, telling me the cops had been at my house the night before to break up a party.

I couldn't speak for a minute, trying to wrap my mind around what she was saying. "A party?" I finally squeaked. "How bad?"

"Lots of loud music and revving engines. I was having a heck of a time trying to keep the boys away from there. I was glad I did when a scuffle broke out on the front lawn. Not bad enough for me to call the cops. But, then, I have teenagers, so I probably didn't take it as seriously as some of the neighbors. I think old Mr. Landrith must have reported it. He was out in his yard, yelling that they were smashing his shrubs."

Randy! He couldn't wait even a day after I left to throw a bash. And those cops were my co-workers, the last people I wanted nosing into my private life. I shouldn't have let him stay. I knew better, knew he'd screw up.

I had my finger poised on his number, ready to call, when I realized he'd be at work. It was his first day, and I needed him to keep that job. Better wait until this evening. Then I'd tell him to pack up his stuff and get out.

My friend Becky, the dispatcher at Galt PD could fill me in on the call-out, tell me how bad it was, but I hesitated. I hadn't wanted anybody at the department to know about my home life, such as it was. Then I shrugged. The chickens were already out of the coop on this one. I glanced at the time. Becky would be off shift now.

"The call came in about one a.m.," she said. "I dispatched a car with two officers. Just a party out of control. Nothing to worry about. But I didn't know you and Randy were back together."

"We're not. It's just...who was in the patrol car you sent out?"

"Grimwell and Hoskins."

"Oh, Lord." Anybody but them, the two worst gossips in the department. "Did they make any arrests?" If it weren't for Randy's new job, I halfway hoped she'd say yes. It would serve Randy right if he had to spend a few days in a jail cell.

"No, just orders to shut it down, along with a warning."

"Let me know if any more calls come in, okay?"

"Will do."

"I suppose the entire squad room is talking about it today."

She laughed. "Only because they don't have anything better to gossip about. I'm getting a call I need to take, Marcie. Gotta go."

Only then did I notice the man sitting in one of the chairs near me. Eric Roberts. How long had he been there? How much had he heard?

Before I could say anything, he'd swivelled his head to watch Grandma Edith come barreling across the room, her lips clamped into a thin line. She rushed past us, out the door.

I grabbed my purse and ran to catch up. "Grandma Edith!" I grabbed her arm. "What's wrong?"

She shook her head. "I'm broke, Marcie. He cleaned me out."

"What? Who?" I guided her toward the car.

"Dan. The checking account is overdrawn. The savings is empty, since I dumped what was left of it into the checking account to cover bills. And the money market—it had almost fifty thousand dollars in it, money it took years to save. Now it's just gone ...disappeared, and the bank doesn't know what he did with it."

I couldn't think of anything to say. Maybe because Randy had put me in that same boat not so long ago. Not for as much money, but the end result was the same.

She was still raging as she drove us back to the mortuary. "What the hell was he doing? Another one of his get-rich-quick schemes? One he couldn't tell me about until after the money started rolling in because I'd put a damper on it? Now I'm left with bills I can't pay, a lot of unexpected expenses, and...blast it!" She pounded the steering wheel and the horn blared. The guy ahead of us rolled down his window and stuck his middle finger in the air.

Ignoring him, Grandma Edith pulled into the mortuary parking lot. "Sorry about that. I just remembered there's something else I can't pay for—the trip to Ireland my sister and I were planning. And I'm pretty sure Cynthia has already booked it." Grandma Edith stared at the door of the mortuary. "Maybe we should just drive away, let Gallagher have the ashes. I don't want them. Not now. I could get out of this town, maybe go back to Sacramento, or to Galt, close to you and Randy."

While I was still trying to process that, especially the 'me and Randy' part, she let out a huge sigh. "But that would take money, something I apparently no longer have."

She got out of the car and I followed her back into the mortuary. James Gallagher looked up from the reception desk and started to rise as we entered the room.

"You'll have to cancel the memorial service," Grandma Edith told him. "I don't have enough money to pay for it."

"But we have a contract. You signed—"

"Before I knew my dearly departed husband took my money with him. You can sue me if you want, Gallagher, but I'm broke. All you'll get for your trouble is attorney fees while I'm filing for bankruptcy."

"But the cremation. You have to pay for that, at least. And the urn." He turned and pointed at it, still displayed on the pedestal.

"I'll write a new check to cover the cremation, but I can't afford the urn. Put the ashes in something less expensive."

He drew himself into a more erect stance, like a marionette obeying a puppet master. "A cheaper urn? I don't have any. We carry only the highest quality products."

I suspected he bought them in bulk from China at a discount. Grandma Edith's thoughts might have been running along those same lines because she shook her head. "You must have some kind of containers around here."

"But you've used this one. It's—I can't sell it to anybody else."

"Of course, you can. Just wash it and polish it up. Nobody will know the difference. Whoever winds up inside it certainly won't care. You probably do it all the time."

He drew his shoulders back even farther and lifted his chin. "I most certainly do not. And I have nothing you can use as a container. You chose this urn and I expect you to pay for it. There's no other way you can take the ashes."

I half expected Grandma Edith to turn and walk out; she'd already told me she didn't want the ashes. Instead, she looked around the room until she spotted a potato chip bag in the wastebasket beside Gallagher's desk. She grabbed it, strode to the pedestal and, lifting the urn, screwed off the lid.

"You...you can't do that!" Gallagher screeched as he took a step toward her. "It's...it's disrespectful to the deceased."

"Really? Well, I'm showing the deceased about as much respect as he showed me when he cleaned out our bank accounts." She lifted the plastic bag of ashes from the urn, dropped it into the potato chip bag, and folded the top down. "I'll send you a check to cover the cremation." She grasped the top of the potato chip bag and stalked out of the building. By the time I caught up, she was almost to the car.

She didn't say anything as we started home through the storm-lashed landscape. I'd been in her shoes—in fact, still was—so I knew her mind would be darting from one expense to another, trying to decide which bills she had to pay, at least in part, whether any could be delayed, and what she could strike out of her budget. Like clothing. Or gas. Or food. An instant weight-loss plan.

Either I was mistaken or she'd thought of a solution I'd never found because she surprised me by smiling. "I just realized that Dan wouldn't have considered what I did disrespectful. He would have thought it was funny, probably reminding me that he liked potato chips and asked whether they were plain or barbecue. He would have preferred barbecue."

She let out a soft sigh. "I wish I could say as much for the town gossips. Emma Kowloski and Jane Portman will be buzzing like flies around molasses when the word gets out. I can just imagine one of those old biddies' shocked expressions." Grandma Edith pitched her voice a notch or two higher. "A potato chip bag? Mercy sakes alive, what is the world coming to? Did you ever hear of such goings on? And what kind of woman would do such a thing? Certainly nobody from Miner's Ridge. We teach our children to respect the dead."

"Right," I said, smiling at her portrayal. "That's why teenagers use the cemetery to make out at night."

Grandma Edith gave me an approving glance. "You know, now that I think about it, James Gallagher isn't likely to tell anybody what happened. People might start wondering if he really did charge too much for his services, if he did re-use urns."

"If he did buy them in bulk from China," I said. "Maybe they'd even wonder whether he was unwilling to work with a grieving widow in financial distress."

We were both smiling by the time she stopped at the cluster mailbox and pulled out what appeared to be several days' mail. She also had a couple of boxes in one of the lockers.

"Probably stuff I ordered for the memorial service." She dumped all of it into the back seat and drove on to the house.

The garbage can was in the middle of the driveway, probably dropped there after pick up. I opened my door. "I'll get it."

By the time I'd pulled it even with the porch, Grandma Edith had put the mail and boxes down beside a couple of other parcels delivered while we were gone, and was unlocking the front door.

As I was putting the garbage can away, I noticed a branch had snapped off one of the rose bushes, probably during the storm. Grandma Edith wouldn't be happy.

I went around to the back and tapped on the patio door. Grandma Edith came to unlock it, sifting through her mail.

"More bills," she muttered, then nodded toward the boxes on the counter. "And stuff from Amazon for the memorial service I can no longer afford. I'll have to send them back."

"Print out return labels, and I'll get them ready to mail," I said. "And, Grandma Edith, a branch is broken on your yellow rose bush."

She sighed and set the mail on the counter beside the boxes. "It's always my favorites that get the wind damage. I'll see what I can do with it later. Right now, I've got to call the newspaper and change the obituary so it says the memorial service is private."

I didn't ask what she meant by that, what she was planning. I suspected she didn't know, that she was just stalling until she could figure something out.

My stomach growled. I looked in the refrigerator, wishing we had stopped in Miner's Ridge for a hamburger. Not that I could afford a meal out, even fast food. Apparently, neither could Grandma Edith. I needed to be more appreciative of the neighbors' offerings. I studied the casseroles for a minute, then closed the refrigerator door and took a look at the apple pie. Adding a glass of milk would give me dairy, fruit, and carbs. Good enough. I started to cut a slice.

Somebody rapped on the door and Grandma Edith went to answer it. Nate Riordan stepped inside. "I thought you'd like to know Cleve's dog is running loose. It took off with your potato chips."

"My potato—oh, crap! I must have left it on the porch." Shoving Nate aside, Grandma Edith ran out the door, yelling at the dog. "Buster, bring that back. Right now!"

The Labrador Retriever hesitated, looked back at her, and decided she wanted to play. He took off again, in a wide circle around her front yard. She ran after him, yelling, threatening. He stopped then and sat still, watching her.

"Good dog. Good Buster." She approached him slowly, holding out her hand. "Let me have the bag, Buster. Nice dog."

He wagged his tail and ran.

I slipped out the door and worked my way around the dog, thinking I might be able to catch him while he was running from Grandma Edith, or at least herd him back toward her. It didn't work; I could swear he loved my entry into the game. He ran past me, just out of reach, and circled back toward Grandma Edith, careful not to get too near. Every time he got close enough, I tried to get a better look at the bag, to see how much damage his teeth were doing. The fold at the top was working loose on one side. How long before the bag ripped apart? Or Buster decided to take it someplace else, maybe find a different playmate?

Grandma Edith turned and yelled at Nate. "There's a piece of ham in the refrigerator. Grab it."

"You're trading ham for half a bag of potato chips?"

"Just do it," she screamed.

He held up his hands. "Okay. Okay, I'm going."

The ham worked. Buster dropped the bag and headed for Nate's outstretched hand. Grandma Edith ran for the bag, which had trailed a thin stream of gray ash over the still-damp lawn. She clamped the bag shut and shuffled her shoes on the grass as Nate came toward her, laughing. "That was fun, but those must be darned good potato chips. I'd have let the mutt have them."

"It's not potato chips. It's...it's other stuff I put in the bag so I could carry all of it inside. Things I bought at the drug store. Personal things."

I don't know what Nate was thinking, but I was wondering why I hadn't seen that piece of ham when I looked in the refrigerator. He raised his eyebrows, then grinned at me. "Nice to see you again, Marcie. How are you doing? Is Randy here?" He wrapped me in his arms for a quick hug.

While I was explaining to Nate about Randy's new job, Grandma Edith escaped into the house. When Nate and I got inside, she was in the kitchen; I could hear a door close, too big to be a cabinet. Probably the pantry.

She turned with a smile when we joined her. "Want some coffee, Nate? Something to take the chill off?"

"Sure." Nate's eyes, almost the color of the storm clouds, were soft when he looked at her. "Are you okay, Edie? I know today had to be tough, trying to make all the arrangements for Dan." He shrugged wide shoulders out of his denim jacket. Even without his cowboy boots, he would have towered at least six inches over her five-foot-nine frame.

"Tougher than you can imagine." She started the coffee brewing and pulled mugs from the cupboard. "I'm almost broke, Nate. Cleaned out." A clap of thunder punctuated the last two words, as though speaking them had unleashed the fury—and perhaps the tinge of fear—building within her eyes.

He leaned against the counter, his ankles crossed. A frown creased his sun-bronzed and weathered forehead, deepening as Grandma Edith told him about our day. "That can't be right, Edie. Dan wouldn't leave you high and dry." But I thought I detected a tentative note in his deep voice, as though he were considering the possibility. "He was still playing poker, wasn't he?"

"At O'Malley's, probably, but not with his poker buddies unless they were meeting somewhere else. I haven't seen any of those guys for at least six months. Why do you ask?"

He brushed a hand through his dark hair. "I don't know. Grasping at straws, I guess, trying to think of anything Dan might have spent money on, and he did love poker."

"Nate, those were all friendly games. There's no way he could have lost that much..." Her eyes widened. "You're thinking he might have found a card room with some high-stakes poker?"

"Hell, Edie, I don't know. I was just...Look, if you need a little help to get over some rough spots, I can probably come up with a little money."

She filled coffee mugs and handed one to Nate. I picked up the other two and carried them to the table. She sat down beside me. "Thanks, Nate, but I'm going to be fine." She motioned to the counter beside him. "I have plenty of food, with more in the freezer. I'm going to plant a big garden this year. Maybe a winter one, too, and freeze the produce. Or do some canning. I'll even get some chickens. You can do a lot with eggs." The pitch of her voice escalated. "Boil them, scramble them, fry them, devil them, make omelets, soufflés, egg salad sandwiches. I could raise fryers, too, and baking hens, and—"

"Grandma Edith, could you really kill a chicken?" I asked, knowing I couldn't. But Grandma Edith was a lot tougher than me.

She shook her head, a smile starting to form. "I'm too chicken." The smile broke into a laugh. "Maybe I'll become a vegetarian."

At the mention of all that food, especially the fryers, I thought about that apple pie again and my stomach rumbled loud enough for Grandma Edith to hear. Neither of us had eaten since breakfast. She glanced at the desserts lined up on the counter, then at Nate. "You want some lunch? Or a piece of pie? Or cookies? We've got a pretty wide selection."

He carried his coffee mug to the sink. "No, thanks. I just came by to see how you're doing, and ask if you need any help." He turned and grinned at us. "And to let you know, in case you haven't heard. Buster isn't the only animal running loose. If you find tame turkeys in your yard, they belong to the Loudons."

"He's raising turkeys now? Why? What on earth does he plan to do with them?"

Nate shrugged. "You'll have to ask him. I don't have a clue. Word is, he fenced off a back section of his lot so they'd be free-range, but the storm brought down part of the fence. So now the turkeys are free-ranging and pooping all over the neighborhood. And, believe me, they leave a ton of it, so be careful where you step."

He pushed away from the sink. "I'd better get going." He bent and gave her cheek a light kiss. "Take care, and call me if there's anything I can do."

"Thanks, Nate. I'll hold you to that."

After he left, we changed into dry clothes, spooned up some more casserole and zapped it, then sat down to eat and plan the rest of the day.

"First things first," Grandma Edith said. "I've got to call Cynthia and see if she can cancel that trip to Ireland. Then we've got to figure out what to do about the memorial service. Once I've got all that nailed down, maybe I'll have time to go through the bank records and see what's going on."

I wandered outside while she called her sister, thinking I might get some exercise to work off the calorie-laden lunch. The storm had moved on, leaving a freshly-washed garden. Butterflies and hummingbirds worked the flower beds while a couple of squirrels scampered down a big oak and up the birdbath. Too bad the patio was such a mess. Dirty plastic chairs, looking as though they hadn't been used in years, were stacked at one end. Leaning on them were shovels and rakes. Every surface, except one small bistro table and its two chairs, was covered: gardening gloves, plant stakes, spray bottles, hand spades, weed diggers—even the parts to something that looked like it might be a sprinkler system.

Grandma Edith came out the door. "Cynthia is going to call the travel agent, but she doesn't think the 'death in the family' escape clause is going to work, since the trip isn't scheduled until late June. I don't suppose you'd like a trip to Ireland? Maybe Randy could go with you. Cynthia says she could sell you our tickets so the two of you could share a room, and she could buy another."

Chapter 6

The closest I was ever going to get to Ireland was my ex-husband's blarney and it wasn't worth enough to get me to the airport. "Grandma Edith, that wouldn't be practical. You see, Randy—"

"Oh," she said, "I forgot. He just started that new job. He won't have any vacation time for a while. And you...you're wasting yours helping me. You're a sweet girl, Marcie. I'm so glad you're my granddaughter."

"Me, too, Grandma Edith." What else could I say? I figured she had enough to worry about already. Either that, or I just couldn't handle her disappointment when she found out about the divorce. Maybe, knowing Randy, that's why he hadn't told her.

"I was just thinking," I said. "Why can't you have the memorial service out here? I've seen that done before. Your yard is big enough, and it's really beautiful."

She looked at the cluttered patio, frowning. "It would take a lot of work."

"Nate said he'd help, and you have plenty of food in the freezer."

Maybe it was the mention of those casseroles and a way to get rid of them that convinced her. She motioned toward the stack of plastic chairs. "We've got all those, and I can round up some more. Maybe borrow a few tables for the food. I'll call Nate and Cynthia and see how much help I can expect."

She went inside and I headed for the back work area. She had plenty of space in the outbuildings to store the junk from the patio if I could just figure out how she had it organized. I dumped the bark from the wheelbarrow and pushed it to the patio. I'd almost filled it when Nate came around the side of the house and joined me. Without saying a word, he grabbed the wheelbarrow and pushed it toward the back gate. I followed him.

"Just dump it," I said when we were on the other side. "I'll stow all of it away while you go back for another load."

We'd been working for several hours when he came out with a couple of cold beers nestled among the wheelbarrow's contents. "Time for a break." He turned over two large plastic buckets and lowered himself onto one.

"I'm worried about your grandma," he said. "She's too proud to ask for help, even if she needs it, and I'm wondering if you could keep an eye on things...let me know how she's doing."

I wasn't sure that was a good idea. For one thing, she'd be furious if she found out. For another, it wasn't any of Nate's—or anybody else's—business, unless she chose to tell them. "Nate, I'm only going to be here for a few days." But I knew he was right; Grandma Edith would starve to death before accepting charity.

"Yeah, you're right." He took a long pull from the beer bottle.

"Do you really think Grandpa Dan could have lost all that money playing poker?" I asked. "I mean, he played so much, I thought he was pretty good."

"Pretty good doesn't cut it when you get into some of those high-stakes games where you're playing against pros." He took another drink of his beer. "And, when it came right down to it, your grandma was a better player than your grandpa."

"You're kidding. I never knew she even played."

"She didn't until he taught her. I remember one night at their house. We had a pretty good bunch, maybe eight people around the table, just neighbors having fun on a Saturday night. It was all draw poker back in those days, or lowball, none of that Texas hold 'em stuff. She kept two cards, so we figured she had a pair—just didn't know how high. After the draw, she kept studying her hand, frowning, and I figured she wasn't sure how good it was. But she kept matching everybody's bets, sometimes raising. I thought maybe she'd hit three of a kind and could be over-betting her hand, but when she laid down her cards she had four. Maybe sevens or eights, I can't remember. Your grandpa shook his head, kind of disgusted like, and told her that anytime she had four of a kind, she should be raising the bets more. I couldn't help laughing when I looked at her stack of chips. I think she had most of his by that time. She hadn't been puzzled at all. She knew exactly what she was doing, keeping everybody in the pot for so long, drawing in all their chips."

"But I thought she didn't play in his poker games."

"Not the ones with his buddies. I don't think she ever wanted to. That was a guy thing. The Saturday nights with neighbors were different, and there was a club your grandparents used to go to. We went with them a few times. Instead of pool tables, it had a couple of poker tables. Friendly games with the locals, but more serious than those penny-ante games at home. Your grandma enjoyed those."

He laughed. "I just remembered. One night, your grandpa wanted to go play poker. This was some years back when money was a little tighter, and they really couldn't afford to play. He decided they'd go anyway, saying the dealer would buy him in, so we all went."

"Buy him in? You mean play for the house? A shill, or whatever you call it?"

"No. Sometimes the dealer would give a good player enough chips to get into the game. If the player lost, it was no big deal."

"Then, why would the dealer do that?"

"I was never much of a poker player, so I'm not sure just how it worked, but I think the dealer got a small percentage of whatever the player won. I could be wrong about that, but you can believe they had a good chance of coming out ahead with a good player or they wouldn't have bought them in."

"Okay. So did they buy Grandpa Dan in? What about Grandma Edith, then? Did she have to just sit and watch?"

Nate laughed again. "Not hardly. The dealer asked them if they were going to play. Dan said they really couldn't afford it that night. The dealer said, 'I'll buy Edith in.'"

I almost choked on my beer, imagining Grandpa Dan's reaction. "So Grandpa Dan had to sit and watch her play. I'll bet that didn't make him happy."

"No, it didn't. More than anything, I think it hurt your grandpa's pride that the dealer thought your grandma was the better player. Of course, after she won a few hands, she gave him enough to get in the game, too."

Nate stood and grabbed the wheelbarrow handles. "Just don't ever get in a poker game with her unless you're planning on losing some money. Come to think of it, don't get in a pool game with her, either. Your grandpa gave up trying to teach her when she couldn't learn bank shots. So she found a pool table at a bowling alley and taught herself. She never could do much with bank shots, but she didn't need to. She was the best cut-shooter I ever saw. If she could see even an edge of a ball, she could slice it into a pocket without scratching." He shook his head, laughing, and pushed the wheelbarrow through the gate.

I wasn't sure I understood exactly what he was telling me, but decided right then that, once we were past the memorial service, I was going to take Grandma Edith out and have her start giving me lessons. I'd love to beat Randy at his favorite game.

We finally got everything moved off the patio and, while I was putting away the last loads, Nate got long-handled brushes from the shed and started cleaning the cement. By the time we finished that, along with washing down the chairs and tables we hadn't moved, it was a little after seven-thirty and the sun was sinking below the trees along the back fence. I turned the water off and was coiling the hose when Grandma Edith came out.

"It looks great," she said. "I think this is going to work out fine. I just talked to Cynthia and Natalie. They're going to help get word out to the family that we're having the service here. I'd forgotten that Joyce and Susan—I don't think you ever met Cynthia's daughters, Marcie—anyway, they run a catering service, so they can bring some food warmers and punch bowls. Cynthia says Robbie, Joyce's boy, has one of those machines with a microphone he uses with his band. Oh, and Cynthia is bringing over some poster boards so we can set up a photo display."

Nate offered to let the neighbors know and said he would ask them to bring some chairs. Grandma Edith tried to talk him into staying for dinner, but I suspect he'd had a glimpse of the casseroles when he got our beer out of the refrigerator. I couldn't blame him for leaving; I just wished I could go with him. Whatever he was planning to eat, I'd lay odds it wasn't a casserole.

He was almost at the door when Grandma Edith asked, "Nate, did you happen to notice anybody coming around my place while Marcie and I were gone this morning?"

He turned toward her, a frown forming between his eyes. "Not that I saw. Why? Is something wrong?"

"Yes. Somebody's been in the house. They tried to pry a drawer open on Dan's desk."

"Maybe I'd better take a look," Nate said.

I followed them to Grandpa Dan's office, a few steps across a short hall from my room. Nate knelt and ran his fingers over the desk drawers. "Looks fresh, all right. No furniture polish in the scratch." He straightened, a smile quirking his lip. "But, then, I don't know how often you polish furniture."

She slapped at his arm. "I'm serious, Nate. That scratch wasn't there yesterday when Natalie left. I cleaned up this room after the kids slept in here, and I would have noticed."

"What time did she leave?" Nate asked.

"Around eleven. Then I worked out in the yard spreading bark until Marcie got here."

"Could somebody have sneaked in then?" I asked, "while you were out back, loading the wheelbarrow?"

She gave her head a slight shake. "Believe me. I've been thinking about this ever since I found that scratch, and I can't see any way. The front door was locked. I suppose somebody could have come through the side gate, but he'd take a big chance of me seeing him on the patio before he could get inside....unless I happened to be on the bank right then." She shook her head again, more emphatically this time. "No, I was back and forth all the time, loading and unloading the wheelbarrow. I would have seen him. Whoever it was, he came in while we were in town today. What I can't figure out is why? I've never known Dan to lock that desk. There's nothing in there that anybody would want."

"Unless it has something to do with the money that's missing," Nate said. "Do you have any idea what Dan kept in there?"

"Just the normal household records, along with some office supplies. Other than that, I don't know, and I can't find the key."

Nate's eyebrows shot up. "You don't have Dan's keys?"

"I do. I just can't find them. They gave them to me at the hospital, but I can't remember what I did with them."

"Grandma Edith," I said, "the back door was locked, too. Remember? You had to let me in after I pulled the garbage can around back." Then I thought about something else: the broken rose branch. Was it under that window? I walked across the room and knelt to examine the latch. "This window isn't locked."

Grandma Edith shook her head. "It has to be. I make sure all of them are latched when I close them in the fall, and I haven't opened any of them yet. I never do until the rains stop and it's time to wash them."

Nate came and stood beside me, looking out into the side yard. "Didn't you say your grandkids slept in here this week?"

Grandma Edith's eyes widened. "You're right. One of the boys must have unlocked that window. But, Nate, it couldn't have been easy to climb in here, with all those roses under the window. Whoever did it must be desperate to find something, and, for the life of me, I can't figure out what he'd be looking for in that desk."

"Maybe it was just a kid," I said, "looking for money or credit cards."

Nate shrugged, but his eyes were troubled. "Apparently, no real damage was done, but be sure everything is locked up. Not just when you leave, but at night, too."

After Nate left, I sank into a chair, watching Grandma Edith fill our plates, so tired I wasn't sure I could make it to the shower. But the heavy work was done; setting everything up for the memorial service would be easy. Even if I stayed long enough to help with the bark, the work shouldn't be hard. Grandma Edith had managed the loaded wheelbarrow with no problem.

She must have been thinking along those same lines. "Things are shaping up nicely. All we have to do now is to clean the house and get those flower beds around the patio weeded. I'm sure glad you're here to lend a hand."

I stifled a groan. Suddenly my place in Galt, even with Randy in it, didn't seem so bad. "Your house looks pretty clean to me."

She raised an eyebrow. Maybe she didn't appreciate the lived-in look as much as I did.

"I think I'd better do the cleaning," she said, "and let you work on the flowerbeds. You do know the difference between a weed and a flower, don't you?"

I resisted the impulse to say "you pull it out and if it comes back, it's a weed," thinking she might not find it amusing. "Only if the flowers are blooming," I admitted, suddenly feeling as inept as a drunk trying to thread a needle.

Grandma Edith closed her eyes and let out a little sigh. "Dandelions bloom, Marcie. You know, those little yellow flowers?"

"Oh, yeah. I know what dandelions look like. I can pull those out." I tried to sound more confident than I felt. I hadn't yet been able to eradicate them from my own yard.

Once we'd decided—or, at least, Grandma Edith had—that she'd clean house the next day while I weeded flowerbeds, I was ready for a hot shower and bed. Grandma Edith said she was going to look through Grandpa Dan's email and social media accounts to see if there were any friends she had missed when she sent out the notification about the memorial service. I left her to it and headed to the guest bath.

The shower It revived me, but I knew I'd be sore the next day. Weeding was not going to be fun. Neither was the conversation I needed to have with Randy. I'd cooled down a little since I talked to Becky at dispatch, but I still wanted Randy out of the house. The trouble was, I also needed him to keep that job and I couldn't push him so far he'd renege on his promise to pay some of the bills.

His phone rang so many times I was already thinking about the message I'd leave when he finally picked up, his voice groggy. "Hi, Marcie. How's Grandma? Is everything okay?"

I didn't know how to answer that question. The woman hadn't slowed down any. She was physically fit and still sharp. But she wasn't just alone now, she was broke, and Grandpa Dan had done that to her. I knew better than most how that felt. "We're doing okay," I finally said. "Were you asleep? It's only ten-thirty."

"Yeah, and I've got to be up at quarter of six to go to work."

"Didn't get much sleep last night, did you? I hear you had quite a party. A rowdy bunch, too. Did you start calling everybody as soon as I left?"

"How did you...Becky!" He almost spat her name. "Why is she blabbing to you? Isn't that sort of information supposed to be confidential?"

"I work there, Randy," I reminded him, "so I would have eventually found out. And from the noise you were making, I don't think your party was exactly a secret."

"It wasn't like that," he protested. "I didn't plan anything. I didn't even call anybody. It's just...well, Billy and Cedric came by with a six-pack to congratulate me on the new job and..."

"And things got out of hand. Let me guess. You ran out of beer and in the process of adding to the supply, a few more friends got invited."

"Yeah, I guess so. But I didn't invite them, babe. I knew I had to get up early for work."

"You did make it to the new job?" I closed my eyes, sending a silent prayer to every deity known to mankind that he hadn't screwed up on the first day.

"'Course I did. And let me tell you, babe, it wasn't easy. Have you ever tried to run a bobcat or a heavy loader when your head hurts so bad you think it's going to fall off? Those suckers make a hell of a racket."

When I didn't answer, he said, "I guess not. Marcie, I need this job, and I really like it. You don't have to worry. I'm going to hang onto it."

"How much damage is there from that party you didn't plan?"

"Uh...not much. And I can fix most of it, with a little help."

"Let me guess. Cedric and Billy, right? With the assistance of a couple of six-packs?"

"I'll make sure it's not a party. I can't put in another day like today. Did I tell you how much that equipment vibrates? I swear my teeth were rattling around in my head. Even my hair hurt."

I couldn't muster up much sympathy. I just hoped the noise and vibration had been miserable enough to keep him from drinking too much, at least during the week. God only knew what would happen over the weekend. Maybe, if things went well here, I could be home by then.

No, I couldn't take my car back until he got paid, almost two weeks from now. Eleven days, to be exact, unless I could come up with a car payment.

Not until I was punching my pillow, trying to make it feel more like my own, did Randy's words sink in. He'd said they could repair most of the damage. I hadn't asked him what they couldn't fix.

I had a hard time relaxing, finally drifting into a troubled sleep, my dreams filled with images from my house. Randy was taking off the screen, making enough noise to set the dog next door to barking. I found the bat, somehow under my mattress instead of inside the closet. I smashed it down on Randy's fingers as he tried to climb in my window. But he wasn't there; he was on the lawn, scuffling with two other men, fighting over a can of beer. It flew up in the air, toward the house next door, followed by the sound of breaking glass. Then Randy morphed back and was crawling through my window. Only it wasn't Randy. It was Eric Roberts. He grinned, looking me up and down as I stood there in my flimsy old nightgown. The scuffling noises had faded to the sound of music, something I couldn't quite place. It was too scratchy, like an old, abused LP, but I started to dance.

My eyes popped open, my dream evaporating as I was finally jarred awake by the racket outside. And this time, I didn't have a bat.

Chapter 7

I crept across the hall to Grandpa Dan's office and the window looking out onto the patio. The sun was up, but barely, judging by the light filtering around the edges of the curtains. Whoever was out there wasn't trying to be quiet. Not wanting to draw attention, I peered through the closed blinds, but could see very little.

I pulled on jeans and a sweatshirt and headed for the kitchen, where I'd have a better view—and access to some kind of weapon.

Grandma Edith was ahead of me. She'd already opened the door onto the patio. I skidded to a stop as soon as the smell hit my nose. Bird droppings—big ones—decorated the brick-colored concrete Nate had scrubbed the evening before, as well as the grass surrounding it, where eight turkeys pecked at the lawn.

Grandma Edith brushed past me, inching her way between the bird droppings, toward the side fence. "We'll have to shoo them out of the yard and, somehow, discourage them from coming back. The problem is, turkeys do pretty much as they please."

I edged up beside her. "How did they get in?"

"Wild turkeys can fly over fences, roost in trees. There's no way to keep them out. But those aren't wild birds. They're domestic, too heavy to scale fences, too broad-breasted. I suspect they belong to Jack Loudon. We must have a hole in the fence, somewhere out back, beyond the shed."

She advanced on the turkeys, yelling and waving her arms. I went out to join her. They scattered, only to mill around in another part of the yard, showing no inclination to leave.

I thought about Buster and the potato chip bag. "Maybe they need some enticement, Grandma Edith."

She stopped, considering, then nodded. "I can try pouring a trail of bird feed to the gate. That might lure them out." Stepping carefully, she headed to the garden shed for a bag of birdseed.

The turkeys liked it. I let out a little sigh of relief as I watched them peck their slow way toward the side gate; this was going to work.
Then Grandma Edith stopped and reversed course, angling toward the back of the lot. Maybe she was leading them to the hole where they'd come in.

It took time, but the turkeys eventually followed her, gobbling up the seed. I joined the procession as she led them into the work area and through the deer-fenced vegetable-garden gate.

"I got to thinking," she said. "Even if we lured them out of the yard, they might not go home. I couldn't have them pooping all over the driveway and walks, maybe even the front porch. It's going to be bad enough, trying to clean up the patio and back lawn."

She turned on a hose and filled a tub with water, led me outside, and latched the gate. As we headed back to the house, she said, "Come on. Let's get some breakfast before we try to tackle this smelly mess."

I didn't have much appetite at that point but figured I'd have even less after cleaning up turkey poop. And I'd learned that, once Grandma Edith got going, it might be a long time between meals.

"How about some bacon and eggs?" she asked. "I can't remember if you like biscuits, but I can make some if you want."

Just like that, my appetite was back.

We had finished eating and I was gathering up the dishes when the doorbell rang. Grandma Edith went to answer it while I loaded the dishwasher, but when I heard raised voices, I decided I'd better find out what was going on.

Jack Loudon was on the front porch, facing off with Grandma Edith. "I don't want to call the cops out here again, Edith, but I know you stole them. I just came from Linda Gray's place. Her yard backs up to yours and she says the turkeys are penned up in your garden. I've spent too much time and money raising those turkeys to let you—"

"I didn't steal them. Why would anybody in their right mind want a bunch of turkeys? I penned them up so they'd stop pooping all over my patio and lawn. We just cleaned all that up yesterday, getting it ready for the memorial service."

Deflated, he took a step back. "Well, I'm sorry about that, but it's not my fault. A tree branch came down during the storm and tore a hole in the fence. I thought they'd come home before dark. They usually roost by then, but they didn't last night and—"

"So why didn't you come looking for them yesterday, before they made a mess of the patio we just cleaned? You had all afternoon."

"Well, I...uh, I thought they'd come back, and I didn't know where to start looking." His face brightened and he gave her a wimpy smile. "But you corralled them for me, and I do appreciate it. If you'll just open the gate enough to let me grab one or two at a time, I can take them off your hands, put them in the trailer, and be on my way." He nodded toward the curb and an old Ford pickup with a wire-mesh enclosure fastened to the bed.

"Let me get this straight," Grandma Edith said. "Your turkeys make a mess of my patio and you don't offer to clean it up. Instead, you expect me to help you round them up?"

"Well, yeah. I guess if you put it that way, but I just need you to stand by the gate and make sure none of them get out when I open it."

Grandma Edith crossed her arms over her chest. "Sure thing, Jack, just as soon as you clean all the turkey poop off my patio and walkways and hose down the lawn."

"I don't...you can't hold them hostage like that. Those are my turkeys."

"Maybe. Maybe not. I didn't see any tags on them. How do I know they're even yours? Did you have them chipped? We can always call animal control to check."

His mouth hung open. "You can't put identification chips in turkeys." Then he looked uncertain. "Can you?"

"Okay, just for the sake of argument, let's say they're your turkeys. Maybe you don't know it, being new to this, but you're legally responsible for your animals and any damage they do. It's up to you to clean up the mess. Once you do that, I'll let you have your turkeys."

"You can't keep them penned up like that. They need water. And food."

"Oh, come on, Jack. There are wild turkeys roaming all over the place. They seem to manage okay without anybody feeding them. I'm sure there are plenty of bugs and grubs in the garden, and the turkeys have water. But I'll admit it's a nuisance, filling up that tub." She shrugged. "If the water runs out, I suppose I can just open the front gate and shoo the gobblers out onto the street."

"No! No, you can't do that. They'd scatter all over." His shoulders slumped. "I guess the least I can do, being a good neighbor, is to bring over my pressure washer."

"Now you're talking. I'll expect you back here in an hour or two."

Grandma Edith closed the door and smiled at me. "Considering the condition of the patio, that garden is probably pretty well-fertilized by now. I won't have to spend any money for manure when I get ready to plant."

She went to take a shower, and I decided to spruce up the kitchen and mark one more chore off the list. I'd finished wiping down the counters and mopping the floor when I realized I hadn't heard Grandma Edith for a while. I put the mop away and went to check on her. She was at Grandpa Dan's desk, her head down on her folded arms.

"Grandma Edith, are you okay?"

She raised her head. "I'm all right. Just...confused, I guess."

"Is it anything I can help you with?"

She glanced at the computer screen. "I doubt it. I can't figure out why Dan's business account was cleaned out, too. Look at all these deposits." She motioned toward the monitor. "His P.I. business must have been doing a lot better than I thought." She sat back in the chair. "I guess he finally found something he liked that earned some decent money."

I came around the desk and looked at the screen. "Wow. Some of those are pretty big, over five thousand. So where did all of it go?"

"That's the big question. I see some substantial cash withdrawals I don't understand and there's no way to track them. He did the same thing with our joint account. I don't think I'm going to figure any of this out until I can get into his client expense files, but I can't find the keys. I think somebody at the hospital gave them to me, along with his phone and wallet, but I don't know what I did with them. They're not in my purse or any of my jacket pockets. I even checked the drawers in his nightstand and dresser, thinking I might have dropped them in there. No luck."

"Have you thought about calling a locksmith—"

The doorbell rang again. "That'll be Jack, ready to clean the patio," Grandma Edith said, as I headed for the door.

Expecting to see Jack Loudon, I was a little surprised to find Eric Roberts standing on the porch. He grinned as he surveyed me, much as he had in last night's dream, those startling blue eyes crinkling at the corners.

"Morning, Marcie. Looks like you've been up and at it for a while."

I resisted the urge to look down at my grubby clothes or run fingers through my messy hair.

"Who is it?" Grandma Edith walked up behind me. "Oh, good morning, Officer Roberts. Is there something we can do for you?" Her normally genial voice didn't sound as welcoming as usual and I wasn't sure whether the catalyst was Eric Roberts, the mystery of Grandpa Dan's locked-up desk, her missing money, or Jack Loudon and the turkey poop. Maybe all four.

"I just stopped by to see how the two of you are getting along and to ask if there's anything I can do to help. And, if you have a few minutes, maybe clear up a couple of questions for me."

Grandma Edith hesitated, not opening the door any wider. "You were just here Sunday afternoon with questions. So, unless something has changed—"

"It has." Smiling, he pushed the door open a little farther. She stood aside. "What's happened?"

He nodded at me, then turned back to Grandma Edith. "I'll get to that, but first I'd like to ask—what made you decide to put bark down on a Sunday afternoon?"

Grandma Edith gave her head a slight shake, as though trying to clear it of extraneous thoughts. "Is the police department now investigating complaints from the town clergy, wondering why I'm not keeping the Sabbath? Because I can't think of any other reason you'd be asking."

His lips quirked into a half-smile. "No, I'm just wondering why you chose that day."

"I didn't particularly choose a day," she said. "I wasn't even thinking about it being Sunday. I just...everything was too quiet after Natalie and the kids left. The house. The neighborhood. I had to do something, stay busy. And that pile of bark was out there. It needed doing."

He nodded as though he understood. "Did you tell anybody you were going to do it?"

She stared at him, a perplexed frown forming. "Tell anybody? Why would I do that? I don't tell anybody when I'm going to make the bed or wash the dishes."

This time, he flashed some teeth when he smiled. "Okay, so nobody knew you were working out there?"

"Well, of course, they knew. Anybody at our end of the street could see me. Some of them asked if they could help. People come down here on walks, too, turning around in front of the Loudon place."

"And he's two doors down from you." Roberts turned to me. "You said that Jack Loudon was the neighborhood busybody, our informant. What did you mean by that?"

Grandma Edith answered for me. "I don't know what else you'd call him. He told you about the pantyhose, didn't he? The so-called bodies in my yard?"

"That's the interesting thing, Mrs. Clifton. He claims the call wasn't his idea. He didn't even know what was going on in your yard until somebody who said he lived a few streets over telephoned him. The caller said he'd walked by and it looked like bodies in your yard. He asked Mr. Loudon to check it out."

Grandma Edith was losing patience. "What in heaven's name does any of this have to do with Dan's death?"

"Not his death. The attempted robbery Sunday afternoon at the bank."

For a brief moment before those last three words, I thought he had somehow heard about Grandpa Dan's jimmied desk. Apparently, she had too, because she didn't speak for a few seconds. Her eyes widened as comprehension dawned. "The bank? On Sunday? That can't be right. Marcie and I were there Monday morning and Lead Bu...Lesley Corringer didn't say anything about a robbery."

"Bank managers never talk about robberies, attempted or otherwise," Roberts said. "It's bad publicity, erodes confidence with depositors." He glanced at the living room. "If we could sit down somewhere..."

Grandma Edith flushed. "Yes. Yes, of course." She nodded toward the seating area. After all of us were settled, Roberts in an armchair, Grandma Edith and me on the sofa, he told us what had happened.

"When the call came in Sunday afternoon about several bodies on your property, the entire force was dispatched to investigate. While we were out of town, somebody took the Jaws of Life from the fenced area behind the police and fire departments and used it on the ATM." He glanced at Grandma Edith. "If you've used the ATM, you know it's around the corner from the entrance, by the drive-up window, pretty much out of view on a Sunday afternoon."

Grandma Edith was sitting on the edge of the sofa. "Did he get anything out of it?"

"No. It seems some kids meet in that empty drive-through every Sunday afternoon to skateboard. They scared him off."

"Did they recognize him?" I asked.

"No. He was wearing a mask and sunglasses, and had a ball cap, pulled down low over his forehead."

Grandma Edith had been quiet through this exchange, looking down at her clasped hands. Now she raised her head to look at Roberts. "You think the call about the 'bodies' on my property was a ploy to get the entire police force out of town so a robbery could take place? But it couldn't have been planned in advance because even I didn't know I was going to lay bark out there until I started. And who could know I'd use those pantyhose?"

Roberts nodded his agreement. "Jack Loudon says the man who called him didn't give him a name. At least, he doesn't remember one. So, the best we can figure is that it was a crime of opportunity. Somebody saw those so-called bodies and hatched the plot. He was probably on his way to town, maybe already standing by the Jaws of Life when he called Mr. Loudon. That would have given him ample time for the robbery if the kids hadn't scared him off."

"What about fingerprints?" I asked. "On the Jaws of Life, not the bodies."

Roberts smiled, then shook his head. "That's one of the things our thief was smart about. He wore gloves."

Grandma Edith rose to her feet. "Thank you, Officer Roberts, for letting us know. I—"

He reached for her hand, patting it. "I was wondering, too, if you have given any more thought to what your husband was doing in the days before the accident, if he said anything that might give us a lead."

She let out a small, almost imperceptible sigh. "If we're going over all this again, I need a cup of coffee, if you don't mind waiting a few minutes."

"I'll make it," I told her. "You talk to Officer Roberts."

"Thank you, Marcie. Just bring the pot out here."

When I got back to the living room with the coffee pot and three mugs, Grandma Edith was telling Roberts, "I don't remember driving to the hospital that night. And while I was there, it was just...I can recall only bits and pieces. The room, the monitors beeping, the doctors and nurses rushing around. I think there was a policeman."

She paused long enough to take a coffee mug from me. "I wish I could be more helpful, but I don't even remember leaving the hospital. I just gradually became aware that I was outside, sitting alone in my car in the middle of a dark parking lot, miles from home, and my husband was dead."

Roberts gave her a sympathetic nod. "It's understandable, Mrs. Clifton. You were undoubtedly in shock. Some of it may come back to you."

But I thought something already had, from the sudden widening of her eyes and her slightly opened mouth. Before I could ask her about it, the phone rang and she excused herself to answer it.

Roberts watched her go, then glanced out the window at the landscaped front yard. "This is a beautiful place. Big, too. Lots of work, especially for a single older woman. Are you planning to stay long, Officer Clifton?"

I almost dropped my cup. "Officer? I'm not—"

"Sure you are. When I first spotted you in front of the house, there was something about the way you moved, the way you noticed things, that should have tipped me off. Then, when I heard your telephone conversation inside the bank...are you here undercover for some reason? Does it have anything to do with your grandfather's death?"

"Whoa!" I held up a palm. "Slow down. I am not a police officer. I'm just a clerk in the Galt Police Department."

He nodded. "I get it. That's your cover. I'm sure, if I call them, they'll verify what you've told me. I just can't figure out what you're investigating unless it has something to do with your grandfather's death. You're from a different town, a different county, so you wouldn't be looking into the card room." He narrowed his eyes. "Unless you're working at the state or federal level, with the Galt Police Department as cover."

"Wow! A promotion from clerk to small-town police officer to state or federal investigator, all in one short conversation. And I didn't even have to take any tests or apply for the job. Have you ever considered writing fiction, Officer Roberts? You have a vivid imagination. The only reason I'm here is to help Grandma Edith."

If anybody had more information about Grandpa Dan's death and the card room, it wasn't me; it was Eric Roberts. "Why would anybody, especially me, be investigating a hit-and-run?" I asked.

He rose to his feet, smiling. "I guess we'll find out, won't we? Nice seeing you again, Marcie Clifton." With that, he got up and walked out the door.

"What the dickens was that all about?" Grandma Edith asked from just inside the door, where she'd apparently been eavesdropping. "You're not a cop, are you, Marcie? I thought you just had a clerical job."

I laughed. "I do. Officer Roberts has a wild imagination. But I can't help wondering what is going on. Grandpa Dan's accident, the missing money, the attempted ATM robbery, somebody trying to pry the desk drawer open—how can any of that be connected?"

"I don't know, but he made me remember something." She headed to the front door.

Chapter 8

As we walked down the front steps, Grandma Edith explained. "That night at the hospital, somebody gave me a bag holding Dan's clothes. I just remembered that I opened the drawstring top and saw his wallet and cell phone inside. The keys had probably slipped down to the bottom."

She opened the Malibu's trunk. Jammed inside, between a couple of insulated grocery totes, was a large white plastic bag with the hospital logo printed on it in big blue letters. I pulled it out and closed the trunk lid. "Where do you want it?"

"I..." She was biting her lip. "Everything inside that bag is going to be...dirty. We can't take it in the house."

I realized then what she was thinking. The clothes were not only going to be dirty; they would probably be bloody and torn. They should have been discarded at the hospital. But medical personnel probably couldn't do that; to avoid liability, they had to make sure Grandma Edith got everything.

Still, we had to go through the bag somewhere and the turkey-pooped patio wasn't an option. Nor, picturing Jack Loudon standing in the street watching us, did I relish the thought of the front porch.

Grandma Edith must have been reading my thoughts. "Not the porch. If any of the neighbors see us, they'll come over to offer condolences or, even worse, bring me another casserole."

She went around to the driver's side of the Malibu, reached inside, and pressed a remote on the visor. The garage had two doors, one double, one single. The big one creaked open, displaying Grandpa Dan's Toyota pickup on the left, close to the wall. Beside it was an older model light-gray Honda.

"I didn't know you had another car," I said, probably with a touch of envy in my voice.

"It's Dan's. He bought it a few months ago from a used-car dealer. He called it his undercover car, claiming it was practically invisible because there are so many Hondas on the road. He liked the color, too, said it would fade into the landscape, day or night."

I wondered how long the car would stay "undercover" in a place like Miner's Ridge. But maybe his business took him out to other towns. Then another thought struck me. "Didn't Grandpa Dan drive one of those vehicles into Miner's Ridge Wednesday night?"

"Yes, his pickup. The police department found it a few days later, parked downtown. They called me after they were through with it, and Nate and Natalie brought it back and parked it." She looked around the cluttered third bay of the garage. "There's room enough for us to work over there, by the freezer."

Once inside the garage, I untied the drawstring. The wallet was on top, but I didn't see the keys or cell phone. They'd probably slid to the bottom. I was going to have to dig through those tattered and blood-stained clothes. I handed the wallet to Grandma Edith, took a deep breath, closed my eyes, and started digging.

My fingers touched the smooth contours of the cell phone. I pulled it out, handed it to her, and dug into the other side of the bag until I found the keys.

Grandma Edith took them from me and turned toward the steps to the kitchen.

"Wait," I said. "What do you want me to do with the rest of...of..." I pointed to the bag.

She let out a soft sigh. "We'll have to go through all of it, won't we? And do a thorough job, so we don't miss anything."

She was right. I didn't have a choice. But it couldn't be any worse than fishing Randy's over-ripe sweaty socks from under the bed, could it?

The search didn't take long. Other than the expected ruined garments, I found only a quarter, deep inside a pocket of the khaki pants, and a blue windbreaker, not as damaged as the rest, probably because the material was stronger. In the jacket's right pocket, I found a scrap of paper. Somebody had scrawled four numbers on it: 5211. I turned it over; there was nothing more. The paper looked as though it had been torn from a napkin. I handed it to Grandma Edith. "Does this mean anything to you?"

She held it up to the light. "No, and that's not Dan's handwriting."

A small zip-lock bag of coins lay near the bottom, on top of the shoes. I pulled it out, then the socks, which had been stuffed inside the shoes. A blue plastic poker chip tumbled onto the concrete. Edith picked it up and added it to her collection.

I shook out the socks and shoes, then the bag, but found nothing else. "That's it. What do you want me to do with all this?"

I don't think she heard me. She had opened Grandpa Dan's wallet. "Look at this. He had over a hundred and forty dollars in here. That should help pay for the cremation. Wait a minute." Her fingers were digging into the wallet's folds. "Here's another hundred. And one on the other side. That makes three hundred and forty-three dollars. Why was he carrying that kind of money around?"

She put the wallet aside and methodically searched through the keys. She held up a small one. "I think this is it. I'm going to try it on the desk."

I held up the bag. "You didn't tell me what to do with this stuff."

"Just throw it in the garbage." She turned to the steps leading into the house. "I don't want to ever see it again."

I stuffed everything back in the bag and tossed it in the garbage can, then went into the kitchen to scrub my hands and arms.

Grandma Edith came in to plug Grandpa Dan's phone into a charger. "I got the desk unlocked and found keys for the file cabinets in the top drawer. Want to help me find out where all that money went? The expense files have to be in there, somewhere. Dan hung onto paper copies of all that stuff to back up his tax deductions."

The oak desk had an extension on one side, creating an "L" shape, with three drawers at each end. Grandma Edith searched those while I tried the file cabinets. I started with the one closest to me, expecting to see folders for household and business expenses. Instead, I was looking at names. Every folder crammed in the drawer had a neatly-printed name on the tab, some male, some female.

Grandma Edith looked up. "Those are his clients. You'll find some big manila envelopes with matching names for some of them. Probably in the bottom of that cabinet. Those hold all the evidence for that client—anything connected to the investigation that won't fit in a folder."

She was right. I found those and moved on to the next cabinet. More bulging manila envelopes. And in the bottom, binoculars, telescopes, flashlights, and other equipment I didn't recognize. "Wow, this looks like high-end stuff. Is that a night vision camera?"

She didn't answer. She had pulled two folders from a drawer and placed them on the desktop.

"Grandma Edith?"

"I've found them. At least, I think there are only two. I'll go through the invoice folder if you want to tackle the American Express statements." She was already running her fingers down the lines of a document.

I settled into a chair on the other side of the desk and opened the American Express folder, not sure what I was looking for. Nothing stood out, demanding attention, other than a lot of charges for restaurants and coffee shops in Grass Valley or Nevada City, and a few in Auburn. I asked Grandma Edith if those were normal.

She nodded, still leafing through pages. "He was probably meeting with clients."

"What about these flower orders?"

She nodded again. "He doesn't do that often. But he says—said—that, in some cases, it helps to build a better connection with a client. You know—if somebody has died or is in the hospital. Milestone birthdays and anniversaries. That sort of thing."

I flipped through pages. "Then there's nothing...wait. There are quite a few more charges from florists and restaurants in December." I turned another page. "November, too."

She sat back in the chair, chewing on her lower lip. "I guess that would make sense, with the increase we saw in his deposits after that. The business was finally taking off."

Her phone rang. I gathered, from her end of the conversation, that it was one of the neighbors. He had a stack of white plastic chairs he could clean up and bring over if she needed them for the memorial service. Grandma Edith told him that would be helpful, to leave them on the front porch. She thanked him and ended the call just as the doorbell rang. When she answered it, I heard her say "Alma."

The woman, who I assumed to be Alma Reitman, said, "I was just thinking, Edith. You're going to need a lot of food for the memorial service. I can easily double or even triple the recipes for some of my casseroles. I'm trying to decide between the tuna casserole and the seven-layer, but if you want both—"

"No!" Grandma Edith's voice had gotten louder. Apparently realizing that, she started over in a softer tone. "Alma, that's sweet of you, but I have so many casseroles in the freezer, I don't think there's room for another. What I could really use are some paper plates and plastic forks. Didn't you have a bunch of that stuff left over from Dick's birthday party?"

"Well, yes. But, Edith, those plates wouldn't be appropriate at all. His birthday party was fishing themed, remember? The plates have a picture of a big bass right in the middle, with a boat in the water behind it."

"That's okay," Grandma Edith said. "Dan liked fishing."
I had to cover my mouth to keep from laughing. Grandpa Dan hated fishing. "Besides," Grandma Edith said, "the bass will be covered with food."

"Not until people fill them up. I think a nice casserole would be better."

"No!" Grandma Edith had raised her voice again. She lowered it. "The event is going to be very informal, so the plates will be fine."

I heard the door close and, a few minutes later, Grandma Edith appeared in the office doorway.

"Liar, liar, pants on fire," I chanted.

She laughed. "I thought about asking her if she could bring booze. Do you think it's too early for a beer?"

"I found something while you were endearing yourself to Alma," I said. "Look at these." I put the forms in front of her. "It looks as though Grandpa Dan was claiming you as an employee. I didn't know you worked for him."

"What?" She grabbed the forms from my hand. "What the—? How far do these go back?"

"I don't know. We'll probably have to look at years of tax statements to find out. But why would he do that, if you didn't know anything about it? It was costing him for payroll taxes."

She snorted. "Because he was Dan Clifton, that's why. A man who never let a scheme get past him. Think about it, Marcie. He would get those payroll taxes back, through me. My social security, my Medicare. And in the meantime, he could charge all kinds of things off as business expenses. My car maintenance and mileage, for example. Probably my clothes!"

"Oh." I couldn't think of anything else to say. Randy truly did inherit his grandfather's genes. Maybe I'd better check my own tax records, at least the ones Randy had filed while we were married.

Grandma Edith sat down at the desk. "I did think about something else when Alma was nattering about casseroles. It must have taken some time for Dan to drain all our bank accounts, so let's look further back at last year's American Express statements."

I didn't find much until October, when there were frequent entries for Stella's Florist in Miner's Ridge and a substantial one for Pahl's Fine Jewelry in Nevada City.

"He must have been planning something for my birthday," Grandma Edith said, taking the page from me. "Maybe that amethyst ring I've wanted for so long." She hesitated then, her fingers tracing the entry. "But why would he have bought something six months early? Dan was a last-minute shopper. And where is it? I searched through all his drawers in the bedroom when I was looking for the keys and wallet."

I nodded toward the file drawers we hadn't yet opened. "Maybe in here somewhere? Or...you said he'd been distracted. Maybe he forgot to pick it up, or had the store hold it so you wouldn't stumble across it. Why don't you call them?"

"Good idea." Grandma Edith looked up the number and called, putting the phone on speaker. "This is Edith Clifton. My husband, Dan Clifton, was killed this week by a hit-and-run driver—"

"Oh, my! I'm so sorry," came the feminine voice on the other end.

Grandma Edith hurried on, past the platitude. "I see from his records that he bought something from your store in October, probably for my birthday. I can't find anything like that in his belongings and it occurred to me that he might not have picked it up yet."

"Um...that long ago? I don't think... Let me check." A pause, then computer keys clicked. "Oh, yes, here it is. Our ten-carat gold tanzanite earrings."

"Tanzanite?" Grandma Edith's voice was sharp. "For a hundred and forty-nine dollars? I never heard of it."

"The earrings are quite lovely, with an intricate gold setting—"

"Do you still have them there, in the store?"

"Let's see." More computer keys clicking. "No. He took them with him, all nicely gift-wrapped."

Grandma Edith ended the call. "That's just like Dan," she muttered. "He never paid attention to anything I said. He probably just walked into the jewelry store, saw something he liked, and bought it, then stashed it somewhere and forgot all about it. I don't even know what tanzanite looks like."

"Why don't you go to the jeweler's website and look for it?" I asked. "Then we'll at least know what we're searching for."

She found the website and scrolled through the merchandise. I spotted them and pointed. "There, Grandma Edith, and that's a nice stone. I like the setting, too."

Saying nothing, she flipped back to the American Express statement. "There's another charge, a big one, the day after he bought those earrings. It's for Giovanni's Italian restaurant, and it's on the same day as one of the Stella's Florist charges." She was silent for almost a full minute. "We haven't been to Giovanni's in years, but it was once our favorite restaurant. You know the kind? Cozy and kind of romantic, at least in the early days."

She slammed her hands down on the desk. "Dan was planning a big evening, all right, but it had nothing to do with me."

She ran to the kitchen and grabbed Grandpa Dan's phone out of the charger. "It's password-protected! When did he put a password on it?"

"You can probably think of it, Grandma Edith. After all, you knew him better than anybody else."

"No. He was hiding something from me. He would use a password I couldn't figure out."

"You can call tech support and get it. Whatever personal question they ask, you'll know the answer."

"Maybe." She headed back toward the office. "But he could be pretty cagey. Maybe he'd give them something I don't know. And I'll only have one shot at this. I'll have to be sure of my answer."

Then, unexpectedly, she laughed. "Dan's memory was never very good, and it was getting worse. If he figured out a fake security question, he'd write it down so he wouldn't forget it. I have to find his password list."

She started with the top left drawer, the one closest to the computer. "Bingo!" She pulled out a list of passwords. It took a while to find the one she was looking for amid the once neatly-typewritten list, now cluttered with hastily scribbled additions. "There it is. The phone password. I won't have to call tech support." She raced back to the kitchen.

The room grew quiet as she scrolled through old voice mails and text messages. Remembering the expensive-looking camera equipment in the file drawer, I went back and locked it, then glanced at the clock. It was past one, but I couldn't face another casserole. I went to the kitchen and eyed the apple pie again. Maybe with a glass of milk. If I put ice cream or cheese on top, I'd have more dairy, making it even healthier.

"My ring!" The words almost exploded out of Grandma Edith's mouth. "My mother's ring!" She ran to her bedroom.

I looked down at the message displayed on the phone: "Thank you, sweetie, for the lovely Mexican fire opal. I love the unusual old-fashioned design."

I rushed after Grandma Edith, who was standing in front of her open jewelry armoire. "It's gone. That ring belonged to my mother and my grandmother before that. Maybe my great-grandmother. I've loved it ever since I was eight years old and first saw the way light flashed on the stone."

She ran her fingers over every row of jewelry, always coming back to the empty spot in the tray. "Dan took it, gave it to somebody else."

I thought she was going to cry and was prepared to wrap my arms around her. Instead, she almost stumbled over the vanity stool in her haste to get out of the bedroom, her voice getting louder. "My mother's ring. You gave away my mother's ring, Dan Clifton. You dirty, thieving son of a rabid skunk! I'm going to kill you!"

I pushed the vanity stool back into place, wondering how you killed somebody who was already dead. I tried to think of something I could say or do that would help, but I was at a loss. Finally, I left her bedroom, headed back toward the kitchen. I was still in the hallway, just opposite the open laundry room door, when I saw her. She was standing in the half-bath beyond the laundry room, a plunger in her hands. The crumpled potato chip bag was in the trash can beside her.

Chapter 9

I crept back toward the office, leaving Grandma Edith to kill her already-dead husband while I dug through his old tax records. A few minutes later, a tap on the back door announced Jack Loudon's arrival.

"I've got the pressure washer," he told Grandma Edith, gesturing toward it. "We'll have all this mess cleaned up before you know it."

"I got a head start on you," Grandma Edith muttered, glancing toward the half-bath. "Let me know when you've finished and I'll help you with the turkeys."

I wasn't sure I'd heard her right. Maybe she still wasn't thinking straight, but it was an offer I wished she hadn't made. I think she did, too, before the afternoon was over.

The turkeys seemed to like the garden well enough to set up residence. They weren't nearly as eager to leave as Jack Loudon would have liked. Only by walking toward them, a few feet apart, arms wide, could we herd one or two into a corner so we could grab them. And all the time I was playing shepherd, I could feel—and smell—the droppings under my shoes. I'd have to throw them away. No, I couldn't afford new ones. I'd have to try to clean them up.

"Why are we doing this?" I asked Grandma Edith.

"Because he'll never catch them by himself." Her voice was more a hiss than a whisper. "And I have to clear them out of here so I can have a celebration of life for a cheating husband."

I decided not to say anything else.

Nate yelled from across his fence, "Need some help?" He was laughing.

Before Grandma Edith could respond, Loudon called, "Yes, please!" His voice had a catch in it, almost breaking in the middle of the last word, reminding me of a little boy I'd once known, trying to contain his tears when he couldn't stop falling off his bike.

Nate came through the garden gate, still laughing, clad in jeans and a Western-style denim shirt with snap buttons. He grabbed a couple of the turkeys Grandma Edith and I had herded into the corner and carried them out through the gate.

Jack Loudon grabbed at one and missed, sending it squawking toward the fence.

"Why are you raising turkeys, anyway?" I asked him.

He gave me a conspiratorial smile. "Eva—that's my wife—she helped me figure it out. Everybody is raising chickens, so there's a surplus of them. But nobody is raising turkeys, so we saw golden opportunity there."

"But people raise chickens for fresh eggs," I said. "What do you get from the turkeys?"

He frowned. "Well, nothing, I guess, except, you know. Thanksgiving. People want free-range poultry, and it's just not available. I mean, a lot of the stuff you get in the stores is marked free-range, but that just means they're let out of their cages for a few minutes every day. The rest of the time, they're penned inside, not moving around much, so they'll fatten up. And people are getting smarter and more health-conscious, so they're looking for something else."

"So you're raising both free-range chickens and turkeys?"

He smiled. "You bet. We've got plenty of space to let them run around on the back of our big lot and they're no trouble."

I tried not to think about what it must be like to walk around on his lot.

He grabbed at a turkey's legs and caught it this time. Holding it, squawking, away from his body, he carried it toward his truck.

Grandma Edith must have been following our conversation because, when he came back, she asked, "Jack, is what you're doing even legal?"

"What? Raising poultry? Sure. We checked."

"No, I mean cleaning turkeys to sell. Don't you need a facility for that, with regular inspections?"

He looked surprised. "Why would we clean them?"

Her lip quirked a little as she shook her head. "I'm not talking about giving them a bath, Jack, but I doubt many people are going to buy a live turkey to butcher and clean. At least, not after the first time. I know I'm not. It's a huge chore just getting all those feathers and pin-feathers off, not to mention killing and gutting them. So I just assumed you're going to do all that yourself and have them all washed and wrapped for your customers. I don't think that kind of commercial operation is legal, even if you have the facilities. Health regulations, all that sort of thing. Especially running a butcher shop in a residential neighborhood."

"Oh." He stared at her, then at the turkey he'd finally caught. "People must buy them. I see them for sale on Craig's List and other places."

"Yeah, I see a lot of stuff, too, but that doesn't mean it's always a good deal. But to each his own. You couldn't pay me enough to kill and clean another turkey. It's almost impossible to hold something that heavy over an open flame, turning it to get all the pin-feathers off."

Nate came back and, with his help, the birds were soon collected and on their way home. I suspected they wouldn't be there long, that the next wild turkey flock coming around would pick up a few domestic cousins.

Nate twisted his foot around to examine the glob on the bottom of his boot. "You should have made Jack hose off the lawn, too."

Grandma Edith sighed. "I thought he did. I'll get to it later. We've got to weed out those flower beds, anyway."

Nate grinned. "I might be persuaded to help, providing the price is right."

"What price?"

"Couple of beers. And maybe a home-cooked dinner?"

"You've got a deal," Grandma Edith said. I suspected she was thinking about all those casseroles collecting in her kitchen, wondering which one might pass if she took it out of the skull-and-crossbones dish and served it with a fresh salad and some dinner rolls.

We'd reached the now clean and dry patio by then. She opened a small refrigerator and pulled out three bottles of water. "I might have to ration the beer after dinner, though. I don't think I'll be able to afford it from here on out."

"Water's healthier, anyway," Nate said.

"Yeah, right." Grandma Edith stretched out a leg to flex her muscles. "You know those little packets of citrus flavoring you put in your water bottles? Do you suppose they have any beer flavors?"

He laughed. "No, but I'll bet somebody could make a fortune if they invented something like that, providing it tasted like the real thing. Not like those fake beers they have now. Think about it. Choose your brand. Coors, Bud, Miller. You probably couldn't do any of the specialty brews, but you could drink all you wanted, stay healthy, and wouldn't have to worry about getting a hangover. Or a DUI."

She laughed, and I watched, fascinated by the rapport between the two of them, how much fun they had together.

"Nate, you should talk to Jack," she said. "He'd probably be willing to go partners with you."

"Jack Loudon? Why?"

Grandma Edith told him about Loudon's plans for the turkeys. Nate choked on his water, spewing it onto his shirt. "Sounds like a guy who's never cleaned a turkey. I doubt he can count on repeat customers."

"You have to keep in mind, Nate—it's a proven fact that half the population has below-average intelligence."

He frowned, thinking about it, then shook his head. "I guess I can't argue with math. But why are so many of them living on our street?"

"Do you think most of them are married to each other?" she asked.

"Guess that's the only way to add to the bottom half of that gene pool," he said.

Later, after we had weeded the flowers and hosed down the lawn, we sat on the patio, drinking Coronas.

"Looks good," Nate said, tilting his bottle toward the yard. "I'll go around to the neighbors tomorrow morning and round up the rest of the chairs."

"Okay." Her eyes on the flowers bordering the patio, she asked, "Nate, what do you think Dan was doing that cost him so much money? You seemed a little hesitant the other day when I told you he'd wiped out all our bank accounts, like you weren't really that surprised."

"No," Nate said, "I was. Surprised, I mean. I just…I guess I was trying to get my head around it. Why he would do something like that. Edie, to be honest, I didn't know Dan that well. You were the one who was over at our place all the time, helping me take care of Sheila."

"But all those years before that, Nate. The four of us were together so much of the time."

"Because you and Sheila were so tight. I think Dan and I were just along for the ride."

Grandma Edith stared at him. "That never occurred to me. It probably didn't to Sheila, either. And Dan…I thought you two were close. He makes friends so easily. He knew everybody in the entire neighborhood. He took all those long walks, knew everybody's name, where they worked, how long they'd lived here, where they came from."

Nate reached over and patted her hand. "Knowing about somebody doesn't mean you have a connection, Edie. Words and sentimental platitudes don't mean shit. Think about how many people post their undying love for their parents on social media, even though they haven't spent a holiday with them in years, visit maybe four or five times a year, and rarely call?"

After a moment of silence, Grandma Edith asked, "Has Jill called lately?"

Nate flushed and looked at me, possibly a little embarrassed. I wished I wasn't there, listening to their conversation.

This time Grandma Edith patted his hand. "Good thing we old geezers have each other. Those kids don't know how much fun they're missing. Who wouldn't want to be part of a turkey roundup?"

She didn't look my way, but I wondered if she was thinking that I hadn't been visiting or calling much, either. Damn Randy! One of us had to tell her that I was no longer her granddaughter.

Grandma Edith rose to her feet. "Let's go inside so I can get dinner started."

Nate glanced at me. "I noticed a few weeds out front. Marcie, why don't you help me tackle those while your grandma is fixing dinner? That should finish everything up and you two can relax for a bit."

I followed him onto the front porch, thinking he wanted to talk to me. Before either of us could say anything, we saw Alma Reitman angling toward us, her too-red cap of dyed hair gleaming in the late-afternoon sun, a sharp contrast to her pale skin. She was balancing something white between both hands.

Nate took a few long strides back to the kitchen. "You know what, Edie? It's been a long day and you must be tired. You need to rest, not have company for dinner. I'll take a rain check, okay?"

Without waiting for an answer, he went out the back door, leaving Grandma Edith to thank Alma for the stack of paper plates she'd brought over, all of them displaying a large bass in the center.

Alma trotted back across the street and Grandma Edith turned to watch Nate leave through our side gate and disappear into his house. "Traitor," she muttered. "It wasn't even a casserole."

I went out and started looking for the weeds Nate had mentioned. She joined me a few minutes later. Hands on hips, she surveyed the yard. "Just a few strays. Not enough to amount to much. Let's get them out and sweep off the porch. Then we'll fix some dinner."

We were cleaning the porch when her phone rang. She listened to the caller, then said, "We'll be right over." Smiling, she shoved the phone in her pocket. "That was Nate. He says he's got three steaks on the grill and is zapping some potatoes and steamed vegetables. He's also opening a bottle of red wine."

I should have declined the invitation, made some excuse so they'd have a chance to talk without me always being around. That would have been the most courteous thing to do. But the thought of those steaks—and the wine—trumped courtesy. "Great!" I said. "I've been wanting to see Nate's back yard."

Chapter 10

I groaned when I tried to get out of bed the next morning. The muscles I'd used in Grandma Edith's yard must be a different set than the ones I exercised in the gym. Hot water didn't help much and I almost limped my way back to my bedroom to get dressed.

Grandma Edith didn't seem to be suffering any pain. She was already at work, reaching her duster high for cobwebs I couldn't even see.

"There's fresh coffee," she said, "and I thought I'd make some blueberry pancakes for breakfast. We have plenty of time to get everything ready. Nate's already been here with the chairs he collected."

Somebody, probably her sister Cynthia, had suggested that Grandma Edith have the memorial service over the weekend when more people could come. She'd disagreed and opted for four o'clock on Wednesday afternoon—today. "Saturday is too long to wait," she had said. "Most everybody except family is from Miner's Ridge, anyway, and it won't matter to the relatives. They'll just leave work a little early or take a day off."

She didn't talk much over breakfast or the kitchen clean-up. I suspected that, with everything Grandpa Dan had done, she didn't care about the memorial service anymore; she just wanted to get it past her.

The day had a strange feel to it. The sun was shining and I saw two squirrels tumbling around on the lawn, but there was nothing to do. Everything—inside and out—was in perfect order, so I hesitated even to pour a cup of coffee or pick up a magazine for fear of disturbing the pristine setting. All I could do was wait.

Grandma Edith was back in the office, going over accounts again, a frown creasing her forehead. I felt like I should be helping her pay some bills, but my house payment would take most of my paycheck.

Randy had called the night before. He couldn't come for the memorial service, but he'd drive up Saturday.

"I hope you're planning on going back the same day," I said, "or else telling Grandma Edith we're not married, because you're not sleeping in my bedroom."

"Aw, babe, I meant to tell her. It just...the time never seemed right, and then Grandpa Dan died and, well...I can bed down on the floor. I promise I won't try to climb into bed with you or—"

I ended the call, cutting him off mid-sentence. I was calmer now, just restless. I wandered back to the office, looking for something to do. I'd never finished with Grandpa Dan's tax records. That should keep me busy for a while.

Grandma Edith looked up at me, smiling. "Cynthia called. The girls have decided to go with her on the Ireland trip, so I don't have to worry about that anymore."

That was good news. Now if I could just find something positive in those tax records.

I found them in a well-organized file drawer, every year's taxes in a separate, clearly marked folder, along with the supporting documents.

Grandma Edith was still at the desk so I settled into a chair and flipped through the folders, one by one. "You've been an employee of Clifton Investigative Services for at least the past eight years," I told her. "That's as far back as his records go."

She looked at me, her expression calm. "I'm not surprised. Anything to make a buck, that was Dan."

Her phone rang. She listened for only a moment before she smiled. "You've reached computer support," she said to the caller. "What exactly is going on?" She took one look at my face and punched the speaker button.

There was a slight pause before the speaker on the other end of the line responded. "Uh...no. This is Microsoft support and there's a problem with your computer."

"Oh, dear," Grandma Edith said in her sweetest voice. "We have a communication problem, don't we? I can tell from your accent that English is not your native language. That's probably why you have your pronouns mixed up. When you're talking about something that belongs to you, the correct word is 'my'. When it belongs to somebody else, it's 'your.' So the word you want is 'my.' My computer."

There was another moment of silence, then the man started over again. "This is Microsoft and there is a problem with your computer."

Grandma Edith sighed. "There, you're still making the same mistake. You're mixing up your pronouns. But never mind. It takes time to learn a new language and English is particularly difficult. Just tell me what's going on with your computer and I'll take care of it for you."

The silence was a little longer this time and the voice a little more flustered. "This is Microsoft—"

"Well, I must say I'm surprised," Grandma Edith said. "I should think a company as big as yours would have its own tech support. I'll be glad to help you, though, if you'll just tell me—"

By that time, the man had reverted to the beginning of his script two or three more times. I was holding a hand over my mouth, laughing so hard I didn't hear the next few exchanges. Grandma Edith put down the phone, a smile of satisfaction on her face.

"That poor man," I sputtered, still laughing. "You had him so confused he didn't know what to say."

"Poor man? He's a crook, trying to scam people out of money. That's the second time this week we've had this conversation, and he still keeps calling. He woke me up at seven-thirty one morning."

"Do you do this sort of thing often?" I asked, nodding toward her phone.

"Only when it's scammers. And when I'm not too busy to talk. Or I'm bored. It's kind of fun. Especially when I can get them to hang up on me. But that usually takes a while."

I was still smiling when I answered the tap on the back door. Grandma Edith's sister had arrived with her work crew. Cynthia's daughters, Joyce and Susan, juggled poster boards and easels. In their mid-forties, they looked enough alike to be twins, both slim, dark-haired, and brown-eyed, like their mother.

Robbie, Joyce's twenty-five-year-old son, followed, carrying some kind of electronics. He was an extraordinarily good-looking young man, his features, coloring, and sturdy build more like his father's, with light-brown hair and hazel eyes.

Amid a flurry of greetings, I offered to help but suspected I was just in the way. They were well-organized, each tackling a specific job. Within a couple of hours, they had transformed Grandma Edith's back yard into a venue. Tables large enough to seat six or eight people, along with their chairs, nestled between flowering plants. Closer to the patio, food warmers and punch bowls lined tables draped with white tablecloths. A big coffee-maker perked. Poster boards displayed photos.

Finding little else to do, I studied the pictures, noting the strong resemblance between Grandpa Dan and Randy. They had the same eyes, the same smile. I got a glimpse of what Randy would look like as he aged, and I wondered if his personality, his behavior, would take the same path as his grandfather's. I was a little relieved that I no longer needed to worry about that; Randy would never have the opportunity to give any of my family heirlooms to another woman.

His brother, Billy, and sisters Natalie and Katie, arrived a little late because Natalie had to pick up Katie at the Sacramento airport. They all hugged Grandma Edith, but Billy hung back while the girls greeted cousins. Both sisters looked a lot like Randy, though Katie's eyes were a deeper shade of blue than his, and Natalie's hair a little darker blonde and not quite as curly.

Billy looked a little rough around the edges. His sun-bleached hair needed trimming and his clothes looked like he might have picked them out of a pile on the floor. But he was here, which was more than I'd expected; Billy rarely showed up for family gatherings.

Natalie worked her way over and gave me a tight hug. "Thanks so much for coming up to be with Grandma. I didn't want to leave her alone, but I had to get the kids back in school. It was sweet of you to come."

Did she mean it was sweet of me because I was no longer family, or had Randy also neglected to tell her about the divorce?

"I had some vacation time coming," I said, "and it's always fun to spend it with Grandma Edith."

Natalie smiled and moved on toward another relative. I turned back to study the pictures and almost jumped when somebody walked up beside me. Eric Roberts. "What are you doing here?"

My voice must have been a little sharper than I intended. He grimaced, then tried a lopsided smile. "Just paying my respects, that's all."

My smile was probably as strained as his. I suspected he was there to ask questions of anybody who might give him some answers. "Is attending memorial services a part of a police officer's official duty in a small community like Miner's Ridge?"

"Sometimes. But that's not always the case. Like you said, it's a small community and sometimes we're just trying to be good neighbors, especially if it's people we like."

He turned away before I could say anything more and worked his way around the yard, chatting with guests.

Slowly, people began to filter into the yard. Nate was standing by the door beside Grandma Edith. She looked around, a frown starting to wrinkle her forehead. I went to join them, wondering what was troubling her.

"Did you get invitations out to the neighbors who might have been Dan's friends?" she asked Nate. "There aren't as many of them here as I expected."

He shrugged. "I tried. A little tough, though, not knowing who they were. I told everybody to pass the word along to anybody Dan knew well." He smiled and dipped his head down to her. "Maybe they heard about Alma's casseroles and decided to stay away."

She poked him in the ribs with her elbow. "Hush. Somebody will hear you." But she smiled.

Taking my hand, she pulled me away from the patio. "Come on. Let's greet our guests, so I can introduce you to those you don't know."

Cynthia grabbed her arm. "Wait, Edie. It'll be better if you stay in one place and let people come to you. We put a 'reserved' sign on the table by the wisteria arbor so you and all your grandchildren could sit together. Is that okay?"

"Yes, if Nate brings me a glass of punch. And tell him to doctor it. He knows what I like and where to find it."

As Grandma Edith and I wended our way toward the table, she made frequent stops, exchanging a few words with family and friends or introducing me to somebody I didn't know. We spent a few minutes with Grandpa Dan's family. One brother, Harry, lived in the Bay Area. The other, Ray, lived in Auburn. Harry had children and grandchildren, but I could never keep all their names straight.

We moved on. Grandma Edith was trying to edge around a small group deep in discussion when she jerked me to a stop. I grabbed her arm and looked down, thinking she had slipped on some turkey poop we'd missed. I didn't see anything. Grandma Edith was staring at the back of a woman's head, not speaking. I was trying to figure out why the sight of that long, auburn hair had stopped her so abruptly when the woman shifted. One of her earrings glimmered in the sunlight slanting through the trees at the back of the yard—the same tanzanite earrings we'd seen on the jeweler's website.

Grandma Edith grabbed the woman's right hand, glanced at it, then craned her neck to see the other hand. She was looking for her missing ring. But this woman wore a diamond wedding and engagement ring on her left hand and a topaz, not the fire opal, on the other.

"What the hell?" The woman, probably in her forties, tried to jerk her hand away as she turned toward us.

The entire group was staring at Grandma Edith as she released her grip on the woman's hand. "I'm sorry," she stammered. "I didn't mean to grab you like that. I...uh...my foot slipped on the grass and I almost lost my balance. I guess I wasn't paying enough attention. I was admiring your beautiful earrings. Where did you get them?"

The woman touched a hand to her ear. "My husband gave them to me. As a birthday present." She nodded toward the man opposite her, who gave Grandma Edith a chilly smile. He'd been facing us; he knew she hadn't slipped on the grass.

Grandma Edith held out her hand to him. "How did you know my husband?"

The frigid smile didn't defrost as he shook hands with her. "You're Dan Clifton's wife?"

"For more than forty-five years. Are you one of his friends?"

"In a manner of speaking. I'm Jerry Pittman, and this is my wife, Daphne. We live two blocks over, on Pine Grove Court. Dan used to come by on his daily walks and he always stopped to visit. As we got to know each other better, he spent a lot of time at our place. I can't tell you how sorry we are about his passing."

His voice was cool, not matching the condolence. Daphne darted a glance at him then said, "We're going to miss Dan. He was a charming man." Her smile looked wary but more genuine than her husband's.

Wondering what that was all about, I followed Grandma Edith to the table by the wisteria arbor, then went back to the patio to get each of us a plate of food.

Cynthia touched my arm. "Marcie, would you mind? The trash cans are filling and we're not sure where Edith keeps the garbage can."

"I'll get it." I grabbed the trash containers, noticing a stack of bass-adorned paper plates. Apparently, either Cynthia or one of her daughters didn't think they were appropriate for the occasion. Of course, they hadn't known the alternative.

As I rounded the corner on my way to the garbage can, I heard a low growl, then saw Buster, Cleve's dog. He had his paws dug in, his teeth clamped to a man's pants at ankle level.

My gaze traveled up to the man's face. I didn't recognize him, but the hospital-logo-imprinted plastic bag he held—the one I'd stuffed with Grandpa Dan's clothes—was all too familiar. And clinging to it, caught in the drawstring top, was the potato chip bag from the mortuary—one that Buster apparently remembered and had claimed as his own.

The man, seeing me, hobbled toward the gate, trying to shake Buster loose. The dog hung on.

I couldn't wrestle the bag away, didn't even want to. Grandma Edith had told me to discard it. But, in the garbage thief's flight, the potato chip bag was slipping loose from the drawstring. Buster wanted that bag. If he got it, I suspected he'd play another game of "catch me if you can," possibly in the midst of Grandma Edith's guests. And I didn't know if any of the contents were still settled in the bottom. Probably not, but I couldn't be sure. Grandma Edith had been a little emotional when she emptied it.

"Stop, thief," I yelled as I ran toward the man, uncertain whether I should grab for the bag or the dog, not sure I could get to either in time. "Help!" I yelled.

Chapter 11

The garbage thief dropped the hospital bag and pushed through the gate. The potato chip bag came loose, floating toward the ground. Buster tried to pull his teeth from the pants leg and turn around. Too late. The gate closed behind him and the man at the same time I caught the potato chip bag.

I was stuffing it inside the hospital bag when Officer Roberts came around the corner, his hand on his holster. His gaze darted from me to the trash bins I'd dropped, to the bag I held. His hand fell from the gun. "You yelled because you need help dumping the trash?"

I was too out of breath to even attempt a laugh. My mind did an Indie 500. The bag I held had a hospital logo on the side. If Roberts noticed it, he would assume the bag held the clothes Grandpa Dan wore the night he was killed. He'd want to search through them for clues. But, if he opened that bag, he'd wonder why a crumpled potato chip bag was stuffed in with the clothes. He'd examine it and find the ash residue inside. I could picture him sending the bag to a big lab in Sacramento have the ashes analyzed.

I twisted the bag around so the logo was against my leg and pointed to it. "There was a man—a thief. He came out of the house with this. I don't know how he got past everybody on the patio."

Roberts hurried toward the gate. "Where is he? Which way did he go?"

"I don't know. I couldn't see over the gate." If Roberts went through it, I'd have a chance to dump the potato chip bag. Maybe. But how could I explain if he saw me pull it out of the bag the 'thief' had carried out of the house?

Roberts opened the gate. "What did he look like?"

"I don't know. All I could see was his back." Did I really want Roberts to catch the man? Possibly have the thief confess to stealing the hospital bag with Grandpa Dan's clothes inside?

"He was tall and skinny," I lied. "And he was kind of dressed up, like maybe he'd been attending the memorial service."

Roberts ran out the gate just as a car started up down the street. I lifted the lid on the garbage can, then had second thoughts. What if somebody else wanted that bag? Best get it inside. And fast, before Roberts came back.

I couldn't take it through the yard with all the people gathered there. But Grandma Edith had locked the front door, not wanting it open to strangers while everybody was in the back yard. I didn't think it had stayed locked. I had seen several people venture out onto the front porch from inside the house. Would they have locked the door again when they went inside? Worse yet, were they still there?

I had to chance it. I pushed through the gate and walked around to the porch. Nobody was on it. I glanced down the street and didn't see Roberts. I hurried up the steps, across the porch, and into the front door.

Somebody could come inside at any minute. I had to get the bag out of sight, but where? I couldn't put it in any of the more public areas or Grandma Edith's room. She might have a heart attack if she saw it back again. I turned toward the open door of my room. Then I heard the toilet flush. Somebody would come out of that bathroom at any minute and could see directly across the hall into my room.

I ducked into Grandpa Dan's office, desperate now to find any place I could stash the bag, at least temporarily. Finally, for lack of anything better, I shoved it into a small closet and shut the door.

When I turned, Roberts was standing in the doorway, watching me.

"The thief got away. I couldn't find anybody matching your description, and we don't know what kind of vehicle he was driving. I can't figure out why he didn't take the stuff he stole out the front door. He was already in the house. Why go out the back, through all those people in the yard?"

"Maybe he meant to but there was somebody on the porch. I saw a couple of women out there earlier."

"Seems pretty risky, taking it through the yard. But then, the guy can't be too bright, trying to pull off a robbery when the place is crawling with people." He gestured toward the closet. "Aren't you going to look inside that bag? See what he took?"

"No, this isn't a good time. I'll have to do it later when everybody is gone. And please don't tell Grandma Edith about the attempted burglary. She's got enough to worry about right now."

He nodded, his eyes thoughtful. "Once you know, I'd like to be informed. It could have something to do with your grandpa."

If he only knew. "Okay, I can do that." I started to brush past him, but he touched my arm.

"I still don't know what you're investigating. Is it something we can work on together?"

"I told you I'm not a cop. I'm just a clerk in the Galt Police Department."

"In that case, would you like to go out for a drink or dinner?" He leaned down, his face inches from mine when somebody came down the hall.

"Marcie?" Katie called. "Do you know where Grandma keeps her big bread basket?"

I jerked back from Roberts, pushed past him, and went to the kitchen to grab the bread basket for Katie. Then I headed outside, working my way toward the table by the wisteria arbor. And with every step, the scent of Roberts's woodsy aftershave lingering, mixing with Grandma Edith's flowers.

I slid onto a bench at the back of the table. Nobody seemed to be aware of my misadventure, and I sat quietly, watching the guests. The Pittmans were still in the same spot where Grandma Edith had accosted Daphne, occasionally joined by other people for brief conversations. One man bent his bald head to listen to something Jerry Pittman said, then glanced our way. Officer Roberts came out the back door and angled his way toward a group near the patio.

While I watched, the faint scent of the fading lilacs wafting toward me on a light breeze, Grandpa Dan's brother Ray detached himself from the rest of the family and came to stand beside Grandma Edith.

He looked much like Grandpa Dan, with the same hazel-blue eyes and graying curly hair. But he was thinner, not quite as tall, and had sharper features. And, unlike Grandpa Dan, I doubted he'd ever been the life of any party.

He cleared his throat. "Edith, I'd wait to ask about this, but we have to leave soon, and I won't have another opportunity. I was wondering if you might have run across a folder or envelope that belongs to me."

We hadn't examined any of the manila envelopes and folders in Grandpa Dan's office; we had been too intent on tracking down the missing money. I was under the impression the folders in the drawers were client files and wondered how any of them could connect to Ray.

"Does it have anything to do with money he was supposed to give you?" Grandma Edith asked.

"Money?" A muscle along Ray's jaw twitched. "Why would you think it's anything like that?"

"Because, when I called to let you know about this gathering, you asked if Dan had paid something. The best I can recall, it had to do with some property management company. Were you and Dan in some venture together?"

"Oh, it was nothing like that, Edie." He averted his eyes. "Just something we bought together, and I was wondering if he'd paid his share."

"What did you buy?"

"Uh...ah...tickets to..." His voice trailed off and he gave her a weak smile. "It's supposed to be a surprise."

Grandma Edith gave him her sweetest smile. "A surprise? Dan was planning something for my birthday?" She turned to me. "Isn't that wonderful, Marcie, everything my husband was doing for my birthday?"

She asked Ray, "Exactly what was he planning? Some big evening with you and Patricia? Maybe with Harry and Laura, too? All three brothers and their wives together for my birthday?"

Ray nodded, his face losing some of its tension. I had a hard time keeping mine straight. If he'd known Grandma Edith as well as I did, he'd have started running when she turned on that too-sweet smile.

"Well," she said, "it can't matter if I know now, Ray, so what was the surprise?"

He'd had a moment or two to pull himself together. "An evening at the Orpheum in San Francisco and dinner afterward."

I held my breath, waiting. Grandma Edith's aversion to San Francisco was almost as strong as that for Harry's wife. She considered her sister-in-law Laura a gossip who exaggerated, and a meddler who delighted in sowing discord throughout the family.

Grandma Edith's face gave none of that away. "Oh, really? What show?"

"I...uh. You know, I can't remember right now."

"I didn't think so. Ray, Dan knew I don't like San Francisco. If he'd planned something like that for my birthday, it would have been in Grass Valley or Sacramento or even Folsom. And it certainly wouldn't have included Harry and Laura. So what's really going on?"

He stood there, not saying anything, then looked over his shoulder at Nate, who was approaching, a drink in each hand and the neck of a beer bottle sticking out of his blazer pocket.

Ray glanced back at Grandma Edith. "Never mind. This isn't the time or place. I'll talk to you later." He turned and, with long strides, headed back to his family.

Nate put our drinks on the table. "Sorry it took so long. Seems like everybody wants to chat. Or, more likely, pump me for information about the investigation." He turned to look at Ray's receding back before settling onto the bench beside Edith. "Dan's brother, right? What did he say to get you so riled up?"

"He lied to me and I don't know why. He keeps hinting at something Dan should have paid and an envelope or a folder belonging to him that he thinks Dan had. There's something really weird going on, Nate. Those guys with him? They've been doing a lot of whispering into each other's ears and glancing toward me."

Nate pulled the Budweiser bottle out of his pocket and twisted the top off. "What guys? I only see one."

Grandma Edith and I both turned to look. Jerry Pittman was still there, but not the man he'd been talking to.

"He's gone," she said. "Do you see him anywhere? He's a bald guy wearing navy slacks and a blue shirt."

"Yeah, I saw him about five minutes ago," Nate said, "going into the house. Probably had to use the bathroom."

Grandma Edith reached for one of the glasses and raised it in a salute to Nate. "Thanks. I need this. If it's not as well doctored as I'd like, be prepared to bring another."

He eyed her drink. "What's going on, Edie? Anything I can help with? Other than running off the lying relatives, of course."

"Only if you can find somebody in this crowd who wouldn't mind saying a few kind words about Dan."

He raised an eyebrow. "That bad, huh?"

"Yeah. That bad."

I didn't know whether they were referring to Grandma Edith's finances, her feelings about Grandpa Dan, or the odd behavior of the guests. During our walk toward the table, I'd sensed conversations abruptly chopped off as we approached.

Grandma Edith confirmed what I'd been thinking. "Nate, at all the rituals for the dead I've ever attended—whether they were called funerals, memorial services, or celebrations of life—people met acquaintances. They chatted and, despite the occasion, sometimes laughed, or at least chuckled quietly. There is little of that here, despite the informal setting. I thought these people were his friends, but I get the feeling very few of them have anything good to say about Dan. I'm not even sure I do. I've been sitting here trying to think about how I start. 'Dan was a charming con man' or maybe 'Dan and I were married for forty-five years and I knew him as well as any stranger I might pass on the street.'"

Searching for something she could use, I said, "He did have a big heart, Grandma Edith."

She squinted her eyes at me, considering. "You're right. Let's see. How about, 'He was generous to a fault, which was bigger than the San Andreas.' Or maybe keep it simple. 'Dan was a generous man. He'd give away your last dollar.'"

Nate looked at me with raised eyebrows, but I shook my head. I couldn't help Grandma Edith with her eulogy. I turned my attention back to her guests, glancing at the Pittmans. Daphne was still in the same group, talking to the woman next to her, but he was heading toward the back door, probably to use a bathroom.

More guests came by to say a few words and offer their condolences. Grandma Edith grew quieter. She was either tiring, worried about her eulogy, or simply wanting the condolences to end. Suspecting the latter, I glanced around the yard to see how many people hadn't yet visited our table. Katie was standing near the patio, talking to Robbie. Another woman was opening the back door to go inside.

I scrambled to my feet. At least three people had gone inside since I noticed Jerry Pittman's absence. He hadn't come out. Neither had the bald man, and the house had only two bathrooms available, three if you counted Grandma Edith's private one.

Chapter 12

I ran for the back door. Katie grabbed at my arm as I hurried by. "Hey, Marcie."

I threw her a hasty smile and wave and kept going, weaving my way around the people on the patio until I reached the back door. I yanked it open and stepped away from the outside hubbub into the quiet kitchen.

Stopping just inside the door, I listened, uncertain which way to go. There were two bathrooms to my left, so I turned that way first. The small bath at the end of the laundry room was occupied. I moved on to Grandma Edith's room. Her door was closed, probably to keep visitors out. I wished I'd thought to close mine. But, then, I didn't have anything worth stealing, and little to rummage through.

I opened Grandma Edith's door and slipped inside. Nobody was there, or in the adjoining bathroom, so I closed the door behind me and headed for the only remaining bathroom, at the other end of the house.

When I got to the dining room, I stopped again to listen. A faint sound reached me from the bathroom next to the office. I crossed the dining room and living room. Muffled sounds came from the office. I stepped into the short hallway just as the closed door to the bathroom opened.

The woman who rushed out bumped me, let out a startled gasp, then stepped back. "I'm sorry. I didn't expect anybody..."

I wasn't listening. The sounds in the office had escalated with the woman's voice, changing to a fast shuffling noise, then a loud scrape, followed by a thump.

I tried to dodge around the well-endowed woman but she moved in the same direction then stopped, laughing. I was in no mood to play the "shall we dance?" game. I shoved her aside and lunged for the office door, opening it to reveal the back of a man in the process of climbing out the window into the side yard. He already had one leg thrown over the window sill.

A thought flashed through my mind that he was the same man who had stolen Grandpa Dan's clothes, that he'd somehow found the bag in the closet and dropped it out the window. But a glance at the open files scattered across the desk told me otherwise.

Other than commanding him to stop, which I had a hunch he'd ignore, I could do nothing but run across the room, grab the leg remaining inside, and hang on. I yelled at the startled woman to get help. Instead, she stared at me, her mouth hanging open, eyes wide.

"Go!" I screamed. "This guy is a thief. There's a cop outside. Get him!"

That prodded her into action. She gave me a quick nod and trotted away.

The man was hanging out the window now, head first, his free foot scrabbling to push against the house for traction. His hands may have grasped something to pull on because he was slipping away, inch by inch. From his profanity-punctuated yelps, I assumed he was grabbing at the branches of Grandma Edith's yellow rose bush. That was going to give him some nasty puncture wounds, though probably not as bad as Grandma Edith would inflict if she caught him after he damaged her roses.

He was wearing dress pants, making my grip less solid than if he'd been wearing jeans. My hands slipped from just below his knee to his shin, then to his ankle and his shiny black loafer.

I managed to get a better grasp around his ankle with both hands, but the man was heavy and gravity was not on my side. I pushed the soles of both my feet against the wall and leaned back with all my weight.

He slipped away so suddenly I lost my balance, falling backward into the bulk of Officer Roberts. He stumbled, took a couple of awkward steps, trying to regain his balance, then went down, carrying me with him.

It was not a romantic moment. The navy-blue dress I'd worn for the memorial service had pulled up around my thighs, and Roberts's arm was holding one of my hands down. The other held a man's black loafer.

I pushed Roberts's arms off me and clambered to my feet, holding the loafer with one hand and tugging at my skirt with the other. I almost fell against the desk and swore when I looked down and saw the broken heel on my strappy patent-leather dress shoe—a favorite pair I couldn't afford to replace.

Nate stood in the doorway, taking in the scene: me, leaning on the desk, pulling my skirt into place; Roberts getting up from the floor; the open drawers on Grandpa Dan's desk and the folders and papers scattered across it. His gaze wandered to the open window, then back to the loafer I still held in one hand.

"Looks like a tough way to catch a man, Marcie."

I gave him a weak smile. "It belongs to Jerry Pittman." I nodded toward the window. "I saw him come in the house earlier, then caught him in here. He lost the shoe when he climbed out of the window."

"Why would Jerry Pittman go through your grandfather's files?" Roberts asked.

"I don't know. Why don't you ask him? With only one shoe, he should be easy to find."

I was right about that. When Roberts went out the front door, he found Pittman sitting in one of the wicker chairs on Grandma Edith's front porch, drinking a beer he'd probably cadged from the refrigerator. Both his black Oxfords were on his feet, neatly tied. Roberts stuck his head back in the door to let me know. "I'll see if I can find somebody missing a shoe."

"Too bad we're not a little farther out in the country," Nate said, grinning. "He'd be easy to track in the dirt."

That made me smile, which was probably Nate's intent. I tossed the loafer to Roberts. "Maybe you can take it around Miner's Ridge and see who it fits."

Nate chimed in. "I doubt you'll find many wicked step-brothers trying to shove a foot into it."

Roberts's lips lifted into a half-smile as he looked down at my broken heel. "I'm more interested in getting closer to a Cinderella, so don't run away."

Nate watched him go then looked back at me, one eyebrow lifting. "That man knows you're married, doesn't he?"

"Nate, I'm not."

"Not what?" A frown was forming between his eyebrows.

"Not married. Randy and I got a divorce, but he's been too chicken to tell Grandma Edith, so she doesn't know. I didn't want to tell her until after...after today."

He studied me for a minute, then nodded. "You're right. That news is going to hit her hard and she has enough to deal with already. But you can't wait too long."

"I know. I'll try to do it by the weekend. Randy plans to come up then."

"Well, just so you know, you can be my granddaughter anytime. I like the way you try to catch a man." He took my arm. "I think we'd better go see how your grandma is doing. If you need a doctored glass of punch first, I can fix one." He winked. "I know where your grandma keeps the good stuff."

"That's the best offer I've had all day, Nate. Maybe all week. But I've got to find another pair of shoes first."

He patted my arm. "I'll fix the drinks while you do that."

I hadn't brought many shoes, so it was either sneakers or my everyday sandals. The sandals won, though they were so old and well-worn, it was a close contest.

When we got back out to the patio, Grandma Edith was holding the microphone, speaking to her guests. We'd missed her eulogy. Neither Nate nor I would ever know what she'd said about Grandpa Dan because we just caught the end of her speech: "I want to thank Jack Loudon for the exemplary job he did cleaning the patio."

At the mention of his name, Loudon broke off the conversation he was having with two other men. He looked startled, then pleased when people gave him approving glances. Some even applauded.

Grandma Edith spread her arms to encompass the space around her. "Isn't it wonderful? I promised him I'd make an announcement today at the end of the memorial service, so he could get his message to all of you good neighbors. He's starting a pressure-washing business and as a new-customer bonus, he's offering a big discount. Fifty percent off for the first ten people who call him."

Loudon, mouth agape, shook his head so hard I thought his brain might rattle around in all that empty space, but Grandma Edith plowed on, reading his phone number aloud from a card she held in her hand. "His prices are some of the most reasonable around, even before the discount, so you don't want to pass this one up, folks. Give him a call."

She handed the microphone to Robbie, smiled, and turned to face us. "I see you two have fixed yourselves another drink. Where's mine?"

Nate grinned. "I liked your eulogy, what I heard of it." He handed me his drink. "Here, hold mine while I fix one for your grandma."

He went back into the house and Katie joined us. "Grandma, I can't stay long this trip. I have to be in D.C. Monday morning, and I want to spend some time with Natalie and Randy before I go. But I'd like to come back when you scatter Grandpa's ashes."

An image of that potato chip bag in the bathroom trash can floated through my head. I tried to keep a straight face as I watched Grandma Edith, wondering how she would handle this.

"Uh...I...well..." She closed her eyes for a few seconds, as though she were gathering her thoughts. "I didn't know you wanted to be here for that, Katie. I wish you'd let me know. You see, I already scattered them."

"Oh! Already? Where?" Katie asked. "I think I'd like to visit the site before I leave if it's not too far."

Grandma Edith patted her shoulder. "You already have, honey. He's right here in the yard."

Katie spun to face the lawn. "Where? Where exactly?"

Grandma Edith pointed toward the back fence. "Over there, by the birdbath. Your grandpa liked to sit out here and watch the birds splashing around. He enjoyed the squirrels, too. That was one of their favorite areas, between the birdbath and the oak tree."

Katie nodded, her eyes misting over a little. "That's so sweet, Grandma."

Grandma Edith put her arm around Katie. "We'll talk some more tonight after everybody leaves."

"I'd love that. I can't stay overnight, much as I'd like to, but it would be nice to have a short visit with just family." She glanced back at the birdbath. "Natalie and I are going to make a quick trip into Miner's Ridge. All the guests will probably be gone by the time we get back." She turned toward me. "Want to go with us, Marcie?"

Did she and Natalie want to talk to me away from Grandma Edith, or was she just being polite? "No. Thanks for the offer, but I think I'll stay and help with the cleanup."

"Okay." She went to find Natalie. Grandma Edith watched her go, then turned toward the door. "What's keeping Nate and my drink?"

I went to help Cynthia and her daughters. They had already begun to discretely put away food and clear tables while the last of the guests made their way out of the yard. Once all of them were gone, the work went quickly, everybody dismantling whatever they had set up earlier. Nate went home and the rest of us got in each other's way as we put away food and washed up chafing dishes and the big percolator. Nobody mentioned my divorce, so I could only assume Randy hadn't told them.

"Let's dish up some of this dessert and take it out on the patio," Grandma Edith said. "Or fix yourself a drink, if you'd prefer."

I opted for a glass of red wine and was pouring another for Robbie when Cynthia opened the back door. "Ooh, look at that."

When I went outside, I could see why Katie and Natalie had gone to town. They'd been doing some shopping. A ring of candles now glowed in a large circle around the birdbath.

I took a big gulp of wine. Grandma Edith made a slight choking sound from somewhere behind me. I turned just in time to see her heading back inside.

Nate was in his back yard, looking over the fence. He beckoned me over. "Why are all those candles out there, over the septic tank?"

I took another drink of my wine and tried a nonchalant shrug. "Who knows?"

He was studying my face, frowning.

"If I were you, I wouldn't ask Grandma Edith," I said. "If she tells you, she'll probably have to kill you."

That made him smile. "I'll wait until you've told her about the divorce and she's intent on killing Randy."

I laughed. "Good night, Nate. I'll talk to you tomorrow."

After everybody finally left that night, I detoured into the office to check the windows. They were securely latched. I turned to leave, then decided I might as well ensure the hospital bag was still safely stowed in the closet.

When I opened the door something—or someone—jumped out, pushing against me to get away. I stumbled back, letting out a loud gasp, too startled to scream. Hair pressed against my mouth and nose. Taking unsteady steps backward, I batted it away so I could breathe. A muffled thunk sounded at my feet. I looked down. A head stared up at me, eyes wide open.

I almost did scream then, before I recognized what lay at my feet: a wig, fastened to an all-too-realistic form. I stared at it, taking long, deep breaths to get my heart rate back to normal, but I couldn't stop my racing mind. Why would either Grandma Edith or Grandpa Dan have a blonde wig? Or any of the other objects in the closet? A long, white cane, like those used by the blind. Several hats, ranging from baseball caps to Stetsons. Different kinds of coats. Uniforms. Boxes with stick-on logos for vehicles, and patches for uniform pockets. Arm and leg braces and a cervical collar. A box containing ragged pants, shirt and jacket, and shoes with a loose sole held on with a wide rubber band.

Finally, once I was breathing normally, I realized they must be disguises Grandpa Dan used for his surveillance operations. All he needed to go with the box of ragged clothes was a shopping cart piled with a worn-out sleeping bag and other junk. I wouldn't be surprised to find one hidden away in the work area out back.

I tried to push the wig deeper onto the shelf, closed the closet door, and picked up the hospital bag. But where to take it? I didn't dare put it in the garbage can again—not until trash pick-up on Monday. Maybe, if I could get it out of the house unnoticed, I could stash it in the trunk of the Camaro, then dump it later, somewhere far from Miner's Ridge. For now, I'd hide it in my bedroom.

While I was pushing it against the wall under the bed, I remembered telling Roberts that I'd let him know what the thief had put into that bag. What was I going to tell him?

I still hadn't figured out the answer to that question when he arrived, a little after ten that night.

"Did you find somebody whose foot..." My voice trailed off. There would be no Cinderella quips tonight. He had put on his professional face, devoid of expression.

"I apologize for the lateness of the hour," he said, "but there's been a new development in the case, one I thought your grandmother would like to know about right away."

"Did you find the man with the missing shoe?"

"No, and the shoe is a common brand, sold in most department stores. Is your grandmother here? I need to speak to her."

I stood aside so he could enter, then followed him into the living room, where Grandma Edith stood, watching us. "Good evening, Officer Roberts. What brings you back so late in the evening?"

He motioned toward the sofa. "Would you mind if we sit down? This could take some time."

She hesitated, perhaps sensing—as did I—that whatever Roberts was about to divulge, he was concerned about its impact on her.

She reached for my hand and pulled me down onto the sofa beside her before turning back to Roberts. "What's going on? What have you come to tell us?"

He lowered himself into a chair. "There's been a new development we need to talk about."

Grandma Edith dipped her head in a slight nod. She was so calm, I think she was already resigned to whatever Roberts had to say.

"We have a witness to your husband's death. She doesn't think it was an accident."

Grandma Edith let go of my hand and rose partway to her feet, one hand pressed to her mouth. Then she faltered and sank back onto the sofa. I put an arm around her, pulling her closer.

Roberts glanced at me, his eyes troubled. "She—the witness—says Mr. Clifton had the signal and was almost across the street, close to the sidewalk when the other car swerved toward him."

One look at Grandma Edith's pale face and I jumped to my feet. "Sit still, Grandma Edith. I'll get you some water."

When I came back, Roberts was again asking her about the night Grandpa Dan died. "If this was a murder and not an accident, it's more critical than ever that we know where he was going that night. He may have said something that could give us a lead."

Grandma Edith shook her head. "I've gone over and over it, and I simply don't remember what we might have said to each other. It didn't seem important at the time. I don't think he told me where he was going. Just that he had to take care of something. That was nothing out of the ordinary."

Roberts let out a small, almost inaudible sigh. "Maybe with the celebration of life over and everything settling down, something will come to you. If it does, no matter how minor it may seem, please call me. Every hour that goes by makes it less likely that we'll ever solve the crime."

I felt like smacking him. Reminding Grandma Edith of the minutes ticking away while she couldn't remember wasn't going to help. But assaulting a police officer wasn't going to help, either, so I did the next best thing and changed the subject. "Tell us about this witness. Why is she just now coming forward?"

"Because she's a seventeen-year-old girl who had sneaked out of the house to see her boyfriend. She'd been grounded, so she didn't want her parents to know. She's spent the past week feeling guilty and finally, after church on Sunday, realized she had to come clean." His lips quirked again in that little half-smile. "She still wanted to know if we could keep it from her parents."

Then the smile disappeared. "A week has gone by without us even suspecting this was a murder. There will be nothing more to find at the scene, and any clues have gone cold. We need every detail your grandmother can dredge up—"

I rose to my feet. "You're right, but she certainly can't do that with you pressuring her. Give her some time to think about it."

"Of course. I'll come back tomorrow."

He put on his cap and walked down the porch steps. This time Grandma Edith didn't comment that he knew more than he was telling us. And a cold shiver ran up my spine, everything that had happened taking on new significance. Had I grappled with a murderer, either by the garbage can or at the office window? And where were those two men now?

Chapter 13

I awoke Thursday morning to a quiet house. Grandma Edith had been tired after Officer Roberts left the night before; maybe she'd slept in, just as I had.

Sleep had evaded me until sometime well after two a.m., my mind jumping from the news of Grandpa Dan's murder to the possibility that one of the men I'd struggled with the day before might have been his killer, then to my unexpected encounter with the wig in Grandpa Dan's office.

Even after my body began to relax, I'd lain awake for a long time, trying to make sense of everything that had happened since I arrived in Miner's Ridge Sunday afternoon. Why would anybody want to murder Grandpa Dan? Why steal his torn and bloody clothes from the garbage can? We'd found nothing unusual in them, other than the piece of paper with the number 5211 scrawled on it, and I could think of no way to learn its meaning. What was the intruder in Grandpa Dan's office looking for that we hadn't found? What had happened to Grandma Edith's money?

I hadn't found any answers during that long, restless night, and more time in bed wasn't going to help. I got up and went to find Grandma Edith.

She wasn't in the house or on the front porch. I glanced out the patio door. She was coming through the gate from the back work area, dusting off her clothes as she strode toward the house. The candles around the septic tank were gone.

"If it's okay with you, I'm going to do some laundry this morning," I told her. "I can do yours, too, and anything else you need done while you just relax. Maybe if you sit out on the patio for a while, enjoying the sun and flowers, something may come to you that Officer Roberts can use."

She shook her head. "I think I'll have a go at some of Dan's client files. I suspect that's more likely to trigger some memories."

Every time I passed her office while I was putting laundry away, she was immersed in files, inputting information into her laptop. I tried not to disturb her, hoping she was right and a relevant memory would surface.

My task didn't take long—I hadn't brought many clothes with me. At loose ends after I finished, I considered moving the hospital bag out to the car but wasn't sure I could get it past the open office door without Grandma Edith noticing. Finally, for lack of anything better to do, I poured a cup of coffee, and took it out to the patio.

I'd barely settled into my chair when Grandma Edith came out, smiling. "How would you like to take a drive?"

I glanced up at the clear blue sky. Did she want to take a ride in the convertible? With the top down? "Grandma Edith, I can't—"

Her smile disappeared. "I suppose you have to get home, back to Randy and your job, and I'm just being selfish. But I wish you could stay a little longer. I need your help."

Visions of car repossessions danced in my head. "No, it's okay. I don't have to get back just yet. What do you have in mind?"

"I want to teach you how to play pool. Eight-ball, to be exact."

I'm sure my mouth dropped open. This wasn't like Grandma Edith, not when there was work to be done. Then I had another vision, of me beating Randy at his own game. "Okay. When?"

"Now, but not in one of the bars in Miner's Ridge. There's an out-of-the-way tavern Dan and I used to go to, years ago. It's a few miles out, on one of the back roads. I hear they still have a pool table and not a lot of people wandering in, especially this early in the day. If you're ready, we can have breakfast there."

"Can we afford to? I mean, I don't have much money and I know you—"

"It's the least we can do, since we'll be using their pool table for most of the day. And I've already packed us a picnic lunch for later."

I understood then. She'd told Roberts she needed some time to think and this was her way of doing it. She wanted to get away from the house and relax, wind down from the past week's stress, doing something she enjoyed.

"Okay," I said. "Give me five minutes to change."

She didn't even glance at the convertible as we headed toward her Malibu. She seemed distracted. Maybe she was remembering something Roberts could use, and I didn't want to disrupt that, so I didn't say anything.

She hadn't exaggerated about the back road. It had two lanes and we seemed to be the only vehicle on it. Brush and trees encroached from both sides, and Grandma Edith had already slowed to make a turn before I saw the weathered-board sign: The Tavern.

"Innovative name," I said.

"It is, in a way. After all, how many taverns do you see in the foothills? In the entire state of California, for that matter? And it was named long before your time. Maybe even mine."

I motioned toward the vegetation alongside the road. "I'm a little surprised anybody finds the place. They must not do much business."

She laughed. "They don't need that sign and they purposely keep the place secluded. Everybody for miles around knows how to get to The Tavern. The owners are just selective about their customers. They don't care much for flatlanders."

"Flatlanders?" Then I got it. People from the valley, mostly urban dwellers.

Grandma Edith slowed as she rounded a curve. A rock structure about the size of a small country church came into view on our left. A sign above the door, not quite as weathered as the one beside the road, told me this was The Tavern. The area at the side of the building nearest us held several picnic tables and benches, along with a built-in grill made of the same river rock as The Tavern. A few yards from them, a path meandered down a gentle slope to a shallow creek.

Grandma Edith parked in the empty packed-dirt lot. We got out and I stood for a moment, admiring the view. "What a great place for a picnic."

"Dan and I used to see a lot of families on Sundays, the kids wading in the creek or playing at the water's edge."

The Tavern's interior was dark, the few windows old and small. Wooden tables and chairs lined one side, near the kitchen. A long bar was on the other side, along with a pool table.

I looked up at the wooden beams. "This place looks like it's been here forever. When was it built?"

She lifted her shoulders in a slight shrug. "I don't know. Probably back to gold-mining days. Are you ready for breakfast?"

A short, plump woman came out from the kitchen carrying a Pyrex coffee decanter, a smile creasing her round face. She was probably in her late fifties or early sixties, with streaks of gray in her dark bun. She filled our cups with coffee. "I just fired up the grill. I've got a batch of blueberry pancakes ready to cook, or I can get you some bacon and eggs with biscuits I just took out of the oven. Or I have ham if you prefer. Fresh, homemade apple butter or peach jam, too."

I was not about to ask for a menu and label myself a flatlander, so I ordered bacon and eggs, scrambled, with biscuits and apple butter.

When it came, it was so good, it almost made up for all those casseroles I'd been eating. I found myself making mental notes, retracing our route, so I could find the place again. I was coming back here.

"What do you know about eight-ball?" Grandma Edith asked as we were eating the last of our meal.

"Not much. I've watched Randy play, so I know each player tries to get all his balls—solids or stripes—into the pockets before the other guy. Then he has to call the pocket he's going to put the eight ball in. If he makes it, he wins the game."

Grandma Edith sipped her coffee. "The white cue ball is the only one that isn't numbered, the only one you're allowed to hit with the cue stick, and the only one that must never go into a pocket. If it does, that's called a scratch, and you lose your turn. If it scratches while you're shooting at the eight, you lose the game."

I nodded. I knew all that.

She pushed her coffee cup aside. "So, are you ready for your first lesson?" Not waiting for an answer, she got up and walked toward the pool table with me trailing behind.

In the next hour, she taught me how to select and hold the cue stick, how to bridge my hand on the table, and how to line up my shots. "Get your head down at table level and find the exact spot that aligns your target ball with a pocket. Then aim the cue ball so it hits that spot."

We didn't rack the balls or play a game. She set up shots for me, watching as I hit the cue ball into them. I was getting a feel for the stick and how hard to hit the cue ball, but wasn't pocketing many balls.

"It'll come in time," she said. "Set up shots and practice. While you're doing that, I'm going to scroll through texts and calls on Dan's phone to see what I can find."

She went back to our table, pulled a pad and pencil out of her purse, and asked for another cup of coffee. I scattered several balls around the table, both solid and stripes, and started practicing.

She seemed so engrossed, I assumed she was no longer paying attention to me. But, every so often when I missed a shot, she'd tell me, "You missed that because you didn't follow through," or "keep your stick level."

Throughout the morning, people—more than I would have expected—filtered into The Tavern for breakfast. The audience made me nervous until I realized few of them were paying any attention to me. That changed with the lunch crowd. Some of them approached the now-open bar and lingered for a few minutes, watching me while they waited for their drink orders.

I missed an easy shot. This time, Grandma Edith didn't call out a correction. "How about a break, Marcie? Could you use some fresh air?"

I put the cue stick back in the wall rack and followed her outside.

"You'll always have people watching you play," she said, as we walked toward the path leading down to the creek. "Try not to take it personally. It's like any sport. They're just interested in the game, wondering if you'll make your next shot."

"I know. It's just...I'm so bad. It would be nice to have a little privacy while I'm learning."

She laughed. "This is about as private a place as you're going to find unless you know somebody who owns a pool table. Bowling alleys are great places to learn, too, if you can find one that has a table."

We'd reached the creek. The water was clear, sparkling in the sunlight, and had enough exposed rocks I could have walked across. People often did. I could see a path on the other side. I wanted to explore it, to see what was over there. No, what I really wanted was to delay my return to the pool table until the crowd was gone.

Grandma Edith, perhaps reading my mind and taking pity on me, turned back toward the parking lot. "Let's go get our picnic lunch."

I pulled the cooler out of the Malibu and carried it to one of the picnic tables. Grandma Edith unpacked sandwiches, cookies, and two cold Coronas.

"I wasn't sure whether I should bring those," she said. "But I figure we're not hurting their sales. We would have just done without, since we can't afford to buy them."

"Grandma Edith, you can't be enjoying yourself too much today, teaching me to play pool and working with Grandpa Dan's phone. So why did you really want to come up here?"

"Maybe to get away from Officer Roberts and the questions I can't answer. Or maybe just to come back to a place with good memories. And I am enjoying myself, teaching you how to play pool. When you get good enough, we can play some games."

I had meant to ask her if she'd thought of anything more about Grandpa Dan but decided to drop it.

The sun was warm on my back and I could hear the faint splash of the creek as it washed over and around rocks. I had a sudden urge to kick off my shoes, roll up my pant legs, and go wading, but Grandma Edith had a different kind of pool in mind. We packed up the cooler, put it away, and went back inside. She set up more shots, and I practiced for another two hours before she called it a day. By that time, I was pocketing most of the straight shots and was learning how to keep a ball running straight down a rail. But I knew from watching Randy's games that few shots were as easy as the ones I was making.

Why was I thinking about Randy's pool game? Exactly when did I plan to beat him? We wouldn't be going out; we weren't together anymore, something I seemed to have trouble remembering since I'd been with Grandma Edith. It was definitely time for me to move on, to get a new life.

Chapter 14

As we sat on the patio late that afternoon, Grandma Edith asked me to dig through Grandpa Dan's business files. "Try to find whatever is causing the break-ins and whether it has anything to do with my missing money. And look for anything with Ray's name on it."

"Grandma Edith, why not let the police do that? I'd be surprised if they don't take those files, anyway. With their experience, they'll find things I might miss."

"Take them? Surely not everything! Those tax records! If they dig into those, I could be responsible for years of back taxes for things I didn't even know Dan was doing, like claiming me as an employee. And I would be responsible. I signed those tax forms. But I never looked at the ones he filled out for his business, something I knew little about."

"I don't think they can prove you weren't an employee," I said. "And I doubt if they'd care."

"You're probably right. They're trying to solve a murder and I don't want to get in the way of that. I want Dan's killer caught. But I also want to find out where my money went if it's at all possible."

"It might be best if you make them get a search warrant."

A frown creased her forehead. "I don't understand. What difference would it make? They'd still see the contents of those files."

"Yes, but if you give them permission, they can use anything they find as evidence. If they get a warrant, they have to specify exactly what they're looking for and, should they run across anything not mentioned in that warrant, it's not admissible in court."

"But wouldn't they list all the files, everything in that office?"

I shrugged. "Maybe, but there's a chance they would hone in on his P.I. files. Or anything pertaining to his murder."

She was quiet for a few minutes while she pulled Grandpa Dan's phone out of her pocket and ran her fingers over its surface. Finally, she set it on the table. "I want you to go through those files before they ask to see them. Look for anything that might lead to my missing money."

"Okay, but wouldn't it be better if we both did that?"

"No. If there is something incriminating in those folders, I don't need to see it. I live in Miner's Ridge, Marcie. I don't want compromising images flashing before my eyes every time I greet somebody I know. You work on the files and I'll get as much as I can off Dan's phone before they confiscate that, too."

Grandpa Dan's files were well-organized with household accounts and tax records separate from his business folders. I ran my fingers over the printed tabs on the folders but found nothing with Ray's name on it.

I pulled out a half dozen folders and sat down to study the contents. They contained reports of his findings, billing statements and ledger-like notes of payments received or in arrears. The amounts surprised me, ranging from hundreds to thousands of dollars, but they did explain the healthy deposits into his business account.

Some of the folders held photographs, apparently evidence for the conclusions he'd reached in his reports. A few showed couples in tight embraces on porches or in dimly lit doorways. Several were of couples walking into hotel or motel rooms. Others were more intimate, ranging from full nudity in an outdoor hot tub to a couple in bathing suits, the woman's top missing, entangled on a pool-side lounge chair.

A few of the pictures seemed innocuous: a man loading boxes into a car, then unloading them into a storage unit; a woman trying to unlock what appeared to be an apartment door, judging by the number "2A" on it; a man walking across a brushy field carrying a five-gallon can; another man engaged in several physical activities. Then I looked at the reports clipped to the photographs: a theft of business inventory; an apartment burglary; a suspected arsonist; and a disability claim.

I went back to the file cabinet, searching for bulky envelopes to match the names on the folder tabs. I didn't find any. Apparently, not every folder had one. I pulled out a random envelope. It contained several thumb drives and audiotapes. I assumed the thumb drives were backups of computer files. The audiotapes could be original recordings, taken from a bugging device. I suspected there would be a player in the drawer where I'd found all the photography equipment, but I didn't look for it. There might be copies somewhere on the computer. We could come back to them later, providing we had time. Instead, I browsed through the rest of the envelopes, hoping to find some connection to that blue poker chip or the number 5211 we'd found on the scrap of paper. I couldn't find either, nor could I find any way to connect the material in those files to Grandma Edith's missing money. I put all the folders and envelopes away and locked the drawers just as the doorbell rang.

I went to answer it and found Officer Roberts standing on the porch, his hat under his arm. I led him into the kitchen. Grandma Edith stood at the counter, making coffee. The pad and pen she'd been using to make notes were nowhere in sight, but Grandpa Dan's phone was still on the table.

She measured coffee into the filter. "Good afternoon, Officer Roberts. I wish I had better news, but I still haven't thought of anything that might help you. Dan seemed...I don't know. Distracted, maybe. Remote. Quieter than usual. Possibly worried. He wasn't talking much, so I really don't know. He was out of the house a lot, especially in the evenings but, with his business, that wasn't unusual." She pushed the button to start the coffee brewing then motioned toward the table. "I had hoped I might find something on my husband's phone, but haven't had any luck there, either."

He picked it up. "Do you mind if I take a look at it?"

"No, of course not."

He slipped it into his pocket, wrote a receipt, and handed it to her. "Maybe something will come to you. If it does, no matter how insignificant it may seem, call me."

"Isn't a detective usually assigned to a murder case?" I asked.

He flushed. "With our small budget, we can barely afford patrol cars and officers. A detective wouldn't have much to do around Miner's Ridge. It would be a waste of resources."

"Yet, just this past week we had a hit-and-run that turned out to be a murder, an attempted bank robbery, and somebody breaking into my husband's desk," Grandma Edith said. "Practically a crime wave."

Either he didn't catch the sarcasm or chose to ignore it. "Don't forget the man Marcie caught—"

"Almost caught. By the leg," I interrupted, to keep him from mentioning the garbage thief. I babbled on, grasping at anything I could think of to change the subject. "So you're going to try to solve all this without an experienced detective?"

"For the time being. We're hoping something in your grandfather's office will help us solve the case quickly. If not, we'll probably have to borrow a detective from the Nevada County Sheriff's Office or the state."

That option was clearly difficult for him to contemplate, but I didn't think a search of the office would help. "I went through some of Grandpa Dan's case files this afternoon. I can understand why the subjects of some of those investigations would break into his desk, trying to get their hands on the files—if they knew they existed. But how would they know? The people paying for the investigations certainly wouldn't have told them."

He drew his eyebrows together. "You're right. And that means the man you caught in the office had to be looking for something else."

Before he could say more, I nodded. "The same logic applies to Grandpa Dan's death. The only people aware of the investigations, other than Grandpa Dan, would be the people who hired him. What possible motive could they have for killing the detective they'd hired?"

"Still, it's the only thing we have, and there was an attempt to break into the desk. It's possible somebody either found out or suspected they were being investigated and didn't want the information to come out." He turned to Grandma Edith. "If it's agreeable with you, I'd like to take a look at those files."

She pulled three mugs from the cabinet and started pouring coffee into them. "You'll need this, then." She handed one mug to him and another to me. "Marcie can show you where his business files are located. And Officer Roberts? I'm sure there's some sensitive information in there. I'd appreciate it if you handled it with discretion. And I'm trusting you not to go through my personal files."

I almost nodded my appreciation. She had decided the safest route was to bank on Officer Roberts's inexperience as a detective and his basic decency. Much as he might be tempted, I doubted he'd look at anything except those business files. Still, I planned to keep an eye on him. After showing him the drawers containing the P.I. files, I left the room, leaving the door open. Grandma Edith might have meant me to stay in the office, but I could watch Officer Roberts from my room well enough to see which cabinets he was accessing.

I didn't want to be alone with him in that small room. Or maybe I did, and my brain, noticing the uptick of my pulse rate when he got too close, was signaling my body to stay clear. Despite my divorce, I hadn't managed to shake Randy loose yet. I didn't need another man in my life, no matter how appealing he might be.

Watching Roberts as he worked his way through the files got me to thinking. Why were we searching the investigation files for leads to Grandma Edith's money? I'd already leafed through the tax material and didn't think I'd find anything there, or even in the household accounts, though they deserved a closer look.

Grandma Edith had been sitting at the desk the first time I'd unlocked a file cabinet. The desk had two drawers, and she had pulled the American Express statements out of the one on the left-hand side. Why was it there, rather than with the other household accounts? And what was in the other drawer, the one on the desk extension?

We needed to find out, but not now. Grandma Edith was calling me to dinner and Officer Roberts was ready to leave.

"Would you walk me out?" he asked.

Assuming he'd found something in the files he wanted to discuss with me before talking to Grandma Edith, I called to her that I'd be just a few minutes. I walked out onto the porch with Roberts, but I wasn't prepared for his question.

"There's a dance at the Grange Hall Saturday night. Would you like to go? With me? We could have dinner somewhere first—"

Despite my brain's frantic signals, I wanted to say yes. I hadn't had much fun since arriving in Miner's Ridge, and I loved to dance. Besides, I reasoned, it would give me a chance to pick Eric Roberts's brain. Then I remembered. Randy was coming on Saturday, and we had to talk to Grandma Edith.

"I'm sorry, I can't. Maybe if—"

He gave me a half-hearted smile. "It's okay. I shouldn't have asked. Not while I'm working on your grandfather's case. And it's obvious that you're here as part of some kind of investigation. I had just hoped we might work together."

"I'm not..."

He reached toward my hair, as though he meant to brush it away from my face, then stopped, his hand in mid-air. "I understand. But once this case is over, I'm going to ask you again."

He turned and walked down the steps, and I went back into the house for dinner.

I had been surprised when Grandma Edith let him have Grandpa Dan's phone, so I asked her about it while we were eating.

"I want to cooperate with them as much as I can," she said. "They can get the information off the phone anytime they want, and I don't need it anymore. I've already made notes of everything, both incoming and outgoing over the past six months. Now I'm going to try to organize it into a spreadsheet so I can sort it by caller, date, or whatever seems to make the most sense. I'm hoping that will give us something we can work with. I'll take my laptop and start putting it together while you're practicing your pool game tomorrow."

"We're going back to The Tavern again? Grandma Edith, why are you so intent on me learning to play pool?"

She arched an eyebrow. "Intent? I thought we were just relaxing, having a little fun together. But if you'd rather not, we can find something else to do. Maybe lay some bark."

"No. No, it's fine. I'm enjoying the lessons and it's a nice drive." But I didn't believe her. She was plotting something, and I was beginning to wonder if scheming came from both lines of Randy's genealogy; I suspected Grandma Edith was as good at it as Grandpa Dan. Maybe better.

Chapter 15

I asked Grandma Edith about the desk files the next morning while she drove to The Tavern. She hadn't looked in the right-hand drawer, either. She'd meant to but stopped when she found the American Express statement.

While we were eating breakfast, she went back to the pool lessons. "One of the most important things to learn is cue-ball English. If you want to keep it from following a ball into the pocket and scratching, hit it low. That stops or slows it. If you want the cue ball to follow, hit it a little high. Both are important for getting position for the next shot. Be careful, though, that you don't dig a trench in the felt on those low shots. Owners frown on repairs caused by careless players."

"So that's English," I said. "I've heard Randy talk about it, but wasn't sure what it meant."

"He probably uses more than top and bottom English, but stick to those for now. The others are tricky and they take time and patience to learn."

It was Friday and more people inhabited The Tavern that afternoon than earlier in the week. I tried to ignore them until two little boys, about four and six, came to watch me. The younger boy, fascinated by the brightly-colored balls, reached up to grab one off the table.

"No. Don't touch," I said, in my best nursery-school-teacher voice.

He drew his hand back and stuck out his lower lip. Was he going to cry? I looked over at the tables, searching for his parents, and settled on a blonde woman with a toddler on her lap. At her feet were a diaper bag and two kids' backpacks. She glanced my way, her attention on the boys, then gave me a quick smile. Apparently reassured that her kids were safe, she returned to an animated conversation with the plump woman across the table from her.

I looked back at the boys just in time to see the youngest kid grab the thirteen ball and duck under the table. His partner in crime crossed his arms and stared at me.

I'd never had much experience with kids. Randy referred to his nephews as "curtain-climbing, crumb-hustling little house apes." I was beginning to appreciate his sentiments.

I didn't need all the balls to practice, so I lined up on the three and drew back my cue stick. A small foot slammed into my shin. I hit the cue ball too low and too hard. While I stared at the felt, praying it hadn't torn, the cue ball bounced off a rail, rose into the air, and plummeted toward the floor, landing with a solid thunk. One of the kids? No, no, no. If it hit one of them in the head, it would probably kill him.

I leaned down so I could see under the table. Both boys grinned back at me, each holding up a ball. They'd won; I couldn't practice without that cue ball. I rubbed my shin, thinking about visiting the bar.

Before I could rise, a man approached the other end of the table and lowered himself to the kids' level, pushing tousled sandy-blond hair out of his eyes. "Hey guys, what are you doing under here? Didn't you hear the ruckus outside? Somebody saw a bear coming up out of the canyon."

The boys scrambled from under the table. The man grabbed the pool balls from their hands as they rose to sprint for the door.

"You can't send them outside," I said. "Not if there's a wild animal out there!"

He grinned. "There's no bear, and mothers may not pay enough attention when their kids are safe inside, but those boys will never get out that door."

He was right. The blonde woman with the toddler lifted him from her lap and plunked him in a chair at the same time she was rising from hers. "You two! Get back here right now. You know you're not allowed outside unless somebody is with you."

"But there's a bear—"

"I don't know where you got that idea, but it's all the more reason to stay inside. Now, do as I say. Get your butts back here."

The kids looked our way, their gazes settling on the man who now stood beside the pool table, holding the cue ball in one hand and the thirteen in the other. They must have decided he wouldn't be the easy target I had been. They followed the woman back to the table.

The man turned to face me, grinning. He was probably somewhere in his late twenties or early thirties, a little stocky, and sun-tanned, with a small mustache a shade darker than his hair.

He put a quarter on the table, pulled a cue stick off the rack and sighted down it to make sure it was straight. I shook my head. "I can't...I'm just learning. I've never played a game." I glanced at Grandma Edith, trying to signal that I didn't know what to do.

She smiled at me. "Go ahead. Playing against somebody will give you some good practice. Just keep in mind that knocking the cue ball off the table is a sure way to lose the game."

Cheeks burning, I turned back to the table. The man put several coins in the slot. "I'm Brad Kinney, and you don't have anything to worry about. I'm not very good, either."

"I'm Marcie Clifton, and I'm serious. I don't know how to rack the balls or how to break."

"Okay, I'll show you." He pulled the triangular rack off the wall and I watched while he dropped the balls inside, pulled them tight, then carefully lifted the rack so he didn't disturb them. "Eight goes in the middle, one ball in front, a stripe in one corner, a solid in the other. Alternate the rest as best you can." He looked up at me from pale blue eyes. "I racked so you get to break. Just aim the cue ball into the little space between the one ball in front and the one beside it. Either side, doesn't matter. Hit it fairly hard and follow through."

I didn't pocket a ball on the break but hadn't expected to. I didn't even scatter them much. They were still in a loose cluster around the eight.

Brad spoke little as he played. He pocketed two stripes, breaking out the cluster of balls a little more before I got a turn. I surprised myself by pocketing two solids and almost making a third.

Brad walked around the table, chalking his cue stick, looking at possible shots, then tried a bank to a corner pocket. He missed, leaving me the easy shot from my prior miss, then a possible shot at the four ball. I missed it, but the cue ball caromed off it into the six and pocketed it.

"Great shot!" a guy from the bar said.

I'm sure my mouth fell open. With that unexpected lucky break, I was ahead of him, four to two.

"I thought you couldn't play," Brad said.

I laughed. "I can't. I wasn't aiming for the six."

He lowered his voice so the guys at the bar couldn't hear. "Never admit you made a slop shot, Marcie. Pretend it's exactly what you planned. Helps to psych out your opposition."

After two more rounds, Brad was down to the eight, but I still had two balls on the table, both positioned so he didn't have a good shot. Finally, he called the right corner pocket beside him, banked the eight to the far end, and brought it back into the pocket.

I think my mouth fell open again. "Wow, I've got to learn to do that!"

"I got lucky," he said, "but it was all I had without risking a scratch. I can show you how if you want to practice a little."

I looked at Grandma Edith for a cue. She nodded and went back to her laptop, so Brad put some more coins in the slot and set up the eight for me to practice a few times. Then we played another game. And another.

"Do you come here often?" he asked. "I don't think I've seen you before."

"No, I'm just visiting." I gestured toward Grandma Edith. "I'll be going back down to the valley in a few days."

"How about tomorrow? Will you be here then?"

I thought about Randy. He was planning to drive up sometime the next day. "I'm not sure."

"Would you call and let me know? Or let me call you? Here." He reached into his pocket for his phone.

We had just exchanged numbers and I was shoving my phone back into my pocket when two men approached the table. One put a quarter on the rail while the other went to the bar for drinks. We'd been challenged to a game and 'ownership' of the table.

Grandma Edith looked up. "About ready to go, Marcie?"

I was reluctant to leave. This was the most fun I'd had since arriving at Grandma Edith's house Sunday afternoon. No, longer than that. But the way I played, we would have lost the table to the two challengers, anyway.

I told Brad Kinney goodbye and followed Grandma Edith to her car.

"You did well with your first games," she said. "The practice is paying off. But, from the number of young men I saw in there today, I think the word is out. A pretty girl is playing pool at The Tavern. You may not find the table as free for practice the next time you come." Then she added, "I suppose you'll make up for it with the games you'll play, because they'll be wanting to partner with you."

She seemed determined that I play as much as possible, no matter what the circumstances, but I realized I no longer cared what she was planning. I was having fun, so I didn't mind waiting until she chose to fill me in on her scheme.

That night, she pulled two Coronas out of the refrigerator. "Let's sit on the porch for a while."

I was a little surprised she'd chosen the porch rather than the more private patio. But maybe she was still remembering the candles over the septic tank.

We settled into the wicker chairs with our beer, looking out over the street and listening to the chirping crickets. It was a balmy night and neighbors were out, some of them walking their dogs. We hadn't been there long before Nate ambled over, carrying his own beer.

I decided to give them some time alone. Slipping back into the house, I went to my bedroom and pulled the hospital bag from under the bed. I'd never have a better chance of getting it into the Camaro.

I took it out the back door and around to the side of the house, where my car was parked. I breathed a little easier once I had the bag stowed in the trunk, and I stood for a moment, listening to the low rumble of Grandma Edith's and Nate's voices. No, there were a couple of others joining in the conversation. I'd forgotten that some of the neighbors tended to gather on Grandma Edith's porch on Friday and

Saturday evenings, catching up on the week's happenings. Few of the houses had front porches, and none as big as hers.

I went back inside and out the front door so I wouldn't call attention to myself. Leaving the remaining wicker chairs for Grandma Edith's visitors, I edged along the wall to the swing at the far end, settled into it, and with a slight push of one foot, started a gentle rocking motion.

From that position, the voices on the porch blended into the evening sounds of a suburban neighborhood. People were arriving home, their vehicle lights briefly sweeping the street before turning into driveways. Tires crunched on gravel and car doors gave a soft thud as they closed. Children laughed; dogs gave excited yips.

Gradually, the hum of voices, sometimes punctuated by a laugh, grew louder as other neighbors joined the gathering on the porch, most carrying their own tall drink containers.

"Hi, Cleve. Nancy," Nate said, as another couple came up the steps. "I don't see Buster. You got him fastened up?"

The woman, Nancy I assumed, let out a sigh. "That dog could get out of Gitmo. He's dug so many holes under the fence, it looks like an excavation site."

"He's smart," Cleve said. "Darned good watchdog."

Nancy snorted. "Sure he is. He sat in the yard and watched while that repair guy loaded the ride-on mower into his van."

"Like I said, he's smart. He knows a repair van when he sees one."

Their laughter was interrupted by another man who came up the steps. "Did you guys hear? They've located the bank robber. He lives on Pine Grove, just a couple of blocks over."

That got my attention. I'd heard that street name before from somebody at the memorial service. While I was trying to remember who, a woman spoke.

"My niece's best friend is dating one of the cops. She said somebody called and told them the guy on Pine Grove was burying something that looked like ammo boxes all over his property. The cops thought he might be from one of those extremist groups or maybe a terrorist, building up a supply of guns and ammunition. Anyway, they went out there with metal detectors and located some of the boxes."

"Was it ammunition?" another woman asked in a shaky voice.

"No. Turns out he's a survivalist. The boxes were full of Spam and toilet paper."

In the laughter that followed, somebody finally thought to pose the question I'd been asking myself: "What did that have to do with the bank robber?"

"Oh, that. Well, from what I heard, the guy was so scared when he saw all those cops swarming in, he figured the jig was up and confessed to the attempted bank robbery before they even started asking him questions."

"Is it anybody we know?" Cleve asked.

"My niece's friend didn't say. I guess the boyfriend couldn't tell her his name."

"Things are getting strange around here," one of the men said. "Somebody told me O'Malley is getting nervous with all these cops investigating. They're thinking about closing the card room for a while."

"Maybe," another man said. "But right now, I think they're just being really careful who they let in that back room. And it's only open on Tuesday nights now."

As I listened, I realized this community didn't need a newspaper; they had the nightly news delivered in person, complete with commentary and opinion polls.

I didn't know most of the people they were discussing. My thoughts were drifting back to home and the Galt Police Department when my brain finally made the connection. Jerry Pittman lived on Pine Grove Court. Was he the inept bank robber? The man who could afford to buy his wife tanzanite earrings for her birthday?

Chapter 16

I opened my eyes the next morning to a deep sense of foreboding and lay still until my brain came fully awake. Randy was coming this afternoon. We would finally tell Grandma Edith about the divorce. I had thought I'd feel relief instead of dread, but I wasn't looking forward to Grandma Edith's reaction.

I didn't know what she had planned for the morning. Maybe working on that long-neglected bark? Or baking something special for the grandson who hadn't visited for so long? I got dressed and went to find her.

She was in the kitchen unloading the dishwasher, stacking plates on the counter.

I grabbed them and put them in a cupboard. "What are we doing today?"

"I thought you might go to The Tavern to practice your pool game this morning."

I shut the cupboard door and turned to look at her. "Me? What about you?"

"There are some things I have to do. And before you ask, no, you can't help me with them." She paused, holding two dessert plates in her hands while she looked into my eyes. "Don't you want to go? I thought you were having fun yesterday."

"I did have fun." Especially after I met Brad Kinney. "But Randy is coming, and I need to...to..." I couldn't think of anything I needed to do.

"Marcie, Randy won't be here until this afternoon. I know you've been apart for almost a week but there's no reason for you to sit around here and wait. I wish you wouldn't hurry back. It's been a while since I had a nice long visit with my grandson."

So I drove to The Tavern alone that morning, feeling almost like a local because I didn't need road signs to find my way. It felt strange, though, eating breakfast without Grandma Edith across the table from me. When I went to the pool table and pushed my coins into the slot, the place seemed empty, too big. Every time I missed a shot, I found myself glancing toward the table where she should be sitting. I was finding it difficult to concentrate, my thoughts straying to her and whatever she was doing. She was up to something and I couldn't figure out why she wouldn't share it with me.

I was about ready to call it quits, drive back and find out, when Brad Kinney walked in the door. He grinned when he saw me at the pool table, came over, and pulled down a cue stick. "I was hoping you'd be here."

"I'm glad to see you, too. I can't get the hang of that bank shot."

A slow smile spread across his face. "Well, if that's the only reason, I'll take what I can get." He walked around behind me. "You set up a tough shot for a beginner." He moved the eight ball a little farther off the rail. "Try it from there."

This time, the ball came off the rail at the right angle, then ran out of steam as it came back down the table. But it was closer than I'd come before.

"Do you want to practice for a while or play a game?" Brad asked.

I opted to play, but our game often stopped while he offered suggestions on making a shot. After our second game, a man slapped a quarter on the rail, challenging us to a game. We lost to him and his partner and, while we played, somebody else had put up their own quarter. We had lost the table.

We took seats at the empty bar. Brad kept up a low commentary, explaining each player's strategy and the shots they were trying to make—and sometimes why they'd missed. He knew more about pool than he'd led me to believe.

We challenged the winners of that game but lost again. Brad started to put another quarter on the table, but I stopped him. "I'm not good enough to play against these guys, and I'm not getting any practice. Let's just watch."

He put the quarter back in his pocket. "It's Saturday and getting a little crowded in here. How about an early lunch? We can order something from the kitchen to take outside."

I should go back to Grandma Edith's. Randy would be there soon. Then I thought about the picnic area and that sparkling creek. Grandma Edith had told me not to hurry back. "That's a great idea."

I locked my purse and phone in the Camaro, dropped the keys in my pocket, and went to help Brad carry our food out to the picnic table: thick hamburgers—possibly the best I'd ever tasted—along with crisp fries and cold soft drinks. Voices and splashing carried up to us from the creek, along with children's laughter. The sun was warm and the little voice that tried to nudge me back toward Grandma Edith's house grew fainter.

Brad was watching me. "You look like you belong here." He flushed. "That's lame. I don't know why I said it like that. You just look so relaxed, so comfortable, like you own this spot."

"I wish I did. It's beautiful." I looked down the slope, toward the children's voices.

"Want to go exploring?" he asked. "See what's on the other side of that stream?"

Even as I thought I shouldn't, that I needed to leave, I found myself nodding. After all, this might be my last visit to The Tavern, my last chance to satisfy my curiosity.

We gathered our lunch wrappings, tossed them in a nearby garbage container, and headed for the well-worn path, working our way down the broad, gentle slope, around children and their watchful parents until we got to the smooth rocks forming a path to the other side.

Brad gestured toward them. "Be careful. They'll be slippery." He grabbed my hand. "I don't think there's enough current to push us off, though."

About halfway across, my foot skidded on a moss-covered spot and I faltered, afraid I was going to fall. The water wasn't deep but those rocks could do a lot of damage.

Then Brad had his arm around me, steadying me until I took the next step. I made it the rest of the way, feeling a surge of relief when I stepped onto dry ground.

The path was fainter and a little steeper on this side of the creek, disappearing as it curved around heavy brush. Brad started up the trail, but I hesitated, thinking about snakes and wild animals, probably because he'd planted the idea of bears in my head the day before. Then it occurred to me that I was going to be out of sight of anybody at The Tavern or the creek, led by a man I'd only met yesterday.

"Marcie?" Brad was looking back at me, his eyes puzzled. "Is something wrong? Did you change your mind?"

"No. I just stopped for a minute to...to look around." What kind of wimp was I? We weren't far from The Tavern and even closer to the people on the other side of the stream. It was only a couple of yards to the top of the bank where we'd be in full view.

When we got there, I drew in a quick breath. Stretching before us was a small meadow framed by evergreens. Clumps of blue wildflowers erupted from the grassy field in profusion, some of them climbing up and over fallen logs. Through a break in the evergreens, I could see a tree-covered ridge and, in the distance beyond it, blue mountains with snowy peaks.

I turned toward Brad. "It's...incredible. And so pristine. Like nobody has been here before us."

"It's forest land," he said. "I suspect only hikers and horseback riders are allowed in here. We can probably find a trail if you want to go farther in."

"No. Not today." But I wanted to, and I might have if I'd known him better. "Maybe someday." I knew I'd be coming back to this spot.

Brad squeezed my hand. "I hope I'm with you when you do." He led me to a log where we could sit and look out over the meadow. "You said the other day that you're just visiting. That you'd be going back down to the valley soon. Where in the valley?"

"Galt. It's a small town about halfway between Sacramento and Stockton."

"I know where it is. I live in Rocklin, about forty-five miles north of you. Not that far." He was quiet for a moment, then asked, "Do you come up to visit your grandmother often?"

And there it was, the subject I constantly tried to avoid. But Brad didn't know any of the people involved; he wasn't from Miner's Ridge. I told him about Grandma Edith and her missing money, about Grandpa Dan's murder, about my divorce, about Randy.

"Have the police solved your grandfather—Mr. Clifton's murder?"

"Not yet. If you lived in Miner's Ridge, you'd know all about it through the underground telegraph."

He laughed at that. "I don't think I've ever been in Miner's Ridge. I'm up here visiting my sister Julie and her husband in Nevada City. They both work during the day, so I'm pretty much on my own. Steve—that's my brother-in-law—told me I should check this place out. I'm glad he did."

"Me, too. You saved me from the juvenile pool-ball pirates."

Brad laughed. "I think they were just trying to get your attention. I'm kind of grateful to them. They gave me an opening."

"How long are you staying with your sister?" I asked.

"About a week. Then I have to get back to work."

"Doing what?"

"I'm a deputy with the Placer County Sheriff's Office."

"Oh!" Why was every man I met in law enforcement? And trailing that thought, before I could even think about filtering my words, I blurted, "Do you repossess cars?"

A puzzled half-smile crossed Brad's face. "No, there are agencies for that sort of thing. Why? Do you need a vehicle repossessed?"

"No." Feeling a flush creep up my neck at my stupid question, I scrambled to my feet. "It's getting late. I'd better go."

Brad stood. "Did I say something wrong? If I did—"

"No. No, it's just...I'm going to be late."

I turned and started down the path with Brad close behind. When we stopped at the edge of the creek, he asked, "Are you going to be here tomorrow?"

"I don't know. It might be difficult." Randy would want to come with me, and I didn't want him at The Tavern. Even if Brad wasn't there, Randy would spoil it for me. It wasn't his kind of place; he'd criticize everything: the poor selection of craft beers, no music, a limited menu, only one ancient pool table. But it was my kind of place. I wasn't going to share it with him.

I was almost halfway across the creek when I caught something in my peripheral vision, coming toward me. I twisted to look. My next step was too short, missing the center of the rock, slipping on the moss-covered side. Windmilling my arms in an attempt to regain my balance, I teetered, then fell, taking Brad with me.

The stream was shallow, so there was no danger of drowning, but the gravel and rocks made for a hard landing. I sat up and pushed hair out of my face before I noticed the mud on my hands. Everybody was staring at us. A young girl splashed toward me in pursuit of the beach ball that had caught my attention at the wrong moment. Brad stood and pulled me to my feet. "Are you hurt?"

"Nothing but my dignity—at least, what's left of it."

I was already wet so, not trusting the rocks, I waded across the rest of the stream. On the other side, I knelt and dipped my hands in the water to remove the mud. Not knowing how much of it I might have transferred to my hair, I brushed wet fingers through the front locks. Some of the kids were laughing, but I was beyond caring.

Brad and I climbed the slope, our shoes squishing with every step. When we got to the top, Brad tilted his head toward The Tavern. "Want to go to the restroom? Try to clean up a little?"

I couldn't think of anything the bathroom could do for me that I hadn't taken care of at the stream, and the last thing I needed was more people staring at me. "Not unless they've got spare clothing inside. I think I'll just head back."

He looked at my wet jeans and polo shirt, plastered to my body. "I don't suppose your job gives you any reason to carry a change of clothes in your car trunk. In my line of work, I've found it prudent to always carry one."

I thought about the hospital bag containing Grandpa Dan's tattered and blood-stained clothes and shook my head. "No, there's nothing."

"I'm pretty sure I've got some plastic garbage bags. They'll at least protect your car seat. Wait here."

He jogged across the parking lot and came back a few minutes later with a box of bags—big ones, the kind you use to collect leaves. I led him to my car, wondering why a deputy sheriff would carry something like that. Then I decided I didn't want to know.

He secured one bag around the driver's seat and slipped another over the back.

I got inside, but he grabbed the door. "Call me sometime tonight, okay? Let me know whether you'll be coming back tomorrow."

"I will."

He closed the door then and gave me a little wave as I started the car and pulled out of the parking lot.

On my way back to Grandma Edith's, I tried to think about my confrontation with Randy—how I'd handle it if he hadn't told Grandma Edith about the divorce. But my thoughts kept slipping back to Brad Kinney. I'd only known the man for two days—less than two days—but I knew I wanted to see him again. And if I went back to The Tavern, I'd wear Bermuda shorts so I could wade across the stream.

I had hoped Grandma Edith and Randy would be on the patio when I got back, allowing me to sneak in the front door and do a quick wardrobe change. But they were on the front porch, watching me as I turned into the driveway.

The plastic bag on the car seat stuck to my butt when I got out of the Camaro. I peeled it away, glad I was out of view of the porch, and went around to face them.

Chapter 17

Randy, sprawled in a wicker chair, didn't move as he watched me walk up the steps. Grandma Edith, eyebrows raised, looked at my wet jeans and polo shirt. "What happened to you?"

"I fell in the creek and, if both of you will excuse me for a few minutes, I need to change clothes. I'll be right back."

Randy raised a Corona to his lips as he surveyed the knit shirt clinging to my body. "You're looking good, babe."

Grandma Edith's gaze moved from me to Randy and back again, a slight frown creasing her forehead. Then she nodded at me. "Hurry up, dear, before you catch cold."

I took off my wet Skechers before I went inside, left them in the tiled entryway, and headed to the bathroom. After a quick shower, I dressed and pulled out the same sandals I'd worn at the end of Grandpa Dan's memorial service. If I couldn't clean up the Skechers, I'd be wearing the beat-up sandals for the rest of my stay.

I grabbed a bottle of cold water from the refrigerator and went back out. Grandma Edith and Randy were deep in conversation. As I slid into one of the wicker chairs, she turned toward me.

"We've been talking about Grandpa Dan's vehicles. He often told me he wanted Randy to have one of them. We helped the girls a little with college expenses, but never did anything for Randy so it seems only fair."

"But, Grandma Edith, you could sell those vehicles. And you need that money more than Randy needs another car."

"I know, but I just wouldn't feel right about it. I'll keep the pickup. It'll be useful for hauling gardening supplies. But I have no use for Dan's surveillance car."

Randy wasn't saying anything, which irritated me. He should be talking his grandmother into selling the Honda. While I would love to have that car, it was too bland, too ordinary for him. He'd sell it within a week.

Then he spoke, his voice more tender than I'd heard it in a long time. "Grandma, I don't need the car. It would just be an added expense, with the high registration costs, smog checks, and maintenance."

"Then sell it. Randy, I can't give you money to make it equal to what we gave the girls. All I have is the car. So, please do something with it." She sounded frustrated.

Randy finally nodded, but I'd never seen him more miserable since the day I told him I was leaving. He'd had that same look on his face then, like he couldn't swallow past the lump in his throat.

Before my sympathies got away from me, I needed to float my idea. "Randy, what if we made a swap? Grandma Edith gives the Honda to you, and you trade it for my Camaro?"

"You'd do that? Let me have the convertible?"

"Well, not exactly. There are a few payments left on it. You know, the ones you agreed to when you traded my Acura for it. But if you don't mind paying those..."

"No, no. That's fine. It would be worth it to have that car. Thanks, Marcie. You're a sweetheart."

"Then it's a deal." The only problem I could see was Randy possibly skipping a payment. Or all of them. But even if I had to finish paying off the loan, I'd be no worse off than I was now, and I'd be rid of the Camaro, which I'd never liked or wanted. Or...I could just let them repossess it.

I asked Grandma Edith how she felt about the trade.

"Whatever works," she said, "but I don't see what difference it makes. In my day, married couples put the titles to their vehicles in both names. They didn't worry about who owned which car."

I plunged into the opening she'd given us. "Uh...Grandma Edith, about married couples—"

She wasn't listening. Her attention was on a car pulling to the curb in front of the house. Officer Roberts got out, followed by another man, probably somewhere in his late forties or early fifties. He looked out of place in a gray suit, a white shirt and a striped red-white-and-blue tie. Short brown hair matched a well-trimmed beard and mustache.

They came up the steps, the gray-suited man a pace or two behind Roberts as he looked around the property.

"Good evening, Officer Roberts." Grandma Edith motioned toward Randy. "This is my grandson, Randy Clifton."

Roberts nodded and introduced the other man as Detective Richard Granger. "He's agreed to come up from Sacramento temporarily to investigate the murder of Mr. Clifton." Roberts didn't look happy about it.

Granger nodded to us as he pulled up a chair beside Grandma Edith. "Okay. I think the best way to start is for you to tell me why Mr. Clifton was downtown last Wednesday night—where he was going, who he might have been meeting, and if he knew that person well."

Grandma Edith sighed, probably tired of answering the same questions again. "I can't be sure, but—"

He smiled at her and patted her hand, then turned his attention to Randy. "Sir, I know you've probably been asked all these questions before, but I'd appreciate it if you could fill me in. Can you think of anybody who would want to hurt your grandfather?"

"I don't know. He was a private investigator. That might have made him some enemies."

I thought it more likely that some of Grandpa Dan's scams would create enemies but nobody was asking me, and I was pretty sure Grandma Edith wouldn't want me to volunteer that opinion.

She was frowning at Granger. "I think Randy is—"

Granger held up his palm toward her. "If you don't mind waiting a few minutes, ma'am...I'll get to you. Right now, I have to talk to this gentleman."

He shifted his chair a little more toward Randy. "Do you know what he was doing in Miner's Ridge that night?"

Randy shrugged as he lifted his beer bottle. "I don't know. I just got here this afternoon."

"Oh, I thought—" Detective Granger looked at me. "Perhaps you can tell me?"

I glanced at Grandma Edith, who was examining her fingernails through narrowed eyes.

"No," I said. "I don't. I didn't get here until Sunday afternoon. The only person who can answer your questions is his wife." I nodded toward Grandma Edith. "So maybe you should talk to her."

She gave him her too-sweet smile as she rose to her feet. "Detective, you'll have to excuse me. You know how it is with us absent-minded old folks. We not only lose most of our brain cells, we can't get through the day without our naps, and I haven't had one this afternoon. Maybe you'd better come back tomorrow."

I couldn't help it; I laughed. So did Randy. Roberts smiled.

It could have been worse. Granger hadn't yet addressed Grandma Edith as "honey" or "sweetie." Maybe that was a female thing.

He flushed. "I'm sorry. I didn't realize...please sit down."

She lowered herself into the chair again. Ignoring Granger, she asked Roberts, "Didn't you share your notes with the detective so he wouldn't have to ask the same questions?"

"We each have to investigate in our own way, Ma'am," Granger said. "By doing that, we can form our own, unbiased opinions. Can you understand how that would work?"

Grandma Edith glared at him. "Despite my lack of a nap, I understand perfectly well, Detective. You're trying to determine whether I give you the same answers each time, if I'm consistent. I'll tell you the same thing I told Officer Roberts. I don't know what case Dan was working, or even if that's what he was doing Wednesday night. He rarely talked to me about his cases. He was often gone in the evenings and in the days before his death he seemed preoccupied, maybe a little worried. That's all I know, other than two failed attempts to break into his desk."

Granger sat back, drawing in a long breath, then narrowed his steel-gray eyes at Grandma Edith. "Where were you Wednesday night at eleven o'clock, Mrs. Clifton?"

She stared at him, her mouth slightly agape. Then she snapped it shut. "I was here, probably in bed. And, before you ask, I was alone. Am

I now a suspect in my husband's murder? Because if I'd planned to kill Dan, I would have done it long ago, not after forty-five years of putting up with his ridiculous get-rich-quick schemes."

Unfazed, Granger studied her for a moment before asking his next question. "Do you know what they were looking for? The people who tried to break into the desk?"

She shook her head. "Not a clue unless it was something in his case files. There's nothing in that desk but office supplies and some household accounts."

"I'd like to take a look at the contents of both it and the file cabinets."

She gave him that sweet smile again. "Don't you need a search warrant for that, Detective?"

He returned the smile. "I do, and I have one right here." He pulled a folded paper from an inner jacket pocket and handed it to her.

She read it, then gave it to me. "Fine. I'm sure you won't mind having my granddaughter observe, to ensure you don't go beyond the limits of this document."

I took a quick peek at the warrant as I followed Roberts and Granger to the office, wondering what Grandma Edith thought they might see that wasn't listed: the desk and "all files." There was nothing else in the office except a pull-out sofa bed, a few small open bookcases, and the closet. Granger glanced at it several times, and I wondered if he wished he'd included everything in that room when he'd asked for the warrant. Too bad they weren't allowed to look in there. I would have enjoyed seeing their reaction if the blonde wig head rolled out at their feet.

A little self-conscious, I stood in the doorway, watching Roberts and Granger work their way through the files. At least, Granger did. Roberts wasn't paying much attention; he'd seen all of them before. Every so often, he looked my way, his eyebrows raised or his shoulders rising in a slight shrug. Never having taken a class on the nuances of body language, I couldn't interpret any of it. Maybe he was signaling "I'm sorry." Or "We could be at the Grange dance right now." Or "Get lost."

The latter seemed like a good option. They had legal access to anything in the room that might prove to be important. So why did Grandma Edith send me in here? To needle Granger for the way he'd dismissed her during his questioning? Or to get me off the porch so she and Randy could talk privately? I didn't know when he had arrived. Maybe they needed a little more time together. He might even tell her about the divorce. No, he'd just learned Grandpa Dan had been murdered. The divorce would be the last thing on his mind.

I wiped perspiration from the back of my neck. It was a warm day for the end of April, and Grandma Edith hadn't yet turned on the air conditioning. The late afternoon sun was shining onto that side of the house and the room was getting warm with three of us in the confined space. Roberts still looked comfortable enough in his short-sleeved khaki uniform, but Granger, in his suit and tie, had beads of perspiration popping out on his flushed forehead and around his neck.

As supervisor of the file search, I made an executive decision. It was late enough to have a Corona. I'd open it, maybe pour it into a frosted glass with a slice of lime. And, to score a few points for Grandma Edith, I'd come back and watch Granger sweat while I sipped my beer. I'd take long, slow drinks, just to make him thirsty. I might even offer him one. He'd have to refuse; he was on duty.

Roberts grinned, apparently thinking my performance was amusing—but, then, he wasn't working that hard. Granger, after one glance, ignored me, pulling out the drawer on the desk extension. I leaned forward, trying to see what was inside. Nothing but pristine new manila envelopes and folders. I could have sworn those had been on the bookshelves earlier.

He opened the other drawer which I knew held the American Express folders, along with perhaps a dozen other files. Those were gone, replaced by two reams of paper and several boxes of printer labels. My gaze went to the empty spot on the bookshelves where those items had rested the day before. Grandma Edith had been busy while I was having fun at The Tavern.

The front door opened and I heard Randy's heavy tread, probably going to the kitchen for another beer. I intercepted him. "You haven't told Grandma Edith about the divorce, have you?"

"No, not yet. I was about to when she started talking about giving me the car. I'll tell her. Just give me a little time."

"Time? You've had all year while we waited for the final papers. And plenty of time since then."

"I know. It's just...well, I thought it would be better to do it in person and..."

I felt like smacking him. "You mean to tell me you haven't been up here in all that time?"

"Well, yeah, a couple of times. But it was her birthday and then Thanksgiving. A lot of other people were here so I never got the chance."

"I should think the perfect time would have been when she asked why I wasn't with you. What did you tell her?"

He gave me a wimpy smile. "I said you were working."

When I stared at him, shaking my head, he added, "I told her you sent your love."

I would have hit him then if Roberts and Granger hadn't come out of the office, carting boxes to their vehicle. Not wanting to be arrested for assault, I dropped my arm to my side.

"I'll tell her. I swear I will. Right after dinner. When she's had a chance to settle down after the cops leave."

I interpreted that to mean I'd be the one doing the telling—probably his plan all along.

Roberts and Granger left, probably to get dinner, if they were as hungry as I was; it had been a long time since my hamburger at The Tavern. So long that the casseroles Grandma Edith pulled out of the freezer didn't look that bad.

She wanted to sit on the front porch for a while after dinner. Randy got a cold beer from the refrigerator, then looked over his shoulder at me. "Want one?"

I started to decline, then changed my mind when I thought about the conversation we were about to have. I needed all the fortification I could get.

I soon discovered that it wasn't easy to have a private conversation at Grandma Edith's house, especially on her front porch. Nate ambled over first, a beer in hand. He'd barely settled into one of the wicker chairs when Alma Reitman and her husband Larry joined us. Alma set a pie on the table and, even with the fading light, I could see high mounds of delicately-browned meringue.

I remembered a story Nate had told me, one from his arsenal of tales about Alma's cooking. He said she'd brought a lemon meringue pie over, his favorite. Against his better judgment, he took a slice. "I should have known better," he said. "She'd forgotten to put the sugar in. I thought I'd never get the taste of that pie out of my mouth."

He was eyeing the pie now as Larry pulled paper plates and plastic forks out of a bag. "Is everybody ready for dessert? It's lemon meringue."

Grandma Edith, Nate, and I all spoke at once:

"I just ate."

"No thanks, I'm full."

"Maybe later."

Randy looked at Nate. "I thought lemon meringue is your favorite."

"It is, but I just had a big dinner."

Alma grabbed the pastry knife. "Well, that's no problem. I'll cut a big piece for you to take home later."

"Thanks," Nate said, "but I'll have to pass. Truth is, I've put on a pound or two and I'm cutting out desserts for a while."

Grandma Edith snorted. Randy shrugged. "Just makes more for the rest of us."

I suspect Grandma Edith wanted to say something, to warn Randy, but couldn't think of a way to do it without being rude. Nate just grinned and winked at me.

I smiled. "Cut him a big piece, Alma. Lemon meringue is his favorite, too."

Larry was the first to take a bite. "Wow, that is great pie."

Nate leaned over and whispered in my ear. "He's been eating her cooking for so many years his taste buds have either died or surrendered."

Grandma Edith poked him. "Hush!"

I don't think Nate noticed. He was watching, almost holding his breath, as Randy's fork deposited a big bite into his mouth.

"You're right," Randy said. "This is really good."

Nate squinted his eyes, frowning as he watched Randy demolish the pie on his plate and ask for a second helping.

"I'm glad you like it," Alma said. "I wasn't sure because store-bought is never as good as home-made. But I didn't have time today. I decided to try that new bakery."

"You should use it all the time," Larry said, his tone hopeful. "Try out some of their other stuff."

"Really?" Alma arched her eyebrows. "You think it's as good as mine?"

Larry had been married to Alma for a long time. "It's close enough, honey. Just think of all the work it'll save, and the neighbors aren't going to mind."

"No, we won't mind," Grandma Edith said.

"Not at all," Nate's eyes were on the pie as Randy cut another slice.

My phone rang. Brad Kinney. Excusing myself, I went into the house.

"I've been sitting here, trying to figure out where you could have gone in those wet clothes," Brad said.

"Just here. I came back to Grandma Edith's to change. I told you that's where I was going."

"But you agreed to call me when you got there, so I could only assume you never arrived. Maybe you found another creek to wade in or another pool table—"

"No, I said I'd call and let you know if I was going up to The Tavern tomorrow to play pool. And I don't think so. Maybe Monday. I'll let you know. After all, I need protection from those pool-ball bandits."

I heard Nate's voice, greeting somebody else who must have arrived. Grandma Edith's porch was a busy place.

Brad asked how things were going with Randy, but I didn't have much to report. We talked for a few more minutes before I told him goodbye, promising I'd call when I knew my plans for Monday. Then I headed for the kitchen to get a bottle of cold water before going back out.

I had the refrigerator door open when I heard footsteps behind me. Probably Randy coming in to get another beer.

A hand touched my shoulder. Startled, I dropped the water bottle. It bounced off the bottom of the refrigerator and rolled toward a cabinet.

"I'll get it," Roberts said, a fraction of a second too late. I was already reaching for the bottle. Our shoulders collided, throwing me off balance. My hands scrabbled for something to hold on to and settled on Roberts's shoulder. He pulled me to my feet.

"Hey—you okay?" Steadying me with an arm around my back, he brushed hair away from my face.

"What the hell do you think you're doing?" Randy's voice boomed behind Roberts. "Get your hands off my wife!"

Chapter 18

Roberts stared at me, his expression blank except for a slight widening of his eyes. He tightened his hold around me for just a moment before his arms dropped and he stepped away.

Past him, Grandma Edith stood, holding the door frame with one hand as though she needed it for support. A frown creased her pale face. "Marcie..."

My gaze slid from her to Roberts's as he turned to walk out of the room. While I watched, both his and Grandma Edith's stricken faces searing into my brain, I told myself I had to control my temper. That was just before my open palm connected with Randy's cheek.

He grabbed my hand. "Marcie, I'm not going to stand here and let you beat up on me just because I object to you and that cop making out in my grandmother's kitchen. I've got an open mind about most things, but—"

"Is that how all your brains leaked out? Through that opening?" I pointed to Grandma Edith. "Tell her. Tell her, Randy. We. Are. Not. Married. Our divorce is final. Has been final for over three months."

Grandma Edith stared at him, her eyes narrowed. "Final? You've been apart for more than a year and you didn't bother to tell me?" She took several steps toward us, then faltered. "You'd filed for divorce before my birthday. You lied to me when you told me she was working—both days. I thought it unusual that a clerk would have to work Thanksgiving day in a police station office. But I didn't question it. My grandson wouldn't lie to me. Would he, Randy?"

She turned to me. "And you. Why did you come? And once you were here, why didn't you tell me?"

"I thought he'd told you over a year ago, when I first filed. Then...Randy said you needed me, that there was nobody else. He'd just started the new job...and I didn't know he hadn't told you..." I was babbling so I slowed down and took a deep breath. "I'm sorry. I should have told you, but you had so much to deal with...Randy said he'd tell you when he got here today."

"And why didn't you?" she asked Randy. "You had a good part of the afternoon—"

"Because I...I didn't know how. You kept talking about how much you loved having Marcie here, how much help she was, how lucky I am to have her, and...and it's hard because I guess I just keep hoping she'll change her mind and come back to me. I'm working on that."

I sighed. "Randy—"

He held up a hand to stop me. "I know. It's stupid. But..." He chewed on his lower lip. "Well, the way I figured it, I'm sticking with a steady job and I'm helping to pay off your bills—"

"My bills? You mean the bills you left me with!"

"Well, yeah, but I'm trying to make things right and you've let me move back into your house."

"Only because I'm gone and you have nowhere else to go! And I'm beginning to realize I was an idiot for agreeing to it."

He stared at the floor. "Okay. I'll find someplace else, but it hasn't been costing you anything, and I've been fixing the place up. Repairing stuff."

Images tried to push their way into my mind of Randy's version of "fixing up." I didn't want to think about what he might be doing to the place. He'd never liked the seventies-era kitchen, but it needed a complete remodel, not whatever he might be doing to it.

"Randy, if there had been the remotest possibility of saving our marriage, I wouldn't have filed for divorce. And nothing happened to change my mind in the year we waited for it to become final. It's over. . It's been over for a long time. I appreciate everything you're doing now, but you need to find a life and let me get on with mine. And stop fixing my house!"

Blinking back tears, I ran to the front porch. I hadn't realized Nate was still sitting there until his voice reached me from the shadows. "If you're looking for Officer Roberts, he took off."

I went back inside, to my room. It was just as well. I'd be leaving all this behind tomorrow. I was going home first thing in the morning. I would throw all Randy's things out of my house. Except maybe the baseball bat. I'd pitch his clothes wherever they landed in the back yard. No, the front, so all the stray cats and dogs in the neighborhood would get a chance to sleep on them. Maybe I'd turn the sprinkler on.

Grandma Edith tapped on my door. "Marcie, may I come in?"

Bracing myself for her anger and disappointment, I said, almost in a whisper, "Yes." Then I tried to clear the lump in my throat so I could repeat the word, louder this time.

She came in and stood still, just inside the door, studying my face.

"I'm sorry, Grandma Edith...it just never seemed to be the right time. I was going to wait until after the memorial service but then we found out Grandpa Dan was murdered. And then we were having so much fun at The Tavern...and Randy wanted me to wait...said he'd tell you this weekend." I was rambling, making excuses for myself, so I stopped and started over.

"Grandma Edith..." The lump was back, bigger than before. "I guess I shouldn't call you that. I'm not your granddaughter anymore."

"No, you're not. I have two, and I don't need another."

I turned away to hide the tears prickling at my eyelids.

"What I need, Marcie, is a friend. One exactly like you. The kind you've been all week." She strode across the room and wrapped her arms around me. "I don't want to lose you."

That did make the tears spill over. "I don't want to lose you, either. I love spending time with you."

"See, that proves you're not a grandchild. They never want to spend time with their grandparents." She smoothed hair back from my face. "You were trying to protect me from more pain and give Randy a chance to do what he should have done last year. I only wish I'd been as smart as you and divorced Dan long ago, before he had a chance to do so much damage. Of course, that wasn't as easily accepted back in my day."

"Grandma Edith, Randy's not a bad man. He's just—"

"Charmingly irresponsible? Always looking for a get-rich-quick scheme, just like his grandfather? I guess we have to cut Randy some slack. The poor boy can't do anything about the genes he inherited. So, what do you say to both of us forgiving him and inviting him to go shopping with us tomorrow?"

"We're going shopping?" My thoughts shifted to my shoes. I needed another pair. They'd have to be cheap, but something I could wear in public that wasn't either ratty or mud-stained.

"Yes," Grandma Edith said. "There's something I want to buy, and I think we should make Randy take us out for breakfast—see him grovel a bit."

I didn't think Randy would go; he'd never shown any interest in buying anything other than beer and my convertible. He surprised me, though, even agreeing to spring for breakfast. He said he needed to find a new pair of jeans. More likely, he was just glad to be back in Grandma Edith's good graces. And maybe mine, though that was still debatable.

We left early the next morning so we'd have time for the breakfast stop before heading for the Walmart out on the highway.

We were barely inside the store when Randy spotted a two-chair bistro set, almost identical to the one I had at home. It sported a big half-price sign. He crouched down to examine it.

I was impatient to find the shoe section. "Randy, why would you want that? You don't even have a house. Besides, it's got a cushion missing and the paint is scraped off one of the chair legs. It's bent a little, see?" I pointed. "It probably wobbles."

He rose to his feet. "That's okay. We don't need the chairs. The table is the only thing that got..." He clamped his mouth shut and averted his eyes.

The pieces fell together. "The party you had at my house. You said you could fix most of the damage. This is what you couldn't fix. Right?"

"It's the same set as yours, Marcie, and it was only the table that got trashed when Cedric fell on it. This way, you'll have three good chairs instead of two. Four, if I can find some paint the same color and a cushion."

He grabbed the tag off the table and we walked to a check-out line. Grandma Edith asked, "How are you going to get it to Galt?"

"If you'll let me borrow Grandpa Dan's pickup to take it home, Billy and I can bring the pickup back next weekend. That way, we could drive both my car and the convertible back to Galt."

She handed him the keys to the Malibu. "Okay, go get it. I guess we can all squeeze into the pickup to go home. But be careful with my car and don't leave us waiting here too long."

The clerk, a young woman in her late teens or early twenties, rang up the purchase and handed the receipt to Randy. He turned to leave, but Grandma Edith stopped him, nodding toward the bistro set. "How are you going to prove that's yours when you come back?"

The woman smiled at her. "Oh, that's no problem, ma'am. He has a receipt."

"Showing he paid for one," Grandma Edith said. "But nothing to prove he left it here."

The clerk gave her a weak smile. "I'm going to print his name on a tag and tape it to the table. See?" She held up a piece of paper with RANDY CLIFTON scribbled on it.

"What if the tag disappears and a different clerk waits on him? One who doesn't know anything about this transaction? How can he prove it's his?"

The woman was losing patience. "You just don't understand, ma'am. He has his receipt."

"Proving only that he paid for it, not that he left it."

The woman was no longer smiling. "I'm trying to explain to you. He has the receipt."

"Then write something on it indicating that he still has to pick it up."

"Fine. Whatever you want." The clerk gave me a sympathetic smile and took the receipt from Randy. "But it's not necessary, sweetie. You just don't understand—"

"Just do it," I said before Grandma Edith could respond, knowing whatever she said wouldn't be pretty. Grandma Edith hated being called "sweetie" or "honey" by strangers. She considered it age-biased condescension. "Just wait until you start getting old," she'd told me. "It'll be a shock when it first happens, usually sometime after you hit sixty. It's as though they're talking to a child."

The clerk sighed, scribbled something on the back of the receipt, and handed it to Randy again.

Grandma Edith leaned over the counter. "Are you wearing some special kind of shoes?"

The woman looked down. "No, just comfortable ones. Why?"

"I was just wondering how you can stay anchored to the floor with all that air in your head."

The clerk blinked and I pulled Grandma Edith away. The next man in line moved up to the counter, chuckling.

"Get me some jeans, thirty-four, thirty-four. You know what kind I like. I'll pay you back," Randy said before he left. Grandma Edith and I found them, then made our way to the shoe department, where I found aisles of shoes, but little seating—padded benches here and there and, finally, a group of four chairs where both Grandma Edith and I could sit. I'd found a pair of inexpensive—but cute—sandals I wanted to try on. I was pulling the first one onto my foot when the scent of stale cigarette smoke and too-strong perfume preceded a woman, probably in her mid-thirties, carrying a pair of black, high-heeled dress shoes. She lowered herself onto the chair at the opposite end—leaving one vacant seat between her and Grandma Edith.

Grandma Edith made a face, rose, and walked to an aisle several yards away, pretending to look at shoes.

Trying to hold my breath, I fastened the straps on the sandals, got up, and walked toward her. "These seem comfortable enough. It'll just take me a couple of minutes to change back into mine and be ready to go."

When I turned toward the chair where I'd left my shoes, I saw that a gangly teenager occupied the seat next to it, holding a pair of new sneakers.

I changed out of the new sandals, and was reaching for the box when the kid took off one of his old shoes, releasing a sweaty-sock miasma that almost made me gag.

Grabbing the box, I jumped to my feet and headed toward Grandma Edith. She wrinkled her nose. "Marcie, I need to get out of here. It smells like young people."

Somebody behind us laughed. I turned to see one of the women who had joined the group on Grandma Edith's porch the night before. "Well said, Edith! I love it!" She gave Grandma Edith a high five.

Grandma Edith winked at the neighbor and pulled me down the aisle. Only then did I get it—all the references I'd read about an "old person smell," usually in fiction. I smiled then, and she grinned back at me. "Come on, let's look at some women's clothes."

"Okay." My paycheck had been deposited into my account Friday, but I couldn't afford to buy clothes. The sandals had been a stretch. But I could help Grandma Edith look for something.

"A shirt," she said. "Something soft. And red."

I couldn't imagine her in a red shirt, but I wasn't about to argue. If anybody could carry it off, it would be Grandma Edith. Maybe she'd joined a red-blouse club, something like the Red Hat Society.

We sorted through the racks until she found a half-dozen she liked. "Here, try these on. And I want to see how they fit."

"What? Me? Grandma Edith, I don't—"

"Hush. I want to buy something for you. To thank you for everything you've done this week. And make you remember me every time you wear it—and maybe give you the urge to come and visit."

That brought tears to my eyes, which made me suspicious. Grandma Edith was rarely sentimental. Then I felt so ashamed of that thought, I modeled each shirt for her and agreed to the one she liked. It was silky, some kind of rayon-poly mix, with a draped neckline. It was definitely not my style and red didn't go well with my auburn hair. Grandma Edith was happy with it, so none of that mattered. I would never wear the shirt again, anyway. Except when I came to visit her, of course.

We still had a little time to kill before Randy came back with the pickup, so we wandered into the food section to do some grocery shopping.

We pushed our carts outside and sat on a bench until Randy arrived in Grandpa Dan's pickup. While he went inside to collect the bistro set, Grandma Edith and I stashed our bags in the extended cab. They filled up one side of the bench seat and floor in back, barely leaving room for me to squeeze in beside them.

Randy came out with two store employees. We watched while they helped him load the bistro set.

"Place the backs of the chairs against the window," he said, reaching for a bungee cord.

"So you can keep an eye on me?" Grandma Edith asked.

"Huh?" Randy's eyebrows shot up. "What are you talking about, Grandma? Marcie will be in the back seat. You'll be in front, right beside me."

"You know perfectly well what I'm talking about." She turned to one of the young men who was jumping down from the pickup bed. "He's going to make me ride up there, on one of those chairs you're putting in the pickup bed. That's why he told you to put the backs against the window. So I'd have room for my legs. Can he do that? Isn't there some law against it?"

The man, eyes narrowed, looked at Randy, who wore a puzzled frown. He cast a pleading glance at me, but I didn't have a clue what Grandma Edith had in mind. She enlightened us when she spoke to the employee again. "He says I talk too much. That I'm a backseat driver, whatever that is, so he's going to make me sit back here. Her, too, if she doesn't like it." She gestured toward me. "And all I did was tell him he was breaking the speed limit. At least three miles over."

The two employees exchanged one of those glances that carried a complete conversation. One of them pulled out a cell phone, probably to call Adult Protective Services.

I was struggling to keep a straight face. Randy, waving his arms as he talked, was trying to explain to his helpers that Grandma Edith was playing a prank on him. "Marcie, help! Tell them what she's doing!"

I couldn't. I was laughing by then, too hard to say anything.

Fortunately, Randy was a good sport who appreciated a prank, even if it was played on him. By the time he and Grandma Edith had convinced the employees it was a harmless joke and we were back on the highway, he was laughing, too. He would be the first to tell Nate about it, then he'd share the story with everybody he met, probably embellishing a little more with each telling.

He didn't stay long after we had lunch and, just before he left, he pulled me aside. "Babe, we have a little problem. The house is in good shape. I got it all fixed up for you to come back home. But, see, I kept thinking we'd get back together and...well, the truth is, I haven't lined up anywhere else to go, and I don't have the money right now. Not if I'm going to pay those back taxes and penalties and make the payment on the convertible."

"No. Absolutely not. You're not staying in the spare bedroom. This is just your way—"

He held up a palm to stop me. "No, I'm not trying to con you this time. You have to believe me. I've been working long hours, racking up lots of overtime. All I do is work and eat and sleep. I'm so tired, I slept until noon before I drove up here. If you can just hang in there a little longer, I'll have enough to get the bills paid and line up something for myself. Not first and last month and deposit yet, but at least a weekly rate at one of those cheap motels. It won't take long. Maybe a couple of weeks."

He looked so sincere, I wanted to believe him, but he had conned me too many times.

Before I could finish shaking my head, he said, "I'd be gone most of the time and when I was there, I'd be sleeping. Honest, babe. I'm being straight with you. I could get all those back bills paid off and we could both start living a normal life again."

I knew I shouldn't trust him, but he was working hard. He liked the job so it wasn't likely he'd quit. And it might be my only shot at getting his help in paying those bills. If it didn't work out, I could always ask him to leave. So I agreed, almost convinced he was being straight with me this time. But knowing Randy, I suspected there was still a con in there somewhere; I just wasn't seeing it.

Chapter 19

The afternoon stretched before us, a warm spring day inviting me outside. I'd mentioned The Tavern to Grandma Edith, but she shook her head. "Too many families there on Sunday afternoons. You couldn't get near the pool table."

I settled into a patio chair to scroll through my email, enjoying the slight breeze ruffling the leaves of the birch trees. Hummingbirds flitted between newly-opened blossoms, competing with bees for nectar. Beyond them, Grandma Edith wandered along the walkways, deadheading a few flowers as she strolled. She seemed at loose ends, her motions aimless. She sat down beside me, watched the hummingbirds for a few minutes, then jumped up to get soft drinks from the kitchen. Fifteen minutes later, she came back, gave me a soda, and made another circle around the garden before she joined me again.

I put my phone down. "What's bugging you?"

She closed her eyes, took a deep breath, then looked out over the garden as she spoke. "While you were at The Tavern yesterday, I went into Miner's Ridge. I meet a group of women there every week to do volunteer work at our food closet."

She paused to sip her drink, then started again, speaking slower this time. "They were different, those women—my supposed friends. Lead Butt Corringer must have spread the word about my empty bank accounts because I can't think of anything else that would make them behave that way. He's the only one who knew about the money, other than you and Nate, and neither of you would say anything."

"What about the funeral director?"

She turned to look at me. "Maybe. I was so upset, I don't remember what I said to him."

"Something like you were showing your dead husband the same respect he'd shown you when he cleaned out your bank accounts. That's right before you put his ashes in the potato—"

"Okay! You don't have to...never mind. So maybe James Gallagher did his share of talking, too. If that's so, they can replace Emma Kowloski and Jane Portman as town gossips of the year. And those women at the food bank...Marcie, they acted so...so smug, like they knew something that made them feel superior. Exchanging knowing looks, that sort of thing. One of them even gave me a hug, like she was trying to comfort me. Irritated the hell out of me."

I tried to suppress a smile; it wasn't funny, but I loved her reaction. "Do you think that's why the people at the memorial service acted so strange? They knew Grandpa Dan had taken all your money?"

"Maybe. But it doesn't explain the attempted desk break-ins. Anyway, after that sympathy party, I didn't stay for lunch and, on the way home, I got to thinking about Ray's behavior that day—the weird questions and lies. He wanted to get his hands on something he thought was in Dan's office. Just like the people who tried to break in."

"But, Grandma Edith, I looked. There was nothing in those file drawers."

"Ah, but neither of us checked that drawer in the desk extension—until yesterday, while you were gone. I found something—a folder and a day planner with Ray's name in them, along with a lot of others."

I sat up straighter. "You moved the contents from those desk drawers and replaced them with office supplies? The paper and manila envelopes and..."

She raised an eyebrow. "Really, Marcie! Wouldn't that get me in trouble with the investigators? Couldn't I go to jail for...for—"

"Obstruction of justice? I don't think you'd go to jail, but..." It took a minute for my brain to get into first gear. "Of course, you didn't move any files. They were in that carton, wherever it is, that they've always been in."

She nodded, smiling her approval at my understanding. "And I won't even know about that box until I find it. Maybe when I'm doing my spring cleaning next month."

"And you want me to take a look at the things you found with Ray's name in them? From the box you won't know about until later?"

She rose to her feet. "I always knew you were a smart girl. They're in my bedroom. Go ahead, while I lock up for the night. Start with the folder. I've rearranged the contents so you can follow them in a logical order."

As soon as I entered Grandma Edith's room, I saw why it had taken her fifteen minutes to get our soft drinks. She'd cleared everything off her vanity top. On it, front and center, was the file folder labeled "Poker." Behind it, to one side, was a day planner. Apparently, she intended to keep both of them in her room, taking no chance on a visitor finding them in one of the more public areas of the house.

I sat on the vanity stool and opened the folder. The top sheet was a hand-drawn chart with eight columns. The one on the left contained six names: Ray, Ernie, Walt, Mike, Lou, and Dan. The others, headed by days of the week, Sunday through Saturday, held only checkmarks, one for each name. Several had been scribbled out and moved to other days.

Grandma Edith had come into the room and was looking over my shoulder. "The best I can make out, each person on that list was assigned a day of the week, which sometimes changed. But for what purpose?"

"I see Ray's name, and Grandpa Dan's. His day is marked as Thursday. Do you know what he was doing that day? Maybe every week?"

"Only the poker games with his buddies. But I didn't think he'd been doing that for a while. Marcie, I don't know. He was gone so much, I assumed he was working cases."

"Do you recognize the other four names?" I had noticed Jerry Pittman wasn't on the list.

"Three of them. His poker buddies. Walt, Ernie, and Lou. They're also married to the women who were showing me so much sympathy yesterday. Maybe they do know something I don't."

"Or maybe—just maybe—they're even more in the dark than you are." I flipped the page over and looked at the sheet underneath. It, too, was a hand-drawn table containing the same names. The headings over the columns were months, not days, and contained a checkmark for every name. That chart made no sense, either, until I noticed a tiny star drawn into the corner of one of them. Under the chart was another star with a notation: Pd half. Will pay rest by his next turn.

More of the same type of charts filled the remainder of the folder, many of them with hand-written notes: Mike out of town all wk. Ernie wants to trade for Sun.

"They were paying a regular monthly fee for something," I said. "And whatever that was, they were assigned one day each week for it."

"And Ray was trying to find out whether something had been paid." Grandma Edith chewed on her bottom lip. "But, according to this"—She pointed at his name on the most recent list—"he had paid. So was he worried about somebody else paying? And why would that bother him?"

I leafed back through those last pages. "The list was growing. There are a few more names each month."

Grandma Edith handed me the day planner. "So much he couldn't get them all on one sheet anymore, so he bought this."

I flipped through the pages until I got to April. Like most such organizers, each daily page had multiple entries. But, unlike other day planners, these consisted of only one word: a name, sometimes with an initial to indicate a surname. Among them, I spotted Dan, Ray, and Jerry. Jerry Pittman?

The entries contained no additional information: no meeting place, subject for discussion, or anything else you would expect. I turned to last Wednesday's page, when Grandpa Dan was killed. His name wasn't there, but it was on Thursday night's schedule, at eight. I noticed then that there was at least a two-hour space between each name, and most of them were clustered around the lunch hour or early evening. Like the hand-drawn charts, an entry was sometimes scribbled out and inserted elsewhere. The schedule, whatever it might be, was flexible.

I flipped back to earlier months and saw the same pattern, only fewer entries. At least a dozen names, possibly more, had been added since January.

I closed the book and handed it to Grandma Edith. "It might have been better to let the detectives see these. I don't see any way to make use of them."

"I do." She opened the day planner again and stabbed her finger at a name. "Ernie. Hilda's husband."

"Who?"

"Hilda. She's one of the smug women. And Ernie is one of Dan's old poker buddies. I know where he lives. He's on the schedule for tonight, and I happen to know Hilda goes to visit her mother every Sunday after church and doesn't get home until late."

"So?" I didn't like where this was going.

"We can follow him. Marcie, this may be our only chance to find out what's going on."

"How can we follow him? Miner's Ridge is small. He would recognize your Malibu. Grandpa Dan's Honda, too."

"What about Randy's car?"

That would have been a good option if I'd been able to find the key. Had he, in typical Randy fashion, forgotten to leave it?

I didn't look for it very hard, thinking the missing key would squelch Grandma Edith's plan, but she wasn't so easily deterred. "We'll take your convertible. The only place it's been since you got here is The Tavern. Not many people will recognize it."

She was right. The Camaro might be flashy, but it wouldn't be familiar to the inhabitants of Miner's Ridge. And I'd never taken the top down since my first rain-soaked attempt. "Okay. Say we follow him. I don't have any surveillance training. Won't he notice and start wondering? Maybe take a closer look at who's in the car?"

"Why would he notice? He wouldn't be expecting anybody to follow him, and he doesn't know you or the car. I can disguise myself somehow. Put a scarf over my hair or..." Her face brightened. "There'll be something in the disguise closet. Let's go look."

She hurried to the office and, before I could warn her, yanked open the closet door. Just as before, the blonde wig I'd so hastily jammed back on the shelf tumbled off and rolled to her feet. She let out a little gasp, her fingers going to cover her chest as she stepped back, then looked down at the wide-open eyes of the mannequin head. "Perfect. I always wanted to be a platinum blonde."

I was tempted to point out that her expiration date for long blonde hair was long past, but thought better of it.

She picked up the wig, removed it from the stand, and closed the closet door. "I've got a shawl, one I bought in Mexico years ago. I don't know why because I never wore it after we left there, but it's big, so I can kind of wrap up in it. Hold on. I'll go get it."

She disappeared into the bedroom and came out a few minutes later with a big orange and turquoise shawl with beads around the edges. I tried to push away the image of her in my yellow Camaro, wearing that shawl and the long, blonde wig. "Don't you think we should find something a little less...less noticeable?"

"It'll be dark. Ernie's not going to notice, even if he happens to look in his rearview mirror. If he does, he's not going to connect anything he sees to me."

She had that right, and I was out of arguments. I went to find a dark shirt to wear with my jeans.

Ernie's house was a modest ranch-style in need of some fresh paint, two blocks off Main Street. Grandma Edith spotted his dark-blue Subaru in the driveway. "He's still here. We'll stake it out and wait for him to leave. Go around the block and find a dark place to park, where we can watch him."

I follow directions well, especially Grandma Edith's, so I drove past the house and turned right at the next corner, toward Main Street. I cruised along and already had my signal on to make the next right turn when lights blinked behind me. A Miner's Ridge police car. Had I missed a stop sign in the dark, one half-hidden by shrubbery?

I finished the turn, pulled to the curb, and rolled down my window.

While the officer got out and approached the car, Grandma Edith scrunched down in the seat, wrapped the shawl around her upper body, and turned her face toward the passenger door.

"Marcie?" Eric Roberts stared in at me. "I recognized your car and thought..." Only then did he notice a figure in the passenger seat. "Is that your husband with you?"

Grandma Edith made a sound—some combination of a laugh and a snort—and shook her head, letting the long blonde strands curtain her face.

Roberts leaned down to take a closer look. I twisted in my seat a little, partially blocking his view. Hoping it was too dark for him to get a good view. "No. I'm not married. This is...is a lady who needs help." That much was true, and I didn't like lying, especially to a cop. But his puzzled look told me I had no choice. "She's...well, she's not feeling well and I'm trying to get her..." Where? He probably knew everybody and every structure in Miner's Ridge. "I think she's a visitor and she can't remember how to get to her motel room."

Now he was going to ask how I'd gotten involved, and I was trying to think up an answer. When he said, "You're not married? But Randy—"

"Is my ex, but he's a little slow to get it. He still thinks ex stands for kisses."

"You're divorced? Then, Marcie..."

Grandma Edith, apparently sensing the conversation was spinning out of control, leaned her face against the window and made the most convincing retching sound I'd heard since the last time Randy had spent the better part of an evening worshiping the commode.

Not smart, Grandma Edith. The logical thing for me to do now would be to get you out of my car. Apparently, she realized that, too, because she added, barely above a whispered croak, "Please. Get me to my motel. And hurry."

I waved at Roberts, rolled up my window, and took off. When I glanced in my rearview mirror he still stood in the same spot, staring after us.

I turned right at the next intersection. "We have to get away from town before he sees the Camaro again. I'm sorry, Grandma Edith, but—"

"There! Follow him!" She was pointing at Ernie's car, pulling out of his driveway on the intersecting street. With that last turn, I'd almost circled the block.

I followed, hoping he wasn't headed into Miner's Ridge, where Officer Roberts might be patrolling. I held my breath when the Subaru turned in that direction, but he went straight through, toward State Highway 20. If he turned west there, he would be going toward Nevada City. East would take him to Norden or Truckee, or possibly on to the Nevada state line. I glanced at the gas gauge. "I hope he's not headed to Reno for some out-of-state gambling."

"Me, too," Grandma Edith said, "because I don't think I can wait that long to find a restroom. I forgot to go before we left."

"I think that's the first rule of stakeouts, Grandma Edith: Go to the bathroom before you leave and every chance you get thereafter. But I don't think Ernie's going to Reno. He wouldn't need an assigned day to do that. At least, not if his agenda is gambling."

He turned west and Grandma Edith let out a little sigh of relief, probably a premature one, since we still didn't know Ernie's destination. We were twelve miles from the little hamlet of Nevada City, famous for its Victorian Christmases. Four more would take us to Grass Valley. Beyond that, who knew?

We followed him along the two-lane winding road, a tunnel enclosed by tall evergreens. The trees gave way to lower foliage as we reached the outskirts of Nevada City. The Subaru kept going, not slowing until we'd passed the city limits sign for Grass Valley. There, Ernie turned onto a street leading into a residential area. I eased off the accelerator; it wouldn't be easy to avoid detection here. I was almost two blocks behind him when he pulled to a stop in front of a house. I couldn't see much in the dusk, other than steps leading up to a small and dimly-lit railed porch.

I should have kept going past him and circled around so he wouldn't notice my headlights going off behind him. But the convertible was too noticeable; he would remember it if he saw it again. I pulled into the driveway of a dark house, hoping nobody was home, and doused the lights. If Ernie noticed, he might think it was somebody just arriving home.

He tapped his horn. A dog yapped in response, but nothing else moved. All of us—Ernie, Grandma Edith, and me—waited. Five minutes, then six, then seven. My stomach grumbled, reminding me that we'd skipped dinner.

"I've gotta go," Grandma Edith said, eyeing the bigger shrubbery along the driveway.

Ernie honked again. A few minutes later, a light came on above the railed porch. A woman came out, closed the door, walked to Ernie's car, and got in. He started the Subaru and I turned on my headlights, ready to follow.

The front door of the house where we were parked jerked open, spilling light across the steps. A burly man stood in the doorway, most of his face hidden behind a bushy and untrimmed beard, mustache, and thick eyebrows. His voice was almost a growl. "What the hell are you doin' in my driveway?" He walked toward us and, though hesitant, I rolled my window partway down.

"I...um...I got lost and...and I didn't think anybody was home so I pulled in to reset my GPS."

"In the dark?" He crossed his arms and leaned toward me. "Lady, I'm not stupid. You one of them A T and F people snoopin' around again?"

"No, nothing like that. We're just—"

"Snoopin'. You tryin' to get in my back yard in the dark? Steal some of my grow?"

I eased the car into reverse. "No, honest. I don't even know what you're talking about. We just got lost and—"

"I want you off my property. Now!" His fist slammed down on the hood. He was yelling, but I couldn't hear what he was saying above all the noise. Grandma Edith was screaming in my ear. "Marcie, look out!"

I'd hit the accelerator and the Camaro was backing down the driveway, way too fast. Ernie was right behind me, coming back up the street.

Chapter 20

The Subaru swerved, its horn blasting as Ernie accelerated past us. Grandma Edith relaxed her fingers from their grip on the dashboard. "I'm pretty sure Ernie will recognize your car if he sees it again."

Keeping that in mind, I hung back as far as I could without losing him. He left the subdivision and drove toward Nevada City again, finally turning into the parking lot of an Italian restaurant. I slowed, giving him plenty of time to get inside the lot, then continued down the street, circled around, and came into the lot from the other side. I spotted his car and found a parking space close enough to watch both the lane next to it and the restaurant's entrance. I'd barely got the convertible parked when Grandma Edith opened the door. "I'm going to the restroom."

"Wait until they're inside, away from the door."

"I can't." She ran, the blonde wig a little askew and the orange-and-turquoise shawl flapping around her shoulders. I scanned the rows where Ernie had parked his car. He and the woman weren't in view yet, so maybe Grandma Edith would have time to get inside a restroom before they saw her. Coming out unobserved might be another story.

Two or three minutes later, Ernie and the woman emerged from the semi-darkness of the lot and walked to the restaurant's entrance. I could only watch as they opened the door, hoping they didn't collide with Grandma Edith.

I tried to ignore my grumbling stomach and the aroma wafting from the restaurant. I envisioned a big mound of spaghetti with meat sauce, accompanied by garlic bread and a fresh green salad. Or maybe cannelloni. Or lasagna. With a glass of red wine.

Fifteen minutes that seemed more like an hour ticked by. What was she doing? Was she in trouble? I couldn't wait any longer; I had to go inside.

As I reached for the door handle, she appeared outside the restaurant door, looking around the lot as though she might have forgotten where we parked. Not surprising, considering her urgent run for the restroom. I tapped the horn and she headed toward me and climbed into the car.

"They didn't see me. Ernie never even looked up, he was so engrossed in that woman he's with. And she's not his daughter, I can tell you that. For one thing, Hilda would have come with him if he planned to meet up with a relative. For another, he's not acting the least bit like a father."

She pulled out her cell phone. "The corridor to the restrooms isn't far from their table, so I got a quick shot. Take a look." She handed me the phone.

She had caught a clear image of a man, about sixty-five, with a fringe of gray hair circling a shiny bald spot. The woman sitting next to him appeared to be in her mid to late thirties with dark, shoulder-length hair. They leaned toward each other, his hand resting over hers on the table.

"That's Ernie Blaylock for sure," Grandma Edith said, "and I don't think Hilda would be so smug if she saw that picture."

"You're not thinking of showing it to her?"

Grandma Edith pursed her lips. "I don't know. Depends on how long she acts so smug."

My stomach growled again, so loud Grandma Edith could hear it. "I'm hungry, too," she said, "but I guess we don't have time to go get anything."

"Where's their table? Can I get in and out without them seeing me?"

"Toward the back, on the left. And you could walk up to them and snap a picture. They wouldn't notice."

I rooted around in the glove compartment for my 49ers baseball cap and pulled it on. "They'll be here for a while. I'm going to go in and order takeout. What do you want?"

"Marcie, this place is upscale, a lot pricier than we can afford. What about some Chinese? Or Mexican?"

I peered through the darkness toward the buildings adjacent to the restaurant. "I don't think there's anything else here."

"There's probably a Burger King or McDonald's somewhere close by. Or a pizza place. A small one wouldn't cost that much. I wonder if they'd deliver to a car?"

I laughed. "What are you going to give them as an address? A yellow Camaro parked in a restaurant parking lot?"

"We could make it work. They're probably used to delivering to strange locations. What if we tell them that we can't afford the Italian food?"

Before I could respond, she laughed. "No, that won't work. They'd ask why, if we want delivery to a car, we can't drive to the pizza place. But maybe...what if we broke down, barely got our vehicle into this lot, are hungry, and can't afford the restaurant?"

"They'd probably hang up on you, thinking it's a prank. Unless you can use your best old-woman voice."

She swatted my arm. "I. Do. Not. Have an old woman voice. What if I give them a credit card number they can run before they deliver? And I'll offer a nice tip."

I was intrigued. If nothing else, I'd get a good laugh. "Okay. But you make the call. I'll park as close to the restaurant entrance as I can."

She pulled out her phone and did a quick search for pizza places. I was pulling into a parking space when she dialed the number. Her end of the conversation was filled with long waits and I could only imagine the expressions of the person on the other end of the call as she wove her tale of our supposed plight. It got even more interesting when she tried to describe the delivery site at the restaurant: "We're in the third row from the front door, on the left-hand side, four cars away from the driving lane. It's a yellow Camaro convertible, but the top's not down. I'll be standing outside, wearing an orange-and-turquoise shawl. With beads."

The silence was longer this time. "No, beads. But it doesn't matter. You probably can't see them in the dark, anyway." She glanced at me and lowered her voice to a husky pitch. "I'm...elderly and I need help. If I don't get something to eat, I'm afraid my blood sugar is going to drop and...oh, good. Thank you. Can you tell your driver to flash his lights when he pulls into the lot? We can flash ours back." Another pause, then, "Bless you. You are truly a good Samaritan."

She ended the call and gave me a satisfied smirk. "I told you we could make it work. You never know until you try."

"Yes, you did, but I didn't know you planned to flash him. And invite him to flash you." She punched my arm again, so pleased with herself, I didn't mention the curiosity that might be aroused inside the restaurant by all the flashing headlights.

After we had demolished the pizza and taken a few sips of our soft drinks, we still had time to take turns in the restroom before settling down to wait. As I sat there, replete with food that didn't come out of Grandma Edith's freezer, my thoughts turned toward my job and home, wondering what Randy had done to "fix up" my house. He would be up early tomorrow morning to work long hours at a job he wanted to keep. If he had put this much effort into our marriage, I might not have filed for divorce. But there were those Grandpa Dan genes to consider, and look where those had got Grandma Edith. No, I was better off with somebody like Eric Roberts: steady, reliable, law-abiding, safe. But not nearly as much fun as Randy or Brad Kinney. And that freight train of thought led me to the realization that I was supposed to call Brad and let him know if I was going to The Tavern tomorrow. I asked Grandma Edith.

"Of course. That is, if you want to. We can't do any more surveillance until tomorrow afternoon."

"Tomorrow? You're planning to do this with everybody on that schedule?"

"Only till we find out what's going on."

I was leaving a message on Brad's phone when Grandma Edith pointed. "Look." She slumped down in her seat. "They're coming out."

I started the car and headed for the same exit I'd come in on, then circled back so I'd be behind Ernie's Subaru when it exited the lot.

For the first five minutes we followed it, I thought he was going back to the house where he'd picked up the woman, but he turned off before he got that far. He led us into, as near as I could determine in the dark, a semi-commercial district. We passed low-lying stucco buildings that might be small businesses. I saw a sign for a dental office and another for a title company. Just past them, Ernie pulled into a small parking lot.

I yanked the ball cap off my head and gave it to Grandma Edith. "I can't drive past him again. He'll recognize the Camaro. I can't suddenly douse the lights, either. You're going to have to follow him on foot while I find a side street and park."

She pulled the blonde wig off, tossed it in the back seat, and pushed her hair up under the cap. "What do I do if I catch him?"

"Don't catch him! Don't even get near him! Try to be a shadow, just close enough so you don't lose him. I'll be there as soon as I get the car parked. And put your phone in airplane mode."

Without another word, she slipped out of the Camaro and headed across the lot. She was enjoying herself way too much.

It took only a few minutes to park in front of a beauty supply store around the corner and walk back to the parking lot, but I didn't see her until she hissed at me from the recesses of a dark doorway. "Over here."

"Where are they? Did you lose them?"

"No, I didn't lose them." From her indignant tone, I knew I'd teetered close to the edge of condescension toward the elderly that she despised. This wasn't the time to tell her I wasn't questioning her mental capacity. I whispered, "Where are they?"

"Inside this building."

I crowded close to her in the entryway. Cupping my hands around my eyes, I leaned close to the unleaded sections of the door's small window and peered inside. The room—or rather foyer—was dimly lit, but I could see a small bank of mailboxes on one wall. The building held at least six or eight units, either offices or apartments. Judging by the lack of a reception desk and the unlikelihood of Ernie and his lady visiting an office at this hour, I assumed the latter.

Impatient, Grandma Edith pushed me aside and peered in. I didn't mind; I was looking for a number on the building, to see if it matched the one scribbled on the paper I'd found in Grandpa Dan's pocket. It wasn't even close: 714, not 5211.

I really hadn't expected it to match, unless the note was an old one he'd forgotten to throw away. He wouldn't have needed a reminder for an address he'd visited so often.

"What are we going to do now?" Grandma Edith asked. "It's getting pretty late, and I'll bet they're going to be in there all night."

"I don't think so. The woman didn't lock her door when she left home, which tells me there's somebody there, maybe a husband waiting for her to get back from her yoga class or dinner with the girls. Otherwise, why not just go back there for the night?"

"So you think he's having an affair with a married woman? That's why he uses the apartment?"

"Probably. But there's nothing more we can do tonight. Let's go home."

She was quiet on the drive and I thought she might have drifted off to sleep until she sat up straighter in the seat. "Marcie, all the men on that list. I think they're having affairs. They need a place to take the women so they all chip in to keep the apartment rented."

I suspected she might be right, but didn't want to get into the implications of that statement, so I said nothing. It didn't take her long, though. "That includes Ray. And Dan. He was part of it."

A big part, I thought. After all, he was keeping the records and, apparently, paying the rent.

I drove in silence for several more miles before she spoke again.

"That's what Ray was so worried about at the celebration of life when he told me the lie about the Orpheum in San Francisco. It had nothing to do with a birthday surprise. He was worried about the apartment rent being paid. But I can't figure out what that apartment has to do with my empty bank accounts. Dan might have given flowers and my ring to some floozy, but not my money."

"You're right." Unless it was a group of women scamming older men. But I didn't see how they could finagle that much money out of them. Miner's Ridge might be a little secluded, but the men weren't stupid—with the possible exception of the garbage thief. And maybe the guy trying to break into the desk during the memorial service when the place was crawling with people. "Maybe I should stay home tomorrow and help you try to figure this out."

"No, you go to The Tavern. I want to spend some time working on the spreadsheet I've been building from Dan's phone calls and his files."

"How do you think the spreadsheet will help?"

"If I've got every possible number Dan might have called and match them up with names, I think I can weed the list down to the woman who has my ring. And my money. I know it's a long shot, but it's all I can think of to do, and I need that money."

Chapter 21

We were almost home but something was niggling at me—a detail we'd overlooked or a connection I hadn't made. I thought about the building we'd just left, the mailboxes on the wall. They might have names on them. More likely apartment numbers. But I didn't see how either would help us. We already had the names we needed and it didn't matter which unit they were using. We could easily find a telephone number for the manager; there couldn't be that many apartment buildings in Grass Valley, and we had the address. But to what end? Unless... "Grandma Edith, do you think there might be something in that apartment that could lead us to your money?"

"It's worth exploring." She was quiet for a moment, then added, "I can't think of a better place for Dan to hide things from me." Her voice had turned a little bitter at the end, something I'd never heard from her before.

"We've got his keys, so we can get inside. Let's look at the schedule for tomorrow—try to find a window when nobody is there."

So my day was planned: The Tavern in the morning, then exploring the apartment. The only thing left in doubt was whether we could get there without being spotted. The convertible would be highly visible during daylight hours and Grandma Edith's Malibu and Grandpa Dan's Honda were too well-known. I'd have to call Randy and ask him where he'd put the key to his car. If he'd left it.

It was past ten by the time I turned into Grandma Edith's street. It had been a long day, starting with our early breakfast and shopping before Randy drove back to Galt. I was tired, ready for a shower and bed.

I was not prepared for Nate, who came over as soon as we headed up the steps. "Edie, somebody broke into your house while you were gone. The cops have already been here and gone. They want you to call them, tell them if anything is missing."

Grandma Edith was staring at him, her shoulders slumping. "Again? I might as well put a welcome mat out. Maybe have a fresh pot of coffee waiting and a plate of cookies." She inspected the front door, unlocked it, and we went inside. "How did they get in?"

"Through the back. They broke the glass in the patio door so they could reach through and unlock it. I didn't hear the noise, just saw what appeared to be a flashlight moving around inside. At first, I thought the power might be off, but mine was still on so I tried to call you. When you didn't answer, I decided I'd better come over and check, make sure you were okay."

Grandma Edith reached for her phone, stared at it, then looked at me. "I forgot to take it out of airplane mode when we started home."

"I heard the back door slam when I walked up on the front porch," Nate said, "then the sound of somebody running out back. I called the cops then. I'll say one thing for our police department. They didn't waste any time getting here, and they did a good job of searching the house and yard to make sure whoever did this was gone."

They hadn't disturbed much in their search. The only indications somebody had been in the house were the broken pane in the door, the shards of glass on the floor and patio, and the open drawers in the office.

"I'd love to have seen his face when he found them empty," I commented to Grandma Edith before I realized she was no longer in the room. She would be checking on the day planner and folder, to make sure they were still safe.

They were. She gave me a slight nod as she came back into the living room. "As far as I can see, there's nothing missing in my bedroom, but I suppose we need to do a thorough search, and we have to clean up all that glass."

Nate shook his head. "I was going to pick up the pieces on the patio, but Officer Roberts said we shouldn't touch it until after you call your insurance agent. I figured it wouldn't be safe for you to stay here until it's repaired, so I've already made up beds for you and Marcie over at my place."

"What am I supposed to do in the meantime? Leave it like this so anybody in town can just walk in and make themselves at home?"

All the time she was speaking, she was studying the doors. "What if I wrapped some wire around those two handles so they won't open? It wouldn't stop anybody from reaching through the broken glass to unwrap the wire, but I doubt they'd want to stay out here that long if I turned on all the backyard lights."

"That could work," Nate said, "depending on how desperate they are. They might unscrew all the light bulbs. But I'll go get the wire if you two want to gather up whatever you need for tonight."

Grandma Edith nodded. "I'm too tired to deal with this right now, anyway. Marcie, take what you need for tomorrow, too, so you don't have to come back over here. Buy breakfast at The Tavern tomorrow. I'll infringe on my good neighbor"—she glanced at Nate—"to give me a cup of coffee in the morning."

"I'll do better than that," Nate said. "Breakfast, then help cleaning up."

She smiled at him. "I'll take breakfast and hope we don't have to wait too long for the insurance people. In the meantime, I'll search the house tomorrow, see if anything is missing."

With that settled, we decamped to Nate's house for the night. I suspected I'd have trouble settling into an unfamiliar bed and quieting my churning mind. That was my last conscious thought before I awoke to sunlight creeping around the edges of the curtains. Apparently, I'd been too tired to let a little glass and another break-in keep me from falling asleep.

I tiptoed out of the house the next morning so I wouldn't wake Nate or Grandma Edith. She must be exhausted; she'd never before slept later than I did. She hadn't that morning, either. As I walked past her front porch on the way to my car, I saw her sitting at one of the wicker tables, her back to the street. I walked up the steps to tell her I was leaving. Apparently, not hearing me, she continued her cell phone conversation. "It gets real bad in the morning, hurting so much I can hardly get out of bed. And when I finally do, my knees almost collapse under me. I need at least one replacement, but I can't afford it and Medicare won't cover all the costs."

I covered my mouth to stifle a gasp. I'd never guessed she was in pain or that she needed medical care she couldn't afford. How had she managed to hide it? And had Grandpa Dan known that when he cleaned out their bank accounts?

"Then, this past week, I got test results back from my doctor," she was saying. "I have kidney disease. He wants me to go on a special diet and stop drinking but, at my age, I've already given up so much, that's really hard."

Oh, my gosh! Why hadn't somebody told me she shouldn't be drinking? And why didn't I know about all her medical conditions? But, even if I did, what could I do? I didn't have money to pay for a knee replacement, and there was no way I could convince her to give up her Corona.

I tuned in again to what she was saying. "You can't imagine the pain. And Tylenol, even extra strength, doesn't help much. But I suppose I'm not as bad off as my neighbor. He's got some kind of strange disease. Makes him throw up a lot. He's lost a bunch of weight."

Who was she talking about? I couldn't think of any sick neighbors. "Grandma Edith—"

She turned to look at me, then held up a forefinger, signaling me to wait. "I think I've got a cold coming on now," she continued. "Or maybe it's the flu. I need some dental work, too. I can't hardly eat these days. I'm down to soup and Jell-O and I don't like either one of them very much."

I slapped a palm over my mouth to smother a laugh, finally realizing she was at it again, trying to get a scammer to hang up on her.

She ended the call and looked up at me, eyebrows raised. "Well, he did say 'How are you?' when I answered the phone."

I bent to kiss her on the cheek. "Grandma Edith, you're incorrigible."

But she did have fun in her own way, I thought as I left the house, and maybe it helped her escape her problems for a little while. She had also found a way to enjoy—almost look forward to—those calls the rest of us found so annoying.

When I got to The Tavern, I wasn't surprised to see Brad Kinney waiting to buy me breakfast.

"So, how did the rest of your weekend go?" he asked as I settled into my chair.

"Grandma Edith now knows I'm not married to her grandson, and we had another break-in. We were gone," I added, seeing his expression shift from surprise to concern, "and we don't think anything was taken."

"Then they were looking for something specific? Something they didn't find?"

I'd forgotten he was a cop. "Marcie, this has to be tied to your grandfather's murder. You and your grandmother probably aren't safe in that house. Why isn't local law enforcement doing something to protect you? If they'd had somebody watching the house, they might have caught him."

Until the seventeen-year-old witness came forward to raise questions about Grandpa Dan's death, it hadn't occurred to me that Grandma Edith and I were in any danger. Even after we'd learned his death wasn't a hit-and-run, the break-ins had been so inept, so targeted toward the desk, I couldn't think of any reason why we would be targeted.

Had the Miner's Ridge Police Department taken a different viewpoint? Was one of their officers watching the house from an unmarked car? Eric Roberts had been an almost daily visitor. Checking on us? He'd even attended Grandpa Dan's celebration of life. But if they were watching, why hadn't they caught the intruder who broke in last night? Unless...I thought of that deep back yard with the work area beyond it. In the darkness, somebody agile enough to climb fences might have come in from the next street, sneaking across Linda Gray's back yard into Grandma Edith's. The structures in her work area would have provided cover until he came through the gate. Then, if he'd avoided the motion lights, it was only a short walk to the patio.

Nate had said the police got there quickly and they'd searched the yard. Had they been watching the front of the house and missed the intruder? I doubted they had enough personnel to watch both the front and back of the property.

"Marcie?" Brad put his hand over mine on the table. "Is everything okay?"

"Yes...yes, of course. I just...I never thought about us being in danger." But as soon as I said the words, I knew we weren't; not really. "Brad, as inept as those potential thieves were, I doubt they mean us harm. That's not their objective. The first time they broke in, we weren't even home. We wouldn't have known they'd been there if not for the scratches they made on the desk when they tried to pry a drawer open."

I started laughing before I could finish telling him about my encounter with the intruder during Grandpa Dan's celebration of life.

Brad laughed, too. "So this cop was going around the neighborhood looking for somebody to fit the missing shoe? And the thief was actually trying to get into the contents of the desk while all those people were there for the memorial service?"

"Exactly. It's kind of creepy, with them working so hard to get their hands on something in that office, but there's no indication they want to hurt us."

Betty—I'd learned her name by now—approached with her Pyrex coffee carafe, filled our cups, and took our breakfast orders. I wanted to tell Brad about the garbage thief while we waited for our food but thought better of it. I didn't think Grandma Edith had told even Nate about Grandpa Dan's ashes and the potato chip bag. While the story might eventually get out, as everything seemed to do in Miner's Ridge, I didn't want to be the source, so I dropped the entire subject of the break-ins.

Neither of us mentioned them again until we'd finished playing pool. Brad fell into step beside me as we headed for the door a little before noon. "Want to go across the creek and explore some of that forest land? I'll make sure we don't fall in this time."

Laughing, I said, "I'd love to. Go exploring, I mean, not fall in. But I can't. Grandma Edith has plans for this afternoon."

"What about tonight? Can you have dinner with me?"

"I wish I could, but—"

"Grandma has plans." He stopped and turned to face me. "Marcie, is this your way of telling me you don't want to go out with me? Because, if it is—"

Without thinking, I reached out and grasped his hand. "No! It's nothing like that. I'd love to have dinner with you. It's just...I came up here to help Grandma Edith, and I never know what that help is going to entail. And I have to be there for her, Brad."

"I get that, but is there any way..." He shook his head. "I like you. A lot. I want to get to know you better, but I have to go home by this weekend."

"Me, too. I shouldn't even stay that long. I'm taking it one day at a time, hoping we can get all Grandma Edith's issues resolved before I leave." And that Randy will be ready to move out of my house. And my life.

"Okay." He reached up, like he was going to touch my cheek, but instead, tucked a strand of hair behind my ear. "How about this? If you can find some time when Grandma Edith doesn't need you, give me a call?"

"I can do that." If I had to, I'd tell Grandma Edith I needed time off to have some fun.

"And Marcie?" Brad said as I opened the car door. "Be careful. You can't be sure the people breaking into your grandmother's house won't harm you. Especially if you catch them in the act."

"I will." I got in and closed the door, knowing if he'd been in that side yard when I'd encountered the inept garbage thief or even in the office with the man climbing out the window, he wouldn't be so concerned.

As I drove back to Grandma Edith's house, safely away from the inexplicable pull of Brad Kinney, reason returned. The last thing I needed was another man in my life. I couldn't even shake loose the one I'd divorced. Why, after more than a year of feeling no interest whatsoever in the opposite sex, was I drawn not just to one, but two other men? And, when I let myself admit it, I kind of liked Randy again.

I had to get away from Miner's Ridge—go back to my life in Galt. That thought depressed me so much, I was almost looking forward to Grandma Edith's plans for the afternoon.

The first thing I saw when I walked onto her porch was the sheet of paper taped to the front door. It was a sign in a large, bold font:
IF YOU'RE LOOKING FOR DAN CLIFTON'S FILES, THEY ARE NOW IN THE CUSTODY OF THE MINER'S RIDGE POLICE DEPARTMENT.

I was laughing as I went inside. "That should stop the intruders. "Do you have one on the back door, too?"

"Since it's not in public view, I got a little more specific. It says, 'Don't bother breaking in. The cops took everything.' The insurance people okayed repairs to the door, but I can't get it fixed until tomorrow. I wired the handles together but it's not going to keep anybody out."

She was right, but neither would a repaired door if anybody really wanted to get in. I suspected the sign might be a bigger deterrent.

"I didn't find anything missing," she continued. "But I did find these." She dangled a set of keys in front of me. "I suspect they're for Randy's car, since they don't belong to me. Unless they're yours?"

"No, they're Randy's." I had mixed feelings about her discovery. While we now had a vehicle that wouldn't be recognized by anybody in Miner's Ridge, I wasn't sure it would get us where we needed to go. Randy had bought the Ford Focus second—or maybe third or fourth—hand. It was temperamental, often refusing to start until Randy tinkered with it. I had never paid much attention to what he was doing under the hood and if Tinkering-101 had been offered in any of my course material, I'd skipped right past it.

Grandma Edith made grilled ham and cheese sandwiches for lunch and said she had packed more food to take with us. "I don't want to order pizza delivered to a parking lot again," she said, looking at me as though I'd been the instigator.

After we ate, I changed from my Bermuda shorts into some jeans, pulled a ball cap over my hair, and grabbed a sweater to ward off the night's chill. Grandma Edith had done some work on her disguise while I was gone. She came out of her bedroom wearing a long-sleeved shirt and a pair of worn bib overalls. They were a close match to the faded blue baseball cap she pulled over her pinned-up hair. To complete the outfit, she'd put on her scuffed-up gardening shoes and donned an oversized pair of sunglasses. The transformation was amazing. She had a body toned by hours of yard work. From a distance, especially in the dark, she could pass as a man.

"I don't think anybody will recognize you," I said. "I'm not sure whether you look like a train engineer, a farmer, or a homeless person."

She looked down at her feet. "Maybe just a prelude. I might as well be homeless if we don't find my money. That Social Security check won't carry me very far. I'm thankful Dan couldn't touch my 401(k), but that won't last long if I have to keep drawing from it."

"But Randy told me you don't have a mortgage. The house is paid for."

"Yes, but not the utilities, the groceries, the house insurance, the car insurance, taxes, and everything else that comes along."

She was right. Somehow, we had to find her money.

Chapter 22

The day planner's schedule listed 'Mike' at two that afternoon, and 'Lou' at eight. That gave us a good window between them to get in and out of the apartment—if the schedule hadn't changed—and that was a pretty substantial "if." There had been plenty of switches in the past, and we had no way of knowing the impact of Grandpa Dan's death.

Grandma Edith had seen Mike with Grandpa Dan but didn't know his last name, nor had she noticed what kind of car he drove. She thought she could identify him if she got close enough, but that meant he would probably recognize her.

To be sure Mike was in that apartment at two, we'd have to be in place to watch him go in. We planned to park in the lot, close enough for Grandma Edith to see his face. Once he entered the building, we'd watch through the door's window until he entered one of the units. After he came out and drove away, we'd go in, with plenty of time to explore before Lou arrived.

It was a good plan, but I hadn't taken Randy into account. The fuel gauge on the Ford hovered over empty. I wasn't sure we could get it to Miner's Ridge's only gas station.

I made it, only to find myself behind a long line of cars. Why would everybody in town be filling their tanks on Monday afternoon?

"They wait till Monday to come into town," Grandma Edith explained, "to avoid the flatlanders visiting on the weekends."

I alternated between watching the gas gauge and the time as I inched forward in line. We could still make it if we hurried.

Finally, we reached the pumps. I filled the tank and we headed toward the highway but, with traffic heavier than I'd expected, we were held up again at the stoplight—probably no more than two minutes, but time we didn't have to spare.

When we were finally back on the road to Grass Valley, I fought the urge to push a little harder on the accelerator. The last thing we needed was a traffic stop.

We rolled into Grass Valley with four minutes to spare and drove past the apartment building. Two cars were parked in the lot. I pulled the Ford into a space where we could watch the door.

Two o'clock came and went. Then five minutes more. Ten. Fifteen. Grandma Edith shifted in her seat. "One of those cars in the lot must be Mike's. He got here before we did."

"Yeah." But we had no way to be sure. We could wait until Mike came out, but that might be never. We had to be sure the schedule was still accurate, that his time hadn't been shifted to the six o'clock slot we'd planned to use. The only way to be sure was to get into that apartment and it had to be me. He'd recognize Grandma Edith.

"But you won't know if it's him," she pointed out.

"No, but we'll at least know somebody is in there. Then, when he comes out, I can identify him as the man in the apartment and you can identify him as Mike."

"But he'll know we're on to him if you go busting in there."

"Maybe not." I had spotted a sidewalk display down the block, an assortment that included wheelbarrows, watering cans, hoses, kiddie wading pools, and other items too small to identify from a distance. "Give me the keys to the apartment."

She handed them over and I trotted to the store. Inside, I did some quick shopping and came out carrying a mop, broom, and plastic bucket. I stopped on the sidewalk long enough to pull a couple of scarves out of the bucket and drop my cap inside. I tied one scarf around my hair and draped the other so it hung out of my back pocket. Then, bucket over my arm and mop and broom in my hands, I headed back down the street.

I reached the lot, passed the Ford and Grandma Edith, who smiled and fluttered her fingers in a little wave of encouragement, and hurried to the building's front door.

Once inside, I tiptoed to the mailboxes, hoping they'd have both names and apartment numbers. No such luck. Keeping an eye out for observers, I worked my way down the hall, tapping on doors. Nobody answered the first two. The third was opened by a man whom I'd apparently awakened—maybe a night shift worker, judging by his surly tone and the door he slammed in my face. I moved along to the next door. Again, nobody answered my tap.

I turned away, ready to try the last two apartments when I heard a noise—a low murmur of voices. Somebody was inside; they just weren't answering the door.

I stood still, listening, but heard nothing more. Somehow, I had to see the man's face, and I knew only one way to do that. Unsure which key fit the door, I fumbled for a few seconds before it opened with a loud creak.

"Who's there?" A rustle, then a man came through an interior door, a sheet wrapped around his waist, trailing behind him.

"Mr. Andrews? You scheduled a cleaning for this afternoon?"

"What? No! No cleaning! You've got the wrong place."

"Oh, okay, sorry." I backed out of the room, closed the door, hurried back to the car, and stowed my cleaning equipment in the trunk.

"He's there," I told Grandma Edith as I opened the car door. "At least, somebody's there. Now we just have to wait. That could take a couple of hours, and we can't stay here. He might recognize me."

"Two people sitting in a car that long would draw too much attention, anyway," Grandma Edith said. She pointed across the street. "That place with the awning. Isn't it a restaurant?"

She was right. We could watch through their wide window while we...ate? "Grandma Edith, we just had lunch."

"We could take home doggie bags. They'd be better than Alma's casseroles."

She had a point. "But we can't just sit there in front of our food for hours before we ask for take-out containers. Besides, I can't afford to eat. Not after buying those cleaning supplies."

I twiddled my thumbs on the steering wheel, trying to think of another option. "Maybe we should get out and shop for a while—work off some of our lunch, then go in the restaurant later for something to drink."

"I don't know about that. I can't see any shops along this street, and I'm not in need of a title company or a dentist. Maybe the lawyer if we get caught in the apartment."

"The way you're dressed, I doubt any of them would let you in the door. Probably not me, either."

We sat there for a while, neither of us saying anything while I tried to think of a way around the problem. Nothing came to me.

Grandma Edith leaned over the back seat. "I've got an idea." She rummaged through a clutter of fast food containers, bottles, cans, and other throw-aways in the back.

A dark green garbage bag covered part of the back seat, probably to hide a stain or rip in the upholstery. She pulled it loose, opened it, and started filling it with empty cans.

"You're going to be a homeless person foraging for cans?"

"Can you think of a better way to wander up and down the street without drawing unwanted attention?"

I couldn't. She would probably become invisible to most people. A few might offer her a little money. Maybe enough to pay for a sandwich.

I didn't think the block would support two homeless people, nor was I as well dressed for the part, so I opted to get out and stroll down the street, pretending I was looking for a particular business. That wouldn't work for long, but neither would the can gathering.

A half-hour later, I'd peered at the sign for every business within viewing distance of the apartment, and had started pretending I was absorbed with my phone. But it was a warm day, I was thirsty, and I wanted—no, needed—something cold to drink.

I crossed the street and met Grandma Edith at the end of the block. We walked to the restaurant together. She set the bag of cans beside the door and we went inside.

The restaurant, wedged in between a couple of office buildings, was long and narrow and had less than a dozen customers. Most of its clientele probably came from the surrounding businesses, and it was well past the lunch hour. As we settled into our seats by the window, I glanced at the wall clock: three-twenty. Forty minutes to wait. Maybe less, since Mike had arrived early. Maybe more, since Lou wasn't scheduled to arrive until eight.

As the waitress approached, I noticed her gaze was moving from Grandma Edith's worn clothing to her battered gardening shoes.

She sniffed and, ignoring Grandma Edith, handed a menu to me. "It's nice of you to do this." She gave a slight nod in Grandma Edith's direction. "But we'd prefer you take any meals you buy for these people outside. Give it to them on the sidewalk."

"What?" I think Grandma Edith and I spoke in unison. Then I got it; she thought I was buying a meal for a homeless person.

While I was trying to make up my mind whether to laugh or protest, Grandma Edith cast a cool stare at the woman. "A menu, please."

The waitress handed one over, and we took our time looking at the limited selections. When she came back, order pad in hand, Grandma Edith asked, "Don't you have another menu? I don't see anything I want on this one. There's no foie gras or caviar. Not even escargot or sea bass."

The waitress shook her head, a befuddled expression on her face. "We don't have any of that stuff. Just salad, soup, sandwiches and a few entrees. That's it."

Grandma Edith wrinkled her nose. "Then, I think I'll skip the food and just have something to drink. You obviously don't have any champagne, but I'm wondering...do you have any halfway decent wine?"

"We don't serve alcoholic beverages."

"Not even beer?" This time, Grandma Edith sounded genuinely shocked.

Feeling a little sorry for the waitress, I ordered a piece of apple pie and iced tea. Grandma Edith sniffed. "I suppose you'll have to bring me the same. I'll try to choke it down."

The pie was better than I expected, but I wasn't hungry. I was picking at it and drinking a second glass of iced tea when the door to the apartment building opened and a woman walked out. Mike's date or somebody else? And would he be close behind her?

I tossed enough money on the table to cover our food, along with a tip for our harassed waitress, and headed for the door. We had a problem. If Mike followed that woman out, we wouldn't be close enough for him to recognize either of us, but we couldn't be sure it was him, either.

I ran across the street, prepared to duck behind a parked car if the man followed her out of the building. The woman, a tall redhead, paused as she opened her car door. "Is something wrong?"

"No! No, I just...I can't find my wallet. I need to pay for my food at the coffee shop and my wallet's not in my purse. I think it may have dropped out." I pointed. "In my car."

"Oh. That's too bad. I hope you find it." She got into her Camry, still watching as I opened the door to the Ford, so I pretended to search until she pulled out of the lot. By that time, Grandma Edith had reached the car and slid into the passenger seat. I got in and barely had time to close the door before Mike walked out of the building. Without a glance in our direction, he got into the only other vehicle in the lot and drove away.

"Finally!" Grandma Edith reached for the door handle. "We can go in now."

"No, let's wait a few minutes, just to make sure one of them doesn't come back to get something they forgot. We have plenty of time."

While we waited, I retrieved the cleaning gear from the trunk, tied the scarf back around my hair, and stuck one corner of the cleaning rag deep into a back pocket.

Why are you doing that?" Grandma Edith asked. "There's nobody in there who will recognize us."

"Just insurance in case anybody questions us being there. It worked pretty well the last time." I nodded down at the bucket. "Besides, this will come in handy if we have to carry something out."

Within minutes, we were inside, and I set down the cleaning equipment. The place looked more like an uninhabited hotel room than an apartment. The air inside was stale and a thin layer of dust covered most of the surfaces.

The few pictures on the walls were hotel grade, as were the bedside lamps and alarm clocks. A basket with a sprawling artificial philodendron was on the dresser opposite the bed.

With the sparse decor, our search shouldn't have taken long, but Grandma Edith, determined to find her money, was thorough. She stripped the bed and made me help her hold the mattress up on each side so she could check underneath. While she was re-making the bed, I looked through drawers. She came along behind me, pulling the drawers out so she could see the bottoms and sides. I looked through cabinets. She took the contents out and examined them. Fortunately, there weren't many, or we might have been there for days. She lifted the lid from the toilet tank and looked inside (for a sealed plastic bag, I presumed).

I wanted to go; we'd been in the apartment long enough, and I didn't want to be caught there. Grandma Edith wasn't so eager. She was on her hands and knees, looking underneath the bed. I turned back to the dresser and ran my fingers through the bottom of the philodendron plant. They struck something odd. I bent and looked into the lens of a tiny camera.

"Grandma Edith, come on! We have to get out of here. Now!" I grabbed her arm and propelled her toward the door. Stopping only long enough to grab the cleaning supplies, I pulled her out of the apartment.

The outer door opened and I heard the tap of high heels and a man's voice. Grandma Edith grabbed me by the shoulders, spun my back to the wall, leaned in, and planted a kiss on my lips. A long kiss.

I struggled. A woman laughed. "Looks like your cleaning crew are pretty friendly. Sure they're not using the room while nobody is here?"

The man's voice, vaguely familiar, responded. "That's not acceptable. I'll talk to the manager."

A door squeaked open, then closed. The voices were gone.

I squirmed away from Grandma Edith. "What was that? What happened?"

"That was Dan's brother, Ray, and he would have recognized both of us if he'd seen our faces. The schedule must have changed."

"Yeah. But they have pictures of us, Grandma Edith. That apartment is bugged."

Grandma Edith was quiet as I drove out of Grass Valley, back toward Miner's Ridge and home. Strange, I thought. I'd been there for little more than a week and Grandma Edith's house felt more like home than my place in Galt. And I'd much rather live with her than Randy.

"We're going to have to tell the cops," she said, her voice resigned. "We're not safe anymore, now that the crooks have our pictures."

I glanced at her, slumped in her seat. "I don't think we need to worry about the crooks, Grandma Edith. From what I'm seeing, most of the people using that apartment already know you. I think the only crook is dead."

Her head jerked up. "Dead? You mean Dan? My husband?"

I didn't say anything, but it didn't take long for her to figure it out. "Of course, it was Dan. He was the one who kept the records. He was a private investigator. He knew how to set up the cameras. But why? This was his own brother, his friends."

"Maybe he had no intention of filming all of them. He could have been targeting one person for a case he was working. It's possible he set up the camera right before he was killed and never had a chance to take it out."

She wrinkled her nose. "It's still unbelievable. I wish we'd never gone in there. I would have been better off not knowing, and we're no closer to finding my money than we were a week ago."

"But we may know why the intruders were so interested in Grandpa Dan's desk. At least one of them must have discovered the camera, and he was looking for the pictures."

Something was bothering me, though. Grandma Edith was right. I couldn't figure out how any of this fit in with her missing money.

Chapter 23

Eric Roberts came over later that evening, and we were all settled in the living room as Grandma Edith told him about the camera we had discovered in the apartment.

He nodded. "We found several possibly incriminating photos tucked away in one of those big manila folders in the bottom of your husband's file cabinets. We would have passed them off as nothing but evidence in a case Mr. Clifton was working if not for the fact that they captured several couples, all taken in the same setting by multiple cameras. That hinted at some kind of illegal operation. Now we know the location of that room."

"Cameras? There were more than one?" Even as I spoke, I realized I should have recognized those "alarm clocks" on each side of the bed; I'd seen them before in the evidence room at the Galt Police Department. "They were getting pictures from three different angles!"

Roberts gave me a strange look. Despite all my denials, he still assumed I was some kind of investigator and should know these things.

He turned to Grandma Edith. "Mrs. Clifton, I know this may be difficult, but do you think...is there any way you could take a look at those pictures? Help us identify all the people in them?"

Grandma Edith's jaw dropped at the same time she started shaking her head. "No! I don't know anything about Dan's cases, but those are neighbors. Dan's friends. Family. I don't want to see any of them that way. I can't—"

"All the people?" I was trying to wrap my mind around the implications of what Roberts had just said. "I thought he was trying to catch images of one person. For a case he was working. That he'd set the camera...cameras up just before he died and never got a chance to take them down."

"No, they'd been in place for weeks and there are at least a dozen couples."

I stared at him, unable to utter my next thought. He did it for me. "Yes," he said. "We can think of only one reason for that. Blackmail."

That would certainly explain why people were acting so weird at the celebration of life—and the attempted raids on Grandpa Dan's office.

Grandma Edith, without saying a word, got up and left the room.

Roberts rose to his feet. "I'm sorry. That was...awkward of me. I should have handled it better. I'll give her a little time, then—"

"No, we're going to do it now."

We both turned to Grandma Edith, walking toward us with the day planner and folder in her arms. "I'm not going to look at those disgusting pictures." She put the day planner and folder on the coffee table. "I found these in some of Dan's things. The names are all here." She hesitated, as though she wanted to say more, then changed her mind. "I'm going to fix myself a drink while you're figuring it all out. Do the two of you want one?"

"I think I will," I said, surprising myself. I rarely drank hard liquor. But, then, I'd never been in a situation quite like this. Roberts nodded, then shook his head. "I'm on duty, but I'd appreciate some coffee if it isn't too much trouble."

It didn't take him long to make sense of Grandpa Dan's records. "This is probably why your husband was killed." He looked up at Grandma Edith, who was setting drinks on the coffee table. "If you'd given these to us earlier, we might have had a better chance—"

"She just found them two days ago," I said, "and she had no reason to think they were connected to Grandpa Dan's death."

Eric Roberts wasn't stupid. He stared at me, a flash of disappointment crossing his face before he donned the mask of professional officer. In a quiet, even tone, he asked, "Then, why did you decide to go exploring? How did you find the apartment? When, exactly, did the two of you decide it might be relevant to the case?"

Grandma Edith let out a long sigh before she lowered herself onto the chair opposite Roberts. "There are some things you need to know—"

"Obviously."

Maybe he had reason to be irritated with us, but Grandma Edith was trying to explain. "You need to cut her some slack," I said. "She—"

Grandma Edith held up a palm. "Let it go, Marcie. I need to tell him what's been going on." And she told him everything, starting with her missing money and over-extended credit cards. Everything, that is, except what she'd done with Grandpa Dan's ashes.

Roberts looked from one of us to the other. "You're not an investigator then?" he asked me.

"No, but I kept trying to tell you that. Why is it important now?"

"Because if you were, you'd have seen..." He glanced at Grandma Edith, who nodded in encouragement. "You'd have realized. If Mr. Clifton's business was successful, with regular deposits, some of them large, being made into his bank accounts, why would he need to blackmail anybody?"

"Because that money was going somewhere faster than he could earn it," I said. "The accounts were empty when he died."

"Which suggests what?" He sat back, watching my face.

"He owed somebody more than he could pay. I can see that. But what? I thought about a gambling debt, but, from what Grandma Edith says, he only played penny-ante poker, no high stakes stuff."

"There's another possibility," Grandma Edith said. "Considering all his get-rich-quick schemes, he might have got into something shady without realizing it."

Roberts took a last drink of his coffee. "Whatever the reason, it's obvious that Dan Clifton, perhaps in desperation, had turned to blackmailing his friends and possibly his own brother."

Grandma Edith, pale-faced, closed her eyes and shook her head. "I can't believe that. Dan had plenty of faults but, in all the years I knew him, he wouldn't do that. I think he got into something over his head. He tended to jump without doing enough checking when he thought he saw an opportunity. But he was loyal to family and friends. He wouldn't have blackmailed them. Especially his brother."

I thought about what he'd done to Grandma Edith: cleaning out her bank accounts, maxing out her credit cards, giving away her mother's ring. He hadn't shown much loyalty to her.

"Maybe he wasn't blackmailing his friends, Mrs. Clifton," Roberts said. "There's a possibility he was selective about the photos he used. We'll know more when we get into his business accounts and find the source of those large deposits."

He picked up his hat and rose. "I wish you'd shared this information with us earlier. If you had, we might have found your money. And possibly your husband's killer. Now, I'm not so sure that's possible."

He gave us a cool nod and walked out of the house. I suspected he wasn't going to be very friendly in the future. It didn't matter; I needed to stop playing detective with Grandma Edith and go home. I told her that the next morning over breakfast.

"Marcie, I can't keep you here if you want to go, but I wish...I still need your help."

I wasn't overly anxious to get back to Galt and deal with Randy. "I can probably stay a few more days. Maybe I'll be better at putting down bark than I've been at finding your money."

"Bark? No, I need you to play pool."

"You want to go back to The Tavern?" I wouldn't mind seeing Brad Kinney again, but I was pretty sure that wasn't what Grandma Edith had in mind. I suspected I was about to learn why she'd taught me to play.

I was right. I also learned why she'd bought me that slinky, low-cut red blouse. I got up from the table. "Grandma Edith, there's no way that can work. We'll both be in plain sight of everybody."

"Yes, it will. Don't you know there's nothing in the world more visible than a pretty young girl? And nothing more invisible than an old woman? They'll be so busy watching you, they won't even notice me."

"No. No way. I'm not going to...to..." I couldn't think of the word I needed, so I gave up and, before I left the kitchen, I'd agreed to her scheme, possibly because a date with Brad Kinney was involved. Two dates, since I had to meet with him to explain the plan.

"I'll have to tell him about the missing money," I said.

She threw up her hands. "Go ahead. Before this is finished, everybody in Miner's Ridge is going to know all about it."

I met Brad at The Tavern Tuesday morning but, instead of playing pool, we crossed the creek, me wading this time, and made our way to the same log where we'd sat three days ago. There, I told him the entire story. Except the part about the ashes. And the garbage thief. "Grandma Edith says there's still one—maybe two—clues we found in Grandpa Dan's pockets. One is the blue poker chip. The other is the piece of napkin with the number 5211 written on it."

"So, somehow or other, your grandmother thinks the poker chip leads to an illegal card room, this O'Malley's. But how does the number on the napkin fit in?"

"That's what she's hoping to find out."

He raised an eyebrow. "And what is my part in all this? Other than finally getting a date with you?"

"I'm supposed to distract the guy guarding the door of that back room so Grandma Edith can slip inside."

"And she doesn't think they'll throw her out?"

"Not once she starts playing. That door is meant to keep the cops out. Brad, you can't do anything about shutting the card room down or I'll never be allowed back in Miner's Ridge."

He grinned. "We can't have that, can we? And the card room is in town—the police department's business. So, even if I worked in this county, I'd leave it to them."

Grandma Edith left first that night, hoping to find a barstool close to the card room door. Brad came to pick me up about a half-hour later. He stood on the porch, staring at me in my tight jeans and sexy red blouse. "Wow! I don't think you're going to have any problem distracting the guy guarding the door. But who's going to guard you?"

I could feel the heat creeping up my neck. "This wasn't my idea. I didn't even know until tonight why Grandma Edith taught me to play pool."

"I'm glad she did. Otherwise, I'd never have met you. But I suspect your nefarious grandmother wants me along for something more than a pool partner. You're going to need protection."

"Hey! I feel uncomfortable enough just thinking about walking into a bar like this. Let's get it over with."

He crooked an arm for me to take. "After you, milady."

O'Malley's was old-fashioned, dark, with nothing as modern as tall pub sets. Beyond the pool tables, a few chairs were scattered along the walls for the players to occupy while they kibitzed their opponents. A bar filled the other side of the room, manned by a single bartender. The place wasn't busy, probably not unusual for a weeknight, and I suspected most of the action would be at the poker game in the back room.

I spotted Grandma Edith on a stool close to that closed door, but I didn't see anybody guarding it. Maybe the bartender did double duty.

Feeling self-conscious, I opted for the short walk to a couple of empty stools closer to our end of the room. As we passed by the first pool table, a player emitted a low whistle. Brad slapped a quarter on the table, then snaked an arm around my waist, pulling me closer. "He's just expressing his appreciation for a pretty girl," he whispered into my ear.

"Yeah, right. More like an appreciation for the tight jeans. Or the red shirt."

He laughed. "Wasn't that part of the plan? How about a beer?" he asked as the bartender approached. "Maybe that will help relax you a little."

"It's probably going to take more than one." I thought about ordering something stronger but decided against it; I was going to need a clear head to pull this off.

I'd finished about half my beer when we were up at the pool table. I glanced Grandma Edith's way, but she didn't look up.

Brad and I went to find pool cues. "Just pretend we're at The Tavern," he whispered, "and if people are watching, it's to see if you make your shot."

Good advice, if I could follow it, but every time I leaned over to make a shot, all I could think about was my tight jeans and the drooping neckline of that red blouse.

Grandma Edith had glanced our way once or twice, but I didn't see any signal that I was to do anything, and it didn't take long for us to lose the game. I was nervous, missing shots I should have made.

We hung up our cue sticks and Brad put another quarter on the table. We went back to our drinks, finished them, and Brad ordered another. Still, nothing was happening around the door to the card room.

It was our turn to play again and the walk to the cue rack seemed longer this time; the natives were getting a little more "appreciative," moving in closer. I was glad Brad was sticking close to my side. "We've got to do something soon," he whispered. "What's the plan?"

Good question. I didn't know if I could knock the cue ball off the table without tearing the felt. Maybe I could drop my cue stick, preferably on one of my admirers' toes. But then I'd have to bend over to pick it up. I couldn't think of a real plan, and Grandma Edith didn't seem to be paying any attention to us; she'd given no signal she was ready to break into that back room. Finally, I realized why; most of the customers—and the bartender—were at that end of the bar. She needed him to be at our end, his attention away from the door for a few minutes.

Something needed to happen soon. Despite the mistakes the other players were making, too busy watching me to take enough time with their shots, we were losing another game. I was no match for these guys, and Brad could carry me for only so long.

Finally, while it was my turn to shoot, he headed for our end of the bar. "Hey, we need a couple of drinks down here."

The bartender strolled down to him, his back turned to Grandma Edith. I was leaning over the pool table, lining up a shot when I felt a hand pat my butt. I jerked the cue stick back, hard, at the same time I pivoted. It connected with something solid. I was ready to swing it at somebody's head, but the guy was already bent over, groaning. Brad caught my arm and pushed me toward my barstool. He pried the cue stick from my hands and walked toward the rack, on the other side of the pool table.

"Hey, man, I'm sorry," the guy's partner said. "He was out of line."

The jerk who had touched me made a quick exit while Brad was hanging up the cue sticks. He stood for a moment, surveying the room, then came back and pulled me from the stool. "Let's get out of here."

"But Grandma Edith, she—"

"Is gone." He gave a slight nod toward her empty barstool, then leaned in to whisper in my ear. "She got inside."

Chapter 24

W e sat in Brad's car, watching the front door of O'Malley's. "Where to now?" he asked. "Are we supposed to wait for her?" I didn't know. We hadn't planned beyond getting Grandma Edith through that door into the back card room. "She's a good player. She may be in there for hours. I guess our job is finished for the night." Still, I was a little unsettled, wondering what she would do if she discovered anything in there. But we couldn't sit there all night. I told Brad he might as well take me home.

"It's early. We could go somewhere else."

"No! I'm not going anywhere until...I have to get out of these clothes."

"Really? Don't you think it's a little soon? After all, it's only our first date."

I planted a playful fist into his shoulder. "Not funny!"

"Ow!" He grabbed the shoulder with his other hand, laughing. "You pack a wicked punch. I wonder how your pool table admirer is faring. I'll bet he'll have a sore gut tomorrow."

I couldn't help laughing. "Served him right. You don't just go around patting—"

"Pretty girls?" He leaned in and kissed me, then pulled back, guarding his face with both hands. "Please, don't hit me!"

My peripheral vision caught a movement outside the car. I leaned closer to the windshield to get a better view. A man stood in the darkened recess of O'Malley's front door, staring at us. Or maybe he was looking at the car, or out across the street; I wasn't sure he could see inside.

I shivered. "Take me back to Grandma Edith's."

After I'd changed into old, comfortable jeans and polo shirt, I asked Brad if he'd like another beer.

"No, better not. I had a couple at O'Malley's, and I still have to drive back to my sister's house."

"Okay, we've got coffee." I opened the refrigerator. "And water."

"And more water," he said, peering over my shoulder, his arm around my waist. It felt good there, right. I wanted to turn so he would kiss me again, but I didn't. There was no point. I had to go back to Galt, and he had to go home to Rocklin. I grabbed a couple of bottles of water and pulled away.

"Marcie..."

"Brad, I'm not into one-night stands. Or short flings. We both have to go back to our jobs soon and, with the distance between them and our work schedules, it would be tough to date."

"It's not that far," he said. "We can call, text, Skype, get together when we can, see where it goes."

We settled on Grandma Edith's living room sofa, Brad's arm around my shoulders, and talked—about our families, our jobs, our lives. I found myself telling him about Randy, the old house I'd inherited from my grandmother, and my boring job at Galt PD.

He told me about the girl he'd almost married and his job with the Placer County Sheriff's Office.

"Why didn't you marry her? The girl?" I asked.

"Because we both realized it wasn't solid. We wanted different things, were headed in different directions. She wanted me to change jobs to something not so dangerous. What she really meant was something where I'd be home every night for dinner. She's a city girl, in the Bay Area now, working for a high-tech company."

"Maybe she knows my dad," I said. "He works for some start-up in Silicon Valley."

Brad squeezed my shoulder. "You didn't say much about him."

"We have very little in common and he...well, he and my mom got a divorce when I was fifteen. I'd grown up in Galt. All my friends were there, so I stayed with my grandmother. It was supposed to be just until I finished the next school year. But then...well, my parents had both moved on. Dad had a girlfriend, and she and I didn't hit it off too well. I tried staying with Mom in L.A. for one semester, but I was miserable. The kids were so different I had trouble making friends and, with a new life and a more challenging job, Mom didn't have much time for me. When my grandmother called and said she was lonely and asked me to come back to Galt, I couldn't pack fast enough. I've been there ever since."

"So you wouldn't consider leaving again?"

I didn't know how to answer that question. My high school friends were still around, most of them now married and busy with families, so I didn't have much of a social life. My job wasn't anything to get excited about. But my house, my safe haven, was almost paid for. All I had to do was get Randy out of it.

"Maybe, if I could stay here, with Grandma Edith," I said. "I've had more fun and excitement in the nine days I've been here than I've had at home in the last nine years."

He squeezed my shoulder again. "I hope I've been part of that fun. And, well, Rocklin is within driving distance to either one, if—"

The front door banged open and Grandma Edith rushed in, a little out of breath. "Marcie, you did a great job tonight. That was quite a distraction—just enough for me to get through that door." She turned to Brad. "And you, Mr...Mr..."

Brad stood and stuck out his hand. "Brad Kinney. From The Tavern."

"Yes, yes, I remember. Thank you for taking such good care of Marcie tonight. You both did a great job." She shifted her attention back to me. "And you have to get rid of that awful red blouse. It really doesn't suit you."

"I don't know," Brad said. "I kind of liked it."

I threw a sofa pillow at him. He ducked and Grandma Edith laughed. "I see you two are getting along well. I did, too. I'd forgotten how much I like to play poker, and I really cleaned up tonight."

She opened her purse and pulled out a small stack of bills. "Enough to buy groceries for a week or two. I think I've found a new source of income." She put her purse down and headed for the kitchen. "Anybody want a beer? I forgot to take my water bottle with me, and I don't drink alcohol while I'm playing poker. I'm parched."

Brad declined because he'd be driving, and I'd had all the beer I wanted for one evening. We both opted for water. Grandma Edith brought it to us, then dug into her pocket for a poker chip and put it on the table. "I want to check something out."

She disappeared into her bedroom and came back a few minutes later holding another poker chip. "This is the one we found in Dan's pocket." She set it on the table beside the other chip. "Can you see any difference between them?"

They were the same shade of blue, with "O'Malley's" inscribed in the middle. I studied the cursive lettering then shook my head. "I don't see anything."

"Pick them up and feel them," she said.

I did. They weighed about the same—practically nothing. I brushed my fingers across both surfaces. The one from Grandpa Dan's pocket had a raised, barely visible ridge encircling the center. I held it up and looked closer. "It's hard to see, but I can definitely feel the difference." I handed them to Brad.

He ran a finger around the edges, then the top of each chip, and nodded. "You're right. But I don't understand the significance. Maybe they just came from two different orders. Or one's older than the other and worn down."

"I would have thought so, too," she said, "except for something odd. That game wasn't high stakes, the size of the pots averaging around twenty-five or thirty bucks. I think most of the players were locals, and they weren't that good. I was winning quite a few hands, but not as much as another guy, Will. I don't remember ever seeing him before. He kept complaining about the game, wishing he could find something with a little higher stakes. I thought it might lead somewhere, so I was agreeing with him."

She took a sip of her Corona. "We played for a while longer, but I was no longer getting good hands, and I was tired of listening to Will gripe, so I cashed out, ready to head home. But then, Will says he wants to cash out, too. And here's where it gets odd. The dealer handed him a blue chip from under the table."

Brad sat up straighter on the sofa. "Maybe it was part of his payout."

"No. I've played enough poker to watch people's hands. He'd already cashed the guy out. This chip came from somewhere else. Then the dealer leaned in and, in a low voice, told Will to talk to the bartender. I left and made a beeline for the bar. I wanted to hear that conversation." She paused to take another drink of her beer.

"And?" I prompted, impatient for the rest of the story. It had Brad's full attention, too. He sat forward on the sofa, frowning.

"All I could hear was 'tomorrow night,' but the bartender wrote something on a napkin and handed it to Will."

"A number," I said. "Like the one on that piece of napkin in Grandpa Dan's pocket." I turned to Brad. "It had the number 5211 on it, but we haven't been able to connect it to anything."

"I followed Will out of the bar," Grandma Edith said. "He got into a white Lexus."

"Did you get a license number?" Brad asked. "If you did, I can get a name and address."

Grandma Edith shook her head. "I couldn't get close enough without him seeing me."

"We should have stuck around," Brad said. "We might have been able to follow him."

There wasn't much to say after that. I walked Brad out to the porch. "Marcie, I promised my sister I'd do something with her tomorrow. I haven't spent much time with her since I've been here. I have to leave Saturday so I'll have a day to get ready for work on Monday. Can we can get together Thursday or Friday? Maybe take a picnic lunch and go hiking in that forest area?"

I needed to get home; I still had to get Randy out of my house before I could go on with my life. I opened my mouth to say no but found myself saying yes. I wanted—no, needed—another day up there.

He smiled and hugged me. "Great. I'll pick you up around noon Thursday." He started to leave, then turned back. "And let me know if anything else comes of tonight's little adventure. That blue chip and piece of paper have me intrigued."

When I went back inside, Grandma Edith was still sitting on the sofa. She patted the cushion beside her. "Sit down. I'd like to talk to you about something before we go to bed."

I lowered myself onto the sofa. "Okay."

"I want to spend as much time as I can with you before you have to leave, but there's something I have to do tomorrow night. So if you want to go out with Brad Kinney—"

"I can't, Grandma Edith. He's spending tomorrow with his sister. Maybe I can help you with whatever you have to do?"

"No! No...I...you can't." She averted her eyes. It wasn't like her to be evasive.

"We're in this together, Grandma Edith. I'm not going to bed until you tell me what's going on."

Her shoulders slumped and she sighed. "Okay. I didn't want to say anything while Brad was here. I did follow that guy, Will, from O'Malley's. I know where he lives, and I plan to follow him again tomorrow night. It may be the only chance I have to find my money."

"Why not tell Brad?"

"He's a cop, Marcie. I suspect this may be an illegal high-stakes poker operation. He might shut it down before I have a chance to find out where my money went."

"Then I'm going with you."

"You can't. It's not going to be easy to get in. I think that poker chip and maybe the number on the napkin are the passports to get inside. I'll take both of them with me. But I'm the only one who can use them because, once inside, I'll have to get into that poker game."

She was right, but I didn't like it. She was going there to snoop around, which could put her in danger. "Keep your cell phone within easy reach, maybe in your pocket. Just in case you run into problems."

She agreed, and we left it at that but I was worried. I wanted to call Brad, or even Eric Roberts, but Grandma Edith was right; they might shut the operation down before she had a chance to discover anything. She might never forgive me.

Chapter 25

Before we went to bed that night, Grandma Edith called Nate and invited him over for breakfast on the patio the next morning. "It'll be nice for you to have a little time with him before you leave. He's been asking me when you're going."

I wasn't sure; so much depended on what Grandma Edith found out that night. I was nervous about her venturing out alone to follow the poker player from O'Malley's. Who knew where he might take her? But it was also possible he wouldn't leave his house tonight. If his destination was an illegal gambling operation, it might, like O'Malley's, be open only one night a week.

If that happened, Grandma Edith would keep following him until he led her to the right place. How long might that take? It was already Wednesday, and I couldn't stay much longer if I wanted to keep my job.

"No later than Saturday morning," I told Nate over a plate of blueberry pancakes, "I'm glad you came over today so we'll have some time to visit."

"I guess you'll be glad to get back to your own place and your friends, but we're sure going to miss you around here."

I thought about Brad Kinney and our hiking trip Thursday in that beautiful forest, and the days I'd spent in Grandma Edith's house. It had gone by too quickly. "I'm going to miss the two of you, too. And, no, I'm not eager to get back to all the problems at home. Not to mention a boring job. This has been a nice vacation."

He looked at me over the rim of his coffee mug. "Marcie, life is too short to spend a single minute of it in a boring job or living somewhere you don't like. If you've enjoyed your time with us so much, why not stay? Find a job up here? I've got more rooms in my house than I'll ever use, and I'd be glad to have the company."

I looked into those gentle, storm-cloud gray eyes, unable to speak around the lump in my throat. Nate Riordan had to be one of the sweetest men I had ever met, and Grandma Edith had told me his daughter rarely called or visited.

"Wait just a minute there," Grandma Edith said. "If she stays, it's going to be with me. She's my granddaughter."

Now I was fighting back tears. I wasn't her granddaughter. Not any more. But I loved her as much as I'd ever loved my own.

Her voice rose an octave, excited now. "Think about it. You could sell your house or rent it out, then pay me room and board. It would solve both our financial problems, and we'd have so much fun together."

Nate put down his coffee mug. "What financial problems? Edie, you told me Dan cleaned out your bank accounts, but I thought you had enough coming in…" He pushed his chair back from the table. "Why didn't you tell me? Let me help?"

"Nate, it's okay. I can get by on my Social Security and 401(k). It'll just be a little tight, and I thought Marcie and me living together would be a nice solution."

"Hell, if you want to live with somebody, why not me? We've got these two houses, side by side. Why not sell or rent one of them and live in the other?" He glanced my way. "Marcie, too."

Grandma Edith sat still, probably not sure just what Nate was proposing. Nor was I, but I thought it a good time to find something else to do. I picked up my dishes to carry them inside. Neither of them said a word as I walked toward the patio door. At least, not one I could hear.

While I was closing the dishwasher, somebody knocked on the door. I opened it to Eric Roberts, standing on the porch, holding his hat in one hand. "Is your grandmother here?"

I led him out to the patio. He stood for a moment, looking at the profusion of California poppies blanketing much of the yard, and drew in a deep breath, probably inhaling the scent of lilacs in the warm breeze.

Grandma Edith gestured toward a chair while I poured him a cup of coffee. He almost visibly relaxed as he sat and looked out over the landscape. "You could make a small fortune if you started charging a fee for entry into this place. Fifteen minutes here is worth more than any tranquilizer ever made."

"Rough morning?" I asked.

"A busy one, and not much sleep last night."

"Did the deposits into Dan's business account lead to something?" Grandma Edith asked.

He shifted his chair toward her. "Yes, they did." He paused to take a sip of coffee, and probably to gather his thoughts. "We traced those large deposits to three men, all of them listed in that day planner of Mr. Clifton's. And he had photos of every one of them, taken in the same apartment you visited in Grass Valley."

"You think my husband was blackmailing them." Grandma Edith's voice was calm and steady, but Nate had put a hand over her trembling fingers.

Roberts, averting his eyes from Grandma Edith's flushed face, nodded. "That also made them prime suspects in the murder."

Grandma Edith let out a little gasp, then took a deep breath. "That's why they've been so desperate to get into Dan's files. They wanted those pictures."

I may have let out a little gasp myself, thinking about the way I'd tried to stop both the garbage thief and the man going out Grandpa Dan's office window. One of them might have been his killer.

I glanced at Nate, who was looking at Grandma Edith, a puzzled frown creasing his forehead as Roberts continued. "The deposits and photos gave us enough evidence to get search warrants for all three properties. We found a dark blue Ford Explorer with front-end damage hidden away on one of them, in an old barn on Walt Gorman's place. Forensics in Sacramento is going over it now, but we're confident it's the car that hit Dan Clifton. Gorman is already in custody."

Grandma Edith sat still, saying nothing. Nor did I, feeling only a surge of relief that she would be safe after I left.

Nate spoke first. "I don't understand a lot of what's going on, other than Dan's murder and something in his bank accounts leading to the car that hit him. Not that it's any of my business. But how could anybody keep a car, apparently one nobody had seen before, in a place as small as Miner's Ridge?"

Roberts gave Nate an approving glance. "We've traced the car. He bought it off a used car lot in Nevada City. We think he had it towed to his place using a back road into his farm and left it there until the night he killed Dan Clifton. We're still trying to track down the towing company."

"How do you know it wasn't one of those other men you mentioned?" Nate asked. "Maybe he had an accomplice. Or even two."

Roberts didn't respond to that, so Nate turned to Grandma Edith. "Edie, you have to come and stay with me until they're sure this guy acted alone. You and Marcie aren't safe here."

Grandma Edith patted his arm. "I appreciate the offer, Nate, but I'm not going to let some chicken-livered low-lives scare me out of my own house."

"Edie, you need to stop being so stubborn. Until they find out how that car got to Miner's Ridge, either move into one of my spare bedrooms or go home with Marcie."

Grandma Edith turned to me. "How do you feel about it? Would you be okay in the house, or would you rather we moved into Nate's for the time being?"

I glanced at both Roberts and Nate, hoping for a clue about how to answer. I would be here for only today and tomorrow. After that, she would be alone in the house.

She was studying my face, waiting. "Grandma Edith, I'll be good with whatever you decide, but if they haven't found the tow truck driver by the time I leave, I think it might be a good idea to go over to Nate's for a while. Or you can come home with me."

Even as I made the offer, I wondered what she would do at my house, away from her friends and neighbors, and with me working all day. I didn't even have a beautiful yard for her to work in and I didn't relish the idea of having her as a witness when I threw her grandson out of my house. But I didn't want either of them to get the idea that he was staying, either.

Roberts reached for his hat. "I've got to get going. I'll let you know as soon as we find out how Gorman got the car to his barn. Mrs. Clifton, let me know if you decide to go elsewhere."

I got up to walk him to the door while Grandma Edith and Nate continued their conversation. We were halfway to the front door when Nate's voice drifted toward us. "Edie, I wish you'd change your mind and bring Marcie over to my place. I thought, if we had enough time, we might convince her to stay in Miner's Ridge after everything settles down."

Roberts's step faltered. "You're thinking about staying in Miner's Ridge?"

I smiled as I shook my head. "Despite the enticing offers and the wonderful time I've had here, I have a house and job to go back to in Galt."

He stopped and turned to face me, his blue gaze intense. "Marcie, if it's a job holding you back, there's going to be an opening at the Department. Our dispatcher is retiring in a couple of weeks, and I'm sure you have more than enough experience to fill the job. I'd be glad to put in a good word for you. If you're interested, that is." His voice softened and dropped almost to a whisper. "I hope you'll consider it. I'd like to get to know you better, and I can't think of a better way than having you in the same office."

Surprised, I couldn't think of anything to say. That didn't seem to bother him. He leaned in closer and said, "Just think about it."

I closed the door behind him, feeling a little guilty because the surge of excitement I'd felt at his words had nothing to do with him, but with the possibility of a job here, where I could stay with Grandma Edith. We could go to The Tavern to play pool, she could teach me to play poker and how to build a beautiful yard. We could walk in that forest land. But not with Brad. He would be going back to Rocklin.

While I was dreaming about the possibilities, Nate approached, on the way back to his house. "Marcie, try to talk some sense into your grandmother. She's not safe here." Then, before I could respond, he leaned in and brushed my cheek with his lips, something I suspected was completely out of character for him.

I did as he asked, but when I mentioned moving to Nate's, she shook her head. "Maybe after I find out where that poker chip and number on the napkin lead me, but I'm too close. I can't quit now."

She had no way of knowing what time Will, the man she'd followed home from O'Malley's, would leave his house for the undisclosed location, so we ate a quick dinner that evening, and she left at five.

"I'll be early," she said, "but I can park somewhere on his block, ready to follow him as soon as he gets in his car."

I must have looked doubtful because she added, "Don't worry. You've shown me how to do this. He won't see me."

Considering our previous surveillance attempts, that did little to reassure me. I didn't like it, but she was going, no matter what I said. All I could do was remind her to keep her phone close, ready to call the minute she had an inkling that something was going wrong.

After she left, silence settled over the house, with nothing to interrupt my thoughts: the hike with Brad Thursday and where that might lead, and whether Grandma Edith and Nate would decide to become roommates. It wasn't hard to imagine the buzz that would send along Miner's Ridge's unofficial news wire. Even if I decided to stay with them, what would I do about my job in Galt, where I at least had some seniority? And what about my house and Randy?

He was sticking to his job, paying the bills just as he'd promised, and showing no indication of slipping back into his past irresponsible behavior. Perhaps because of that, I had to get him out of my house before he wormed his way back into my life.

Every thought I had of him and my house seemed to channel straight to his brain because he called me.

"Me and Billy are coming up Friday night after work to bring Grandpa Dan's pickup back and get my car. We're not going to stay, though. I figure you'll be coming home Saturday or Sunday, and I want to see the look on your face when you get here. I have a surprise for you, babe, one that's going to blow your mind."

More often than not, Randy's surprises did blow my mind. And my bank account. And my blood pressure. "What kind of surprise?"

He laughed. "One you're going to love, but I can't tell you now or it won't be a surprise. Just be prepared for something big."

I drew in a deep breath, trying to control my too-rapid heartbeat. We weren't married anymore, so he couldn't trade in my car or get a mortgage on my place. So it could only mean he'd done something to the house and I was probably going to kill him.

Chapter 26

Eventually, my brain clogged with too many unanswered questions, I took a shower, grabbed a beer, and sought oblivion in whatever Netflix or Hulu had to offer. There was no point in going to bed; I wouldn't sleep until Grandma Edith was home.

At least, that's what I thought until my eyes popped open at the sound of quick footsteps on the front porch.

I'd dozed off and my brain, still fuzzy from my nap, took a few seconds to click into gear. I jumped to my feet, looking around the room for a hiding place or a weapon and not finding either. Then the door swung open and Grandma Edith walked in, frowning at me. "What's wrong? Has something happened?"

I could only shake my head, not trusting my voice, and more than a little embarrassed.

She sank onto the sofa. "We'll have to go back tomorrow."

I sat down beside her. "Back where? And why?"

"I couldn't find anything. When I tried to poke around, every door was locked or occupied. And there's plenty going on in that place—flashy women hanging all over the poker players or serving them drinks. A bar, hidden away in another room—one with no stools for drinkers. I suspect drinks are spiked or drugged, judging by the sloppy way some of those players started betting after they'd had a few."

"So you didn't learn anything about the poker chip or the number on that piece of paper?"

"Oh, yeah. That part was pretty simple. It's a big house, tucked away off a dirt road out in the country, surrounded by a wrought-iron fence, at least ten feet high. The number is a code to unlock the gate. I had to hang back too far once, and didn't see Will go inside, so I parked in a dark area, got out, and worked my way up to some bushes close to the front door. I waited there for somebody else to come along, so I could see how it worked. It didn't take long. When the guy knocked on the door, a light came on so I could see him hand over a chip. The guard, or whatever he was, felt it, then nodded, handed it back, and let the guy in."

"The ridge around the middle. Grandma Edith, none of this sounds like an amateur gambling operation. You should call Eric Roberts."

She shook her head. "I don't have anything solid. Besides, it's county out there, not city, so he'd probably turn it over to the Sheriff's Office. I may have stumbled onto an illegal gambling operation but, if I get the Sheriff's Office involved, I'll have to tell them where those chips with the ridges originated. That could not only endanger O'Malley's, but give our city police department a black eye for not closing it down."

"So I'm assuming you used Grandpa Dan's blue chip to get inside. Grandma Edith..." I didn't know how to finish that sentence. She had more courage than I, but what she'd done was so foolhardy it scared me.

She patted my arm. "I need a beer. My water bottle ran dry and, even if I normally drank alcohol while I played, I would have had second thoughts about doing it tonight."

She went to the kitchen, brought back two Coronas, and handed one to me. "After I began to suspect the players were being drugged, I took a bathroom break. I figured it would give me a chance to refill my water bottle and snoop around a little. That's when I found out I couldn't get into any of the other rooms. I went back and played a little longer. Some of the players were cashing out, I don't know if they were tapped out or suspecting something was wrong, but they were being short-changed by the cashier, too drugged or drunk to notice. The strange thing is, they didn't always go alone. Some of the women working there went with them."

She took a healthy slug of her beer. "By that time, the dealer and cashier were giving me some strange looks, maybe suspicious because I wasn't drinking anything they offered. I decided I'd better get out of there and go back during the daytime, while there's not a game in progress."

"But if they're not open for business, how do you plan to get in?"

She smiled, a fiendish grin. "I left a window unlocked in the bathroom."

I knew I wasn't going to dissuade her; that's what made life with Grandma Edith so interesting, but she scared me sometimes. We couldn't go out to that house alone, with nobody knowing where we were, but Nate would insist on calling the police. And they would contact the Nevada County Sheriff's Office.

I must have been around Grandma Edith long enough for her to read my mind because she shook her head. "You can't tell anybody. If they get in our way, I'll never have a chance to find my money."

She didn't explain why she thought her money would still be there—if it ever was—and no amount of arguing could change her mind. Resigned, I went to bed that night and had nightmares about gangsters with machine guns chasing me through endless corridors of a dark house with all the doors locked so there was nowhere to hide.

The next morning, groggy after a restless night, I finished a quick breakfast as I watched Grandma Edith digging out the all-too-familiar plastic bucket, mop, broom, and cleaning rags.

"They worked before," she said to my questioning look. "If we're caught in there, we can always claim we've been hired to clean the place."

I didn't bother pointing out that whoever caught us trespassing would probably be familiar with their house cleaners. I'd learned that Grandma Edith, smart as she was, often operated on overly-optimistic hope rather than logic. So, dressed in my faded jeans and denim shirt, I followed her directions as I drove Randy's old Ford Focus to the gambling house, hoping we didn't have to depend on it for a quick getaway.

The house was about ten miles northeast of Miner's Ridge, off a winding two-lane road that intersected with another that was unpaved. We followed it through a canopy of tall pines and oaks to the wrought-iron gate, where I entered the 5211 code. I drove around to the back and parked in a grove of cedar trees, edging as far in as possible, hoping to make the car less visible.

The house was old, rambling, with weathered green siding. It seemed to be deserted, which was fortunate since the old-fashioned vertical-paned window Grandma Edith pointed out was so high I had to scout around for a chair to stand on. It had seen better days, portions of the wood decaying from dry rot. Grandma Edith did her best to hold it steady while I pushed up the window, holding my breath for the sound of an alarm, then realized there wouldn't be one; a window was already open. And why would the operators of an illegal establishment install anything that might bring law enforcement snooping around the premises?

I clambered inside, landing on a countertop, one foot in the sink and the other knocking over a bottle of liquid soap. I froze but heard nothing. I counted off a long three minutes before bending to untangle my pants leg from the faucet, still listening for anybody coming to investigate the noise. I heard nothing and, knowing Grandma Edith would be huffing with impatience, I went in search of a door I could unlock.

"Took you long enough," she muttered, handing me the mop and broom. "I thought somebody had grabbed you. I was about to call Roberts."

"Oh, now you're considering the cops? So they can arrest me for breaking and entering?"

"We didn't break anything, and the window was already open." She glanced at my face, probably reading my mind again. "Never mind. Let's check out some of those rooms I couldn't get into last night. And put some water and soap in that bucket, just in case. You should probably get the mop wet, too, and wring it out, so it'll look like we've been using it."

By the time I'd filled the bucket, she had found a bedroom to explore. It was small, containing only a dresser, queen-size bed, and two nightstands topped with table lamps. She pointed down the hall. "Check out that bathroom. And don't forget to look in the toilet tank."

I did as instructed but, as I raised the lid, I wondered what she thought I might find. Bundles of cash zipped into a plastic bag? Drugs? The combination to a safe? Maybe the key to a safety deposit box?

It didn't take me long to finish; there was little to find. I headed back to the bedroom to help Grandma Edith.

She was running her fingers over the sides and bottom of a drawer she'd taken from the dresser and I again wondered what she expected to find. Then I noticed something else, only because I'd seen them before. I waved my arm at Grandma Edith until I had her attention, then pointed. "Hidden cameras."

She scurried out of the room. "Maybe they're only turned on at night, when they have games."

I didn't comment; there wasn't any point. It was too late to worry about them now, and the cameras were aimed at the beds. She might not have come within their range.

Grandma Edith, resigned, was still determined to continue the search, but she insisted I check the bathrooms and hallways, staying out of range of any cameras. And, if I hadn't been so spooked by that time, I probably would have appreciated her somewhat tardy attempt to protect me.

We moved along the corridor, the water sloshing in the bucket, and found four more bedrooms, all minimally furnished, and all with hidden cameras aimed at the beds.

"A blackmail setup," I murmured.

"Helped along with spiked drinks and maybe some drugs," Grandma Edith said. "Let's check out the bar."

The wide hallway emptied into a huge room, at least thirty feet long and twenty wide, with a high ceiling. Dark wainscoting covered the lower portion of the beige walls. Four round felt-covered tables filled the space, each large enough for at least eight poker players. Near the end, a long desk-cabinet combination fronted the room. As we drew closer, I noticed a chair behind it.

"I'll check out that area," Grandma Edith said. "It's where the players cashed out, so there may be a safe. I want you to take a look at the bar." She nodded toward double wooden doors opening on the left, revealing a smaller, windowless room. It had been divided in half with a counter

and a small, swinging door at one end. "There's not much space back
there." She took the mop and bucket and handed me the broom. "It's
not designed for customers. All the drinks are served to the poker tables
by trashy-looking women."

Broom in hand, I pushed through the half-gate, flinching at the
squeak it emitted. The room was too small, the space behind the counter
cramped. Not normally claustrophobic, I felt the windowless walls
closing in on me. We'd been in that house too long; we needed to get
out. But, to accomplish that, I had a job to do, and there were no
cameras in that confined space.

I didn't find anything suspicious among the bottles on the top
shelves after a thorough search—unless you counted the number of
cheap brands. I guess it made sense; if their objective was to get their
customers drunk, cheap would do the job at less cost, once the taste
buds had been sufficiently numbed.

Grandma Edith wasn't visible; all I could see was the mop handle,
leaning against the cabinets. What could be taking her so long? Had she
moved on to another area while I had my back turned? No, surely not;
she would have told me—and taken the mop and bucket with her. I went
back to my search.

The shelves under the counter held little of interest: the normal bar
supplies, along with racks of poker chips, a couple of desk calculators,
and a black metal box, about twelve by eight inches, fastened with a
combination lock through the hasp. As I set it on the counter to show
Grandma Edith, I noticed a row of small bottles behind it. None had
labels, but several had GHB imprinted with a marking pen. Date rape
drugs. I had pulled one of the others forward, trying to find some kind
of mark, when I heard the footsteps.

Grandma Edith, coming to join me? No, this was a woman, her heels
clicking on the wooden floors, echoing through the big room. I raised
my head just enough to peer over the counter. The only thing I could see
from that tiny space was the desk-cabinet combo, almost directly across
from me. Grandma Edith still wasn't visible and, wherever she'd gone, I
couldn't warn her that we had company.

I crawled to the half-door and peered through the small crack where
the two sides met. A woman stood beside one of the poker tables,

staring at the desk-cabinet combo at the end of the room. She wore skinny jeans and red, strappy shoes that matched a skimpy halter top. The incongruous effect, in that deserted house in mid-morning, was further heightened by mahogany-tinted hair so perfectly styled, it looked as though she'd just stepped out of a salon.

Did she know I was there? Had she seen Randy's Ford, where I'd tried to hide it in the trees? Or had she seen Grandma Edith on the cameras and come to investigate?

I crouched lower, trying to regulate my breathing as thoughts churned through my mind, every one of them trying to gain my immediate attention. Who was the woman and what was she doing here? Was she a threat to us? Did she have a weapon? Could she see me and, if she did, what kind of a story could I come up with to explain my presence?

She was moving again, the steady tap-tap-tap coming closer. She stopped, then turned toward the bar, her steps faster now.

As I scooted away from the half-door, my paralyzed brain could not move beyond one thought: She had seen the box I'd placed on the counter and knew something was wrong.

The steps kept coming, closer now. I reached for a bottle, then hesitated. Could I actually hit the woman with it? Possibly kill her, not knowing whether she meant me harm?

My fingers closed around the broom handle.

Chapter 27

T he woman leaned over the bar. "Get up!"

She had something in her hand I couldn't identify from my position on the floor, but she was pointing it at me. I struggled to stand. A little off-balance, I lurched to the left. Gripping the handle, I swung the broom. The gun the woman had held clattered to the floor, followed by a cascade of water. Where did that come from?

The perfect hairdo disappeared under the mop bucket Grandma Edith still held. Water drenched the red halter top, spattering me.

"Grab her other arm!" Grandma Edith barked as she pried the fingers of one of the woman's hands away from the bucket rim around her neck.

I did as I was told.

The woman, gasping and sobbing, thrashed her head back and forth, trying to dislodge the bucket while we pushed her to the closest poker table. There, we used our bandana 'cleaning rags' to tie her well-manicured hands to a chair.

Grandma Edith paused for a moment after she finished, then stood back, smiling as she pointed at the metal box. "Grab that and let's get out of here."

By that time, I had so much adrenaline coursing through my system, I don't know if we closed the door behind us. Everything became a blur: running to the Ford, scrambling inside, starting it, and barreling out of the gate. I only remember asking Grandma Edith, "Do you think it's okay to leave her like that?"

"If she can't get herself loose, somebody will find her when they open up for business tonight. But I think she's going to need a new hairdo before she greets customers."

We had reached the paved road before my fight-or-flight reaction had settled into something resembling normal. "It was a complete waste of time, wasn't it? We could have been killed for nothing."

Grandma Edith patted my arm. "Not for nothing." She held up her right hand, spreading her fingers wide to show off what circled one finger. "She was wearing my mother's ring. We got it back."

"So she's the woman Grandpa Dan was sending flowers to? The one he bought those tanzanite earrings for?"

She wrinkled her nose as though she smelled something rotten. "I thought he had better taste. It's embarrassing."

"So, if she's the woman, you know where your money went. Do you think some of it's in that box?"

She sighed then and, for the first time all week, she looked her age, tired and a little fragile. "I can only hope it at least gives me a way to find it." She turned to look out the passenger window. I knew her well enough by then to drop the subject. We drove the rest of the way back to Miner's Ridge in silence.

I wasn't sure I should leave her for my date with Brad. I would be late, anyway. Our excursion had left me dirty and water-spattered. I needed a shower and clean clothes, and I felt too tired to make the effort. But it might be our last date for a while; we were both leaving Saturday morning.

When I started to call, to let him know I'd be late, I noticed I had a message from him, sent while my phone was in airplane mode. Hi, Marcie. Sorry, but I can't make it to The Tavern. Something came up at work and I don't know when I'll be free. I'll call or come by as soon as I can.

Why was I so disappointed? A few minutes earlier, I had felt too tired to go. And why had something come up at work? He was on vacation until Monday morning. Maybe a break in a case he'd been working? I'd seen it happen once or twice at the Galt Police Department.

I went to find Grandma Edith. She was on the patio, fingering the combination lock. "I think Dan had some bolt cutters, if I can just find them." She picked up the box, running her fingers over its dimensions. "How much money do you think it would hold?"

"What makes you think it's money? Maybe it's drugs. Or more photos, kept up front to use as leverage, reminding their customers why they had to pay up."

"No. Not in the poker area. Think about it. Those games end late. They'd lock the cash up overnight."

"But wouldn't they take it with them? Or at least pick it up the next morning?"

She frowned. "We don't even know for sure what's in it. Let's find those bolt cutters."

As she lowered the box to the table, she shifted her hands across the bottom. "Wait. What's this?" She held the box above her head to get a better view, running her fingers across one spot. "I can't see. It feels like scratches, but they're not straight. Here, take a look."

She was right. When exposed to the sunlight, a series of numbers stood out, silver against the black finish: 21913. I read them off to Grandma Edith, but neither of us could make sense of them. I started to put the box down when I noticed something else. The numbers were unevenly spaced, several close together, others farther apart: two one space nine space one three. "Grandma Edith, do you think this could be the combination to the lock?"

She looked at me as though I'd just dropped beneath that fifty percent IQ level. "Nobody is that stupid, Marcie."

"Unless they have a hard time remembering numbers."

"But these are the guys who are cashing in chips and settling up with customers." Then she laughed. "I guess they didn't have to be very accurate with how much they cheated, did they? Let's try it."

She dialed in the combination as I read it off to her. The lock didn't open.

She tried it again. "Well, like I said, nobody's that stupid. I'll get the bolt cutters."

"Wait! Maybe they were just a smidgeon short of stupid. What if they carved it in there backward. Try it in reverse: All the way around, then right thirty-one, left nine, right twelve."

The lock opened. Grandma Edith raised the lid to expose stacks of currency, everything from ones to hundreds. "Looks like I found part of my money."

She was right; Grandpa Dan had drained their accounts to pay these same blackmailers, so the money was hers. But law enforcement might not see it that way. They'd take it as evidence.

She was quiet for a few minutes. Then, without saying another word, she locked the box, picked it up, and, without inviting me to join her, carried it out to the work area. I went back to my room, putting as much space between me and that box as possible, wondering whether those cameras at the old house had been operational. Even if they had, I doubted they could have caught a clear image of Grandma Edith, since they were aimed at the beds. The woman with the gun hadn't seen either of us, so we were probably safe.

Brad still hadn't called by that evening, and I considered going home the next morning, a day earlier than I'd planned. Grandma Edith no longer needed me. But Randy and Billy were still in my house, I was reluctant to leave Miner's Ridge, and there was still a chance Brad might call and we could have one more day together, I considered going to The Tavern alone, but it wouldn't be much fun to play pool without him. I decided to wait one more day.

I found a text from him the next morning, one he'd sent a little after midnight: Still hung up. I'll try to call later. But he still hadn't called by noon, and the afternoon stretched ahead of me with nothing to do until Randy and Billy arrived that evening. Everything was packed, and I'd cleaned my room.

I wandered into the yard and found Grandma Edith on her knees, weeding a flower bed. She looked up at me, her face vibrant again under her wide-brimmed hat. "How about lunch? I'm sure there's something in the freezer we can zap."

I was hungry but at the thought of one of Alma's casseroles, the growl in my stomach plummeted to a whimper. "I could use a peanut butter and jelly sandwich."

She laughed as she rose to her feet and tossed her gloves onto a bench. "I don't think any of Alma's casseroles are left. One of those intruders must have stolen them. How about a grilled cheese sandwich?"

We headed for the kitchen and, while I buttered bread and she sliced cheese, I asked, "Do you suppose they'll report that metal box to the cops?"

She turned to look at me, a slice of cheese in one hand. "What box?"

I shook my head. "Never mind. It must have been a bad dream."

She nodded as she placed the cheese on a piece of bread. "You seem to have a lot of those. Next thing we know, you'll be having nightmares about an old house somewhere in the country. You think it's the beer? Maybe you shouldn't drink any right before bedtime."

I shrugged. "I kind of like my dreams. Lots of adventure to spice up my life. Who knew mops and brooms could be so much fun?"

We carried our sandwiches, along with tall glasses of iced tea, out to the patio table so we could watch the hummingbirds and butterflies as they flitted from blossom to blossom, gathering nectar. As I sat there, looking out over the profusion of California poppies, a lump started to form in my throat. I would miss this yard, this patio, this house. Most of all, I would miss Grandma Edith and Nate. I turned so I could look into her eyes. "Grandma Edith, are you going to be okay?"

"I'll be just fine. I've got it all figured out. I came into quite a bit of money recently, enough to start replenishing my savings account, and I found a new income source, one I'm going to enjoy—playing poker at O'Malley's every week." She paused long enough to take a sip of her iced tea. "And, just to keep my mind sharp, I'm going into business for myself."

"Business?" I tried to think of something she could do at her age but was at a loss. "Doing what?"

"Being a private detective."

"I...you...what did you say? How can you—"

She patted my arm. "I've been doing it for years, according to our tax records. I already have all the equipment and those disguises in the closet, not to mention client files. And you'll have to admit, I'm pretty good at this sleuthing business."

"But you have to be licensed, trained."

"I already checked all that out, Marcie. Clifton Investigative Services already has a license. And all the training required is to work for a licensed agency for three years. I have proof through those tax records that I've already done that." She paused again, probably giving me an opportunity to say something, but my brain was too numb. I couldn't come up with a single word.

"I'll admit, I may need a little formal training," she said, "but I can start bringing in money right away with some of the cases I'll solve while I'm taking classes."

"What cases?" I croaked.

"Oh, I didn't tell you." She pulled her phone out of a pocket and scrolled through it. "Take a look at these."

I looked, then wished I hadn't. "When did you get these...these awful photos? And who are the people in them?" Then the light dawned. "They're from that house, aren't they? The people they drugged, posed in compromising positions?"

She gave me a smug smile. "I found them in those cabinets in the poker room. I didn't want to take the originals. They'd be missed. So I took pictures of them."

"That's why I didn't see you. I thought you'd deserted me."

"I'd never do that. I had the photos from that file spread out on the floor, snapping pictures as fast as I could when the bimbo showed up."

"That file? There was more than one?"

"A bunch of them, all with photos mounted on paper with a space underneath for names, telephone numbers, addresses, and dates—I presume when the pictures were taken. I only worked my way through the folder from Miner's Ridge and part of the one for Grass Valley. And when all those wives hire me to investigate, I'll be able to tell them exactly what happened and where their money went, because a record of payments was on the back of each picture."

"You said wives. So the incriminating photos are all of men?"

"The ones I saw were. Maybe because women weren't available. You have to be a better-than-average poker player to get into that place, and most women aren't that interested in the game."

She glanced at the pictures again. "What I can't figure out is why Dan was still seeing that woman—buying flowers and gifts, taking her out to dinner. He had to know she'd led him into that mess—that she was responsible for the blackmail."

I had been wondering about that, too. "If she worked for the people at that house, they'd want to protect her identity. So maybe they were careful to keep her face from appearing in the photos, and he never knew. Or they might have paid other women for the poses, once he was drugged."

"Like lingerie models, only without the underwear? But I think you're right. Whoever took the pictures was capturing clear images of the men's faces, but not the women's. And that would explain why he was still going to the apartment. He was meeting her there."

"Maybe. What's puzzling me is why he still had that poker chip and gate code in his pocket. Why would he go back to that place? And would they have even let him in once they had what they wanted?"

She thought about that. "Do you suppose...Marcie, what if he was trying to do the same thing we did? Get in there just long enough to unlock a window or door so he could go back later and find the pictures? The guy guarding the door probably wouldn't have known to keep him out as long as he had that poker chip."

I suspected she was right; Grandpa Dan would have been desperate and may have seen that as his only option. But wouldn't every other person who had been victimized? To avoid that, it should have been standard procedure to retrieve the chip and gate code at the same time the photos were taken—when the victims were drugged. Somehow, they had missed Grandpa Dan's. And that probably explained the garbage thief. I wondered if he'd checked that trash can every week, looking for those clothes.

Grandma Edith was scrolling through the images again, frowning. "These women are going to be hard to find. But, with a little help from you, we can figure it out."

"Me?"

"Marcie, I have an idea I'd like to run by you."

Surprised, I could only nod, but that was enough for her to launch into her proposal, one she'd obviously been thinking about for some time. She wanted me to apply for the dispatcher job at Miner's Ridge PD, stay with her, and help with her new business.

"It would be perfect," she said. "You'd have a regular income, along with a source in the police department."

"I'm not sure that would be ethical."

"Sure, it would. Private investigators do that all the time. Look at Kinsey Millhone. She even dated a couple of cops."

"Kinsey...oh, you're talking about the character in Sue Grafton's books."

Her look that time was one of disappointment, maybe mixed with a touch of disapproval. "Marcie, how are you ever going to learn anything worthwhile if you don't read?"

Chapter 28

When the neighbors started drifting over to the porch that evening, I watched Grandma Edith's face, wondering if she recognized any of them from the photos she'd taken. I'd had only a glance at those on her cell phone, but she'd placed each of them on the floor of that house to snap pictures.

When I mulled over her proposal, I considered those images. How could we hope to find the women who were responsible? Even if Grandma Edith had access to the victims' bank accounts—which she didn't—I could see no way to track gifts and dinner dates back to anybody... unless she tried to become a regular at the poker place to somehow connect the women there to the men in the photos.

Surely, she wouldn't try that; it would be too dangerous. But when had that ever dissuaded Grandma Edith? I couldn't even discuss it with her, try to convince her not to try, because I might be planting a seed she hadn't yet considered.

I decided I had only one option. I'd talk to Nate, tell him the entire story, swearing him to secrecy, and trust that he had more influence over her than I.

While I was plotting a way to get him away from the group long enough to fill him in, I tuned in to snippets of conversation, including conjecture about the bank robber. The woman whose niece had a friend who dated a Miner's Ridge cop said the robber was desperate to pay off a gambling debt, that he was about to lose his property. Another, who picked up her information from her beauty salon clients, said the guy was being blackmailed.

Grandma Edith didn't look my way, nor did she offer an opinion, even when the conversation turned to the signs she'd posted on her front and back doors. She didn't know why anybody would want Dan's files and the police department hadn't found the people who'd broken into his office.

That dampened the mood. The conversation became more subdued, nobody mentioning the damaged Ford Explorer found in Walt Gorman's barn or his arrest for Grandpa Dan's murder. The party broke up a little earlier than usual, and I wondered if all the recent events and those still to come would change these Friday and Saturday night gatherings.

No, Grandma Edith wouldn't allow that. The underground news source would be too valuable in her new line of work. That thought jarred me back to my plan. When Nate got up to leave, I rose, too. "I'll walk you home, Nate, so I can say goodbye. I'll be leaving early in the morning."

But I'd missed my chance. Randy and Billy had arrived in Grandpa Dan's pickup to take the old Ford Focus and the Camaro convertible back to Galt. Billy was out of the cab and bounding up the steps before I could do more than whisper in Nate's ear that I'd call him later.

Billy grabbed Grandma Edith in a rib-bruising hug which she endured for less than a second before she pushed him away. "If you're looking to inherit my property, Billy, you're about a dozen visits too late."

Randy trudged up the steps behind him. "Hi, Grandma." He gave her a gentle hug, looking over her shoulder at me. "Marcie."

Grandma Edith led them inside to warm up some dinner while I picked up bottles and plates and carried them inside.

I watched Randy and Billy as they ate, filling Grandma Edith in with news of their siblings between bites. Randy looked tired and a little restless.

Grandma Edith noticed, too. "Why don't you spend the night and get a fresh start in the morning? I can pull out the bed in the office, and Billy can sleep on the couch."

He pushed back from the table and carried his plate to the sink. "No, I want to get back. I still have some work to do—"

"Before Marcie gets back," Billy interrupted. "We still have to paint—"

"Billy!" Randy looked like he wanted to throttle his brother. "I told you not to—"

"The appliances are already in and—"

"Billy!" Randy thundered. "I told you not to say anything. I wanted it to be a surprise. And put that beer back in the fridge. You have to drive the Ford back."

He let out a deep breath, his shoulders slumped as he turned toward me. "I've been remodeling your kitchen. I didn't tell you because...well, I wanted to see your expression when you walked in."

I put my hands over my face, not sure whether I wanted to hide tears, rage, or simple frustration. What had he done?

He pulled my hands away. "It's nice, Marcie. Stainless steel appliances, new vinyl, some good countertop I found on sale. No more yellow and avocado. I promise you, you're going to like it."

"Why?" I couldn't think of anything else to say.

"Because I owe you. I talked you into that mortgage on your house. I traded in your car for that Camaro you never liked, and I left you with all those bills. I'm just trying to make it up to you."

"It looks great," Billy said. "We've been working on it every night after he gets off work, and I've been there during the day when the appliances and the counter were installed and the floor repaired. They did a good job."

"But why are you doing it now?" Randy was so earnest, I couldn't bring myself to utter the question I really wanted to ask: what did he want?

We'd been together long enough that he probably knew what I was thinking. "I'm just trying to make things right, Marcie. I don't expect you to...to do anything. Except maybe, if you can see your way to letting me and Billy rent your spare rooms for a while. If you did, we could work on the rest of the house. And I'd stay out of your way. Out of your life. I promise."

I didn't know how to respond to that. I was in unfamiliar territory. This was not the Randy I'd grown to resent so much, the man I thought I knew.

Grandma Edith, ever practical, answered for me. "Well, now that you don't have to go back to surprise her tomorrow, I'll fix some beds for you."

Randy rose to his feet. "No. I'm going to finish painting that kitchen tonight. I want it finished when she sees it tomorrow." He reached for my hand and gave it a gentle squeeze. "Then you can make up your mind about the rest."

I was still thinking about him, wondering if he really could have changed that much since our divorce, when Brad finally called. He was back in Rocklin, still working a case. "I'm so sorry, Marcie. I wanted that last day with you, but it will be too late to drive to Miner's Ridge when I get off work tonight. Is there a chance you could meet me for breakfast tomorrow, on your drive back down to Galt? You'll have to come through Rocklin and Roseville and there's a restaurant right off the freeway, Brookfields."

I agreed to meet him at ten the next morning, but that was before Eric Roberts showed up a little before nine, just as I was loading my suitcase into the car.

"I'm glad I caught you before you left. I brought an application for the dispatcher job, in case you're interested." He started toward the porch steps, then stopped, looking over his shoulder. "I have some news for your grandmother you might be interested in hearing."

I stowed the suitcase, followed him up the steps, and opened the door. "Grandma Edith, Officer Roberts is here to see you."

He took off his hat and motioned toward the sofa. "You might want to sit down."

Once we were seated, he leaned toward Grandma Edith. "We got a call this morning from the Placer County Sheriff's Office. They raided a gambling house Thursday night and found evidence that your husband had been there, possibly drugged and posed for compromising photos, along with a number of other victims. We think they were being blackmailed, which explains where your money went."

Grandma Edith, not looking at me, murmured, "Oh, my!"

"I know it's something of a shock," Roberts said, "but we've been suspecting something like this all along. Placer County will keep us informed, and I'll let you know more as soon as I can. Right now, all I can tell you is that a crime ring has been operating a number of illegal gambling establishments hidden away in remote areas all over the state. I don't know at this point how many of them are also running blackmail schemes, but I suspect several."

My mind was racing. "They called you? Why would they do that? We're not in Placer County."

"You're forgetting that Placer County runs all the way from Roseville up to Tahoe. The house they raided was only a few miles over the county line, out in the country, off a dirt road. Apparently, it's been in operation for quite a while."

Brad Kinney worked for Placer County. Was this the case he'd been called in on? While he was on vacation? But he'd sent me that message yesterday morning, while Grandma Edith and I were at that same house. It had to be the same place if they'd found Grandpa Dan's pictures there. How could he have known about it so soon?

I had a lot of time to think about it on the drive to Roseville. By the time I'd found Brookfields, the pieces had all fallen into place.

"You used me," I told Brad. "All the time you were there—that we were at The Tavern—you were working, weren't you? Trying to find that gambling house somewhere in the area. I told you about Grandpa Dan cleaning out Grandma Edith's bank accounts and his gambling. And that night at O'Malley's—you were on the job then, too, weren't you?"

"It wasn't like that, Marcie. Not at first. I liked you. I wanted to spend more time with you. We had fun at O'Malley's. I still want—"

I blinked, my eyes stinging. I was not going to let him see how much he'd hurt me. "I liked you, too. I trusted you. That night, when Grandma Edith came home, we handed it all to you, didn't we? The poker chip, the number for the gate. And knowing Grandma Edith, you followed her that night when she went to Will's house."

"Yes, I suspected she'd lead me to the place, but I...Marcie, it didn't—"

"So then all you had to do was to follow Will. Just like Grandma Edith did the next night. Did you tail her, Brad, watch her open that gate and drive inside?"

"She shouldn't have been there. I was afraid she'd get hurt. Or that she'd take you there and...Marcie, these people are dangerous. You and your grandmother shouldn't have been involved."

I rose from my seat. "Yet our involvement led you straight to them, didn't it? You wouldn't have found that house if not for me and Grandma Edith."

I grabbed my purse then and fled, knowing tears were too close to the surface. He couldn't follow me—at least not right away. He was a cop; he couldn't leave without paying for the coffee he'd ordered, that we'd never drank.

I was in my car and on my way out of the lot before he got to the door. I took one last glance, knowing I'd never see Brad Kinney again.

He was a cop. He couldn't share information. But he'd lied to me, telling me he was on vacation, letting me share personal information because he suspected it would lead to his objective.

When would I ever learn to stop making men the center of my life? I'd been fooled again, letting instinct rule me, rather than logic, learning nothing from Grandma Edith's experience with Grandpa Dan and my marriage to Randy. Why was I always drawn to charming, charismatic men who proved to have no substance?

Well, no more. I'd go home, kick Randy and Billy out of my house and go back to my job.

My dull, boring job.

No, I wouldn't. I was going to fill out that application for the dispatcher job in Miner's Ridge. I suspected Eric Roberts would put in a good word for me. I'd take Grandma Edith up on her offer. Randy could rent the house in Galt from me or I could sell it.

Even as I made that decision, I realized the dispatcher job wouldn't be very interesting either. Not in Miner's Ridge. But I could take some classes, learn more, maybe eventually qualify for a position as a police officer.

I smiled. That kind of training would really help me as a private investigator.

Notes From the Author

Word-of-mouth is crucial for any author to be successful. If you enjoyed this book, please consider leaving a review on Amazon. Even a line or two would be a tremendous help.

While you're there, take a look at my books in the Callender & Wagner series:

Love, Murder and a Good Bottle of Wine
Snowbound
Haunted by the Innocent
Little Boy Gone

The series is unlike most mysteries and thrillers, in that it does not contain profanity-laced dialogue, graphic sex scenes, or extreme violence. Instead, the reader gets character-driven novels with unexpected twists, a dash of humor, and intriguing, page-turning plots.

My website at chrisphipps.com has more information about my books and a little about my life. There's also a place where you can sign up for my mailing list, to get advance information about sales and new book publication dates. You can also follow me on Facebook. I am too busy writing to spend much time on either site, though, so the best way to contact me is by email at chris@chrisphipps.com.